Stone Barrington gains an adversary that he can't seem to shake in the electrifying new adventure from the #1 *New York Times*–bestselling author.

Stone Barrington's latest lady friend is full of surprises, both good and ill. A sensual woman with unexpected desires, Stone finds her revelations in the boudoir extremely agreeable. But on the other hand, she also has some unfinished business with a temperamental man who believes Stone is an intolerable obstacle in the way of his goals.

In a cat-and-mouse game that trails from sun-drenched Bel-Air to a peaceful European estate and the wild New Mexican desert, Stone and his friend remain just one step ahead of their opponent. But their pursuer is not a man who can stand to be thwarted, and tensions are mounting . . . and may soon reach the boiling point.

Praise for the Stone Barrington Novels
Dishonorable Intentions

"Diverting."   —*Publishers Weekly*

Family Jewels

"Tony trappings, colorful characters, and a magnificent McGuffin . . . Dry-witted dialogue keeps the tone light and drives this glossy, modern take on the classic detective story."   —*Publishers Weekly*

Scandalous Behavior

"Addictive . . . Pick [*Scandalous Behavior*] up at your peril. You can get hooked."   —*Lincoln Journal Star*

Standup Guy

"Stuart Woods still owns an imagination that simply won't quit . . . This is yet another edge-of-your-seat adventure."   —*Suspense Magazine*

Doing Hard Time

"Longtime Woods fans who have seen Teddy [Fay] evolve from a villain to something of a lovable antihero will enjoy watching the former enemies work together in this exciting yarn. Is this the beginning of a beautiful partnership? Let's hope so."   —*Booklist*

Unintended Consequences

"Since 1981, readers have not been able to get their fill of Stuart Woods' *New York Times*–bestselling novels of suspense."   —*Orlando Sentinel*

Collateral Damage

"High-octane . . . Woods's blend of exciting action, sophisticated gadgetry, and last-minute heroics doesn't disappoint."   —*Publishers Weekly*

Severe Clear

"Stuart Woods has proven time and time again that he's a master of suspense who keeps his readers frantically turning the pages."   —Bookreporter.com

Books by Stuart Woods

Dishonorable Intentions

Stuart Woods

G. P. PUTNAM'S SONS   New York

G. P. PUTNAM'S SONS
Publishers Since 1838
An imprint of Penguin Random House LLC
375 Hudson Street
New York, New York 10014

The Library of Congress has catalogued the G. P. Putnam's Sons hardcover
edition as follows:

Names: Woods, Stuart, author.
Title: Dishonorable intentions / Stuart Woods.
Description: New York : G.P. Putnam's Sons, [2016]
Identifiers: LCCN 2016010830| ISBN 9780399573910 (print) |
ISBN 9780399573934 (ePub)
Subjects: LCSH: Barrington, Stone (Fictitious character)—Fiction. | Private
investigators—Fiction. | BISAC: FICTION / Suspense. | FICTION /
Thrillers. | FICTION / Action & Adventure. | GSAFD: Suspense fiction. |
Adventure fiction.
Classification: LCC PS3573.O642 D59 2016 | DDC 813/.54—dc23
LC record available at https://lccn.loc.gov/2016010830

First G. P. Putnam's Sons hardcover edition / June 2016
First G. P. Putnam's Sons premium edition / February 2017
G. P. Putnam's Sons premium edition ISBN: 9780399573927

Printed in the United States of America
1   3   5   7   9   10   8   6   4   2

This book is for Karen and Bob Copeland.

Dishonorable Intentions

1

S tone Barrington spotted the Santa Fe airport ten miles out. "Albuquerque Center, November One, Two, Three, Tango Foxtrot has the airport in sight."

"N123TF, contact the tower on 119.5. Good day to you."

"Good day." He tuned into the channel. "Santa Fe tower, N123TF nine miles to the north at ten thousand. Request straight in for runway two zero."

"N123TF, I have you in sight. Cleared for the visual to two zero."

"Tango Fox, cleared for the visual." Stone lined up on the runway, reduced power, put in his first notch of flaps, and dialed in eight thousand feet. The autopilot began the descent. Five miles out, he dropped the landing gear, slowing the airplane further, then put in 35 degrees of flaps and let the airplane slow to approach speed.

At the sound of the gear lowering, Bob, Stone's trusty yellow Labrador retriever, left his bed in the passenger compartment, jumped up on a seat, and looked out the window.

At five hundred feet above ground level, Stone slowed to reference speed of 107 knots, crossed the runway threshold, and settled smoothly onto the tarmac. As he put in the final notch of flaps to dump lift and began to brake, he spotted the Aston Martin parked on the ramp outside Landmark Aviation and the tall blond woman in sweater and slacks leaning against it.

He turned off the runway, stopped, and ran his after-landing checklist, then called the tower and was cleared to taxi to the ramp. A lineman waved him in next to the Aston Martin, then chocked the nosewheel. Stone pulled the throttles to the shutoff position and waited for the engines to spool down before turning off the main switch, which shut down the instrument panel. He struggled out of his seat, opened the cabin door, grabbed his briefcase, kicked down the folding stairs, and allowed Bob to deplane first.

Gala Wilde met them at the bottom of the steps, planted an enthusiastic kiss on Stone's lips, and scratched Bob's back. "Welcome back," she said. "We've got dinner at seven at the Eagles' house." Gala was the sister of Mrs. Ed Eagle, Susannah Wilde.

Stone retrieved his overnight bag from the forward luggage compartment and tossed it into the rear of the Aston Martin along with his briefcase, which used nearly all of the available luggage space, then got into the passenger seat and let Bob crowd in beside him. "I'm ready for a drink," he said.

"Sadly, I don't keep the stuff in the car, so you'll have to wait another twenty minutes."

"I'll try, but I may get the shakes. Flying always makes me thirsty."

She started the engine, which emitted a pleasing, guttural noise, then waited for the gate to open. "Good flight?"

"Boring flight—the best kind. I read the *Times* and did the crossword."

"Good crossword?"

"Saturdays are always a bitch. They're the most fun."

"Thank you, I think."

Stone laughed. "That wasn't a personal reference."

Twenty minutes later they pulled into the driveway of her house in the village of Tesuque, on the northern rim of Santa Fe. He grabbed his luggage and followed her to the master suite, while Bob paused to inspect the grass, then followed. Stone dumped his bags in the master bedroom and followed her into the kitchen sitting room, where a leather-covered rolling bar held a nest of bottles. Bob settled for Tesuque well water.

"Knob Creek?"

"Of course."

"Have you tried their rye?"

"Didn't know there was one."

"There is. Shall I pour you one?"

"Go ahead, I'll be brave."

She handed him a glass and poured herself one. They both sipped.

"That's really good," Stone said. "I haven't drunk a lot of rye."

"I hadn't either, until I discovered it at a bourbon bar at a restaurant in town." She sank down beside him on the sofa. A cheery fire of piñon wood crackled in the fireplace.

"A bourbon bar? Never seen one of those, but it sounds like a good idea. What's happening with your screenplay?"

"The plan is for Ben Bacchetti to sign his first production order on Monday morning, and it's my screenplay."

"He'll be signing it as head of production," Stone said. "Leo Goldman isn't quite ready to relinquish his title as CEO. He's unwell, though, so it might only be a matter of months before he moves over."

"How does Peter feel about losing his production partner?"

"He's not losing him, Ben will still produce their pictures personally, at least until he becomes CEO."

"He'll be a busy fellow."

"He seems to like it that way. Peter says Ben always got bored while they were waiting for production approval. That won't be a problem anymore. By the way, I'm joining the Centurion board on Monday morning."

"What do you know about motion pictures?"

"Well, I've seen a lot of them. That seems to be the only qualification of half the movie executives in L.A."

"You're right about that."

"Of course, Peter's trust and I, combined, are the largest stockholders of the company."

"I suppose he inherited his stock from Vance Calder." Calder was the late movie star who had been Peter's stepfather. His mother, Arrington, had married Calder while pregnant with Stone's son.

"He did."

"How about you?"

"I've been buying the stock for years from people who were required to divest on retirement. It adds up over time."

"What are the duties of a director of the company?"

"Four board meetings a year, plus an occasional special meeting, when circumstances require."

"And for that you get what?"

"Money and the use of the corporate jet at half the company's cost."

"But you have your own jet."

"True, but it's nice to have access to a brand-new Gulfstream 650 when traveling long distances, and they might even let me fly right seat sometimes. I'm getting qualified in it."

"And how long will that take?"

"A month or more, but it will be fun, as well as hard work. I've already done three weeks of it. They'll let me finish up when I can find the time."

"I get the impression that your time is pretty much your own," she said.

"It's surprising how much law you can practice with an iPhone and a computer. I've even attended board meetings on Skype, while at my house in England."

"I'm looking forward to seeing that house."

"That can be arranged."

"Well, it's not as though the production company is glad to see me after they've started shooting. They regard the writer as excess baggage once the production order is signed."

"Will you start a new one soon?"

"I'm always working, and I have a good idea for a new one."

"Think you can write in England?"

"I don't see why not." She looked at her watch. "We've got an hour before dinner. Do you think we could find something to do until then?"

"My intentions are thoroughly dishonorable," he said, kissing her.

"Sofa or bed?"

"It's a big sofa."

Buttons, snaps, and garments came undone.

2

Stone was asleep, curled up behind Gala, when a noise woke him. It wasn't much of a noise, so he began drifting off again, then there was a loud crash. Bob was snoring away, ignoring his role in security management.

Gala woke, too. "What was that?"

"I don't know. Do you have a gun in the house?"

"Bedside table, top drawer. There's one in the chamber."

There was another noise, loud enough to waken even Bob. He began growling, but he didn't move.

Stone got up and trotted noiselessly across the kitchen and into the master suite. He found the gun, a Colt Government .380; he opened the slide slightly to be sure there was a round chambered. The noise came again. He tiptoed to the door opening onto a patio and silently opened it, stepping outside in his bare feet.

A scraping noise came from his left, sounding like somebody trying to get in through a window or door. The evening desert chill hit him, and he realized he was naked. He crept to the corner of the house and looked around it, just as an outdoor security light came on. The intruder blinked in the harsh light, then stared at Stone.

Stone found himself staring back at a large black bear, no more than ten feet from where he stood. The bear uttered a low, threatening noise. Stone screamed wordlessly at him, while jumping up and down and waving his arms. The bear seemed to reevaluate his threat, while watching Stone with curiosity.

"Okay," Stone said to the bear, "I can't shout any louder than that. How about this?" He pointed the gun and pulled the trigger twice, hitting the tree he had been aiming at.

The bear thought better of things, spun around, and hurried off into the darkness.

"Well done," a voice behind him said.

Startled, Stone spun around. Gala stood in the door, as naked as he. Bob peeked out from behind her. "Did you invite that guy over for drinks?"

Gala laughed. "They sometimes come down the mountain and into the village. When I had the new roof put on, the roofers found bear scat up there."

Stone suddenly realized he was cold and stepped inside, shivering.

"Dinner is in twenty minutes," Gala said. "We'd better get dressed."

They arrived at the residence of Ed and Susannah Eagle fashionably late.

"I'm sorry we were late," Stone said, "but we had an intruder."

"An intruder?" Ed asked.

"Biggest black bear you ever saw."

"Did he get into the house?"

"No, I fired a couple of shots into a tree, and he thought better of it."

Ed handed them both a Knob Creek on the rocks. "Susannah is finishing dinner. Use this as a stopgap." He waved them to a living room sofa. "You don't ever want one of those things to get into the house, Gala, they can destroy it in minutes."

"I'll keep that in mind, Ed."

"Didn't you bring Bob?"

"I thought he needed his rest. I think the bear scared him to death."

"Stone, can we hitch a ride to L.A. with you tomorrow? My airplane blew a couple of current limiters, and we had to order replacements from Wichita."

"Of course."

"Anyway, I've wanted a chance to fly your airplane."

"You'll love it. My cockpit is identical to your M2's, except for a single cockpit switch."

Susannah came into the room and greeted them both with hugs and kisses. "Dinner will be ready in half an hour," she said, accepting a drink from her husband. "We're looking forward to your party Monday night, Stone."

Stone was throwing a large party at his house at the Arrington for Ben Bacchetti. "It's going to be mostly studio people," he said.

"Why aren't Dino and Viv with you?"

"Dino had a thing he couldn't avoid. They're flying in commercial tomorrow."

"Will Mary Ann be there, too?"

Mary Ann Bianci was Dino's ex-wife and Ben's mother.

"Oh, sure."

"That should be exciting."

"Mary Ann has been behaving herself, since her father died. The experience seems to have mellowed her."

"I'm so glad to hear it. I remember when she could be a horrible bitch."

"If she gets started, we'll throw a bag over her and push her into the pool."

"That, I'd like to see. Who from the studio is coming?" Susannah asked.

"I left that to Ben and Peter. They tell me we'll be thirty for dinner. We'll do a buffet around the pool."

"Will the President and the President be there?"

"The Lees will be in town to meet with the Japanese prime minister. They'll be occupying the presidential cottage, but I don't expect to see them during their visit."

"How's their baby doing?"

"I've met him only once, and he seems to be behaving like a baby should. He's cheerful enough."

Dinner was beef and plenty of it, washed down with a couple of bottles of the Caymus Special Selection Cabernet. It was nearly midnight when the party broke up, and Stone and Gala returned to her house.

"Shall I inspect for bears?" Stone asked as they got out of the car.

"Not without the gun," Gala replied. "It's back in the bedside drawer."

She let them into the house. Stone collected the gun and walked back onto the patio off the master suite. The outside lights automatically sensed his presence and came on. He moved carefully around the rear exterior of the house. Something rustled in the bushes, but nothing big enough for a bear; however, he managed to step in something that was too much for a dog or a coyote. He had to get paper towels from the kitchen to clean it off his shoe.

Gala was looking out of sorts when he returned. He cleared the weapon and returned it to its drawer. "I'll clean the gun for you tomorrow." He looked at her closely. "Something the matter?"

"A phone message from my ex-husband," Gala said wearily. "He wants to see me when we're in L.A."

"You don't have to see him."

"If I don't, he'll just keep calling. I'll have a drink with him and get it over with."

"Whatever you say."

"I just can't imagine what he could want. He's gotten everything the settlement entitled him to. The last thing he demanded was a case of old wine that he forgot to include."

"I hope you drank it."

"No, I shipped it to him."

"But he keeps asking for things?"

"That's his pattern."

"You'll have to call an end to that. I'll help, if I can. You can introduce me as your new attorney."

"That's a thought. Let's see how it goes in L.A."

They made love again and were soon asleep. Why did beautiful women always seem to have grumpy ex-husbands? he wondered as he drifted off.

3

Stone was served a sumptuous breakfast in bed, while watching his favorite Sunday-morning shows, which Gala had TiVo-ed for him. To his surprise, CBS News *Sunday Morning* had a feature on Boris Tirov, Gala's ex-husband.

"I heard about this a couple of weeks ago," Gala said, "but I forgot about it. We may as well watch it."

In an interview conducted next to his large pool overlooking Malibu Beach, Tirov, a handsome, fit-looking fellow of around fifty, waxed eloquent about his success in the film business, commenting graciously on some of the people he'd worked with.

"I understand you're leaving Sony and taking your production company to Centurion," the interviewer said.

"I'm afraid I can't comment about that," Tirov replied.

"Would such an announcement come as a surprise to Sony?" he was asked.

Boris chuckled. "It might come as a surprise to Centurion."

"How long ago was this interview filmed?" Stone asked.

"At least a couple of weeks ago, maybe longer. I'm a bit surprised—Boris would seem to be a better fit at one of the bigger studios than at Centurion, which is a more gentlemanly place."

"Would you like him not to be at Centurion?"

"From the sound of it, it's probably too late for that. At least he won't be in management, so he won't be able to interfere with my new deal at Centurion."

"How many pictures is your deal for?"

"Three, but it's a writing deal, not a production deal. I don't have a company to move there and take up a lot of office space, the way Boris does. I'll get a small bungalow, and that's good enough for me, since I do most of my work at home or while traveling."

"If Boris's deal isn't signed and sealed, I may be able to have some effect on it after tomorrow, when I'm appointed to the board."

"Don't do anything on my account," Gala said. "It would just get back to Boris and make things more difficult for me."

"Whatever you say," Stone replied, downing the rest of his orange juice and pouring himself some coffee. "I'll stay out of it."

"That would probably be best."

Stone turned to the Sunday *New York Times*, and in the Arts section immediately found a story about Boris Tirov's move from Sony to Centurion. He handed it to

Gala. "Looks like he's serious enough to give the story to the *Times*. Or is that just a PR move, to make Sony think twice about his deal there?"

"Could be," she said. "Boris has done that sort of thing before."

Stone picked up his iPhone, looked up the name of the CEO of Centurion, Leo Goldman Jr., and pressed the button.

"Good morning, Stone," Leo said. "Nice to hear from you on a Sunday."

"Sorry about that, Leo. I just wondered if you'd seen the story in the *Times* about Boris Tirov leaving Sony for Centurion."

"Yes, I did see that, and it was a surprise, since the board is not scheduled to consider that deal until tomorrow. You'll be there, won't you?"

"I will be."

"Do you have a view on the Tirov move?"

"I find it a little premature to announce a deal that is still awaiting board approval."

"Tell me, Stone, is it possible that you are calling from Santa Fe?"

"Entirely possible."

"I thought perhaps you might be. There'll be time for a full discussion of the Tirov deal at tomorrow's meeting. See you there."

"Goodbye, Leo." Stone hung up. "Boris's deal is before the board tomorrow. I think Leo was annoyed that it was in today's *Times*."

"Oh."

"And he figured out that I am here with you."

"How did he do that?"

"The grapevine, I suppose."

"Does he know what we did in bed last night?"

"He'd better not."

"Oh, good, then it's not so bad, is it?"

"I suppose not. How would you like to see the board's decision go tomorrow?"

"I don't have an opinion," Gala said primly.

"An ex-wife without an opinion on her husband's business? I've never heard of such a thing. I believe you told me that you've already received everything due to you under your settlement?"

"That's correct."

"Then the board's decision won't affect you."

"Not in that way."

"Is there some other way that it might affect you?"

"I hope it won't be uncomfortable for me, working on the same lot as Boris."

"I see."

"I'm glad."

Stone turned back to his *Times*.

4

S tone set down at Santa Monica Airport with Ed Eagle in the right seat, and they, along with Susannah and Gala, were met by chauffeur-driven Bentleys from the Arrington. Half an hour later they were deposited in front of Stone's house on the hotel property, and their luggage was being taken to the master suite, while the Eagles were settled into a guest suite.

"This is lovely," Gala said, looking around the house. "And it looks as if it has always been here."

"That was my instruction to the builder and the interior designer."

They settled into the library and were brought refreshments by a butler.

"Tell me how this Arrington group came into existence," Gala said. "Ed told me something about it, but I'm hazy on the details."

"My late wife, Arrington, was previously married to Vance Calder."

"I knew that part. She's Peter's mother?"

"Yes. When Vance died, Arrington and Peter's trust inherited his property, which included eighteen acres of Bel-Air. I and a group of investors formed the group, and Arrington sold us the land, with the provision that we would build her a permanent residence on the property."

"What happened to Calder's old house? I was there once, and it was beautiful."

"It was expanded and became what is now the reception center and the executive offices. When Arrington died, I inherited her house, still uncompleted, from her estate. Any further questions?"

"So Peter is Vance's son?"

"No, Arrington and I were an item before she met Vance, and on our last night together she became pregnant, although she didn't know it until a bit later. She met Calder, was infatuated with him, and they ran off and got married. Peter was the result of that pregnancy. He and I didn't really become acquainted until after Vance's death. Fortunately, the relationship took, and we've been close since that time."

"Thank you, I think I've got it all now."

"You're welcome."

There was a bustling in the front hall, and Dino and Viv Bacchetti entered the room. "I heard booze was being served in here," Dino said.

Stone introduced the Bacchettis to Gala, and booze was served.

"What are we doing for dinner?" Dino asked.

"The chef is preparing some of his delicacies for us," Stone replied.

"That works for me," Dino said.

"Gala, would you like to see the rest of the house? Perhaps Viv would show you around."

"Love to," Gala said, and the two women left, carrying their drinks.

"How was your flight?" Stone asked.

"Not as good as yours was," Dino replied. "Even first class doesn't cut it, compared to Stone Airlines."

"It warms the cockles of my heart to hear you say so. I'll be happy to give you a lift home."

"Apart from the party for Ben, have you got business out here?"

"I'm being seated on the board of Centurion Studios tomorrow morning at ten AM, followed by a luncheon in the studio canteen."

"What time is the party tomorrow night?"

"People are invited for drinks at six, followed by dinner. L.A. is an early town."

"Suits me, I've got three hours of jet lag to deal with." Dino peered closely at Stone. "You don't seem to be thrilled by this board appointment."

"I am appropriately thrilled," Stone said, "but on the agenda for my first board meeting is the approval of a production deal between Gala's ex-husband, one Boris Tirov, and Centurion. She's uneasy about having him on the same lot—she just signed to write three scripts for the studio. I'm uneasy about it, too, and I've been trying to figure out how I can torpedo Tirov's deal without appearing to."

"Ah, I see you're acquiring the habits of the denizens here, already plotting against somebody."

"I'm not plotting against him, this is just business."

"That's what they always say just before they pull the trigger."

"I haven't shared my concerns with any other board members, though I spoke briefly with Leo Goldman after I saw the announcement of the deal in the *New York Times* today."

"It's already in the *Times*, and the board hasn't approved it, yet?"

"I think that may count against Mr. Tirov. He's making television appearances, too."

"Maybe you won't have to slip the knife in, then."

"Maybe not, though I'll do it if I have to."

"Having had a look at Gala, I can see why. She's a knockout, just as beautiful as her sister, and younger."

"All that you say is true," Stone replied.

The women returned, and they schmoozed until dinnertime.

5

On Monday morning, Stone had breakfast with his party, then hopped into an Arrington Bentley for the twenty-minute drive to Centurion Studios and his board meeting. Traffic was moving briskly at mid-morning as the car moved onto the freeway, and Stone settled in with the *New York Times* as the car motored smoothly along the route. Then it came to a full stop.

"What's going on?" Stone asked the driver.

"I don't know, Mr. Barrington. The GPS has a lot of red symbols ahead. Let me see what I can find out on the radio." He fiddled with the tuning knob, and the two men listened to reports of a multivehicle pileup on the 405.

"This sounds bad," the driver said.

Stone checked his watch. "My board meeting starts in fifteen minutes."

"I think all we can do is just wait it out," the driver said.

"How about if I hoof it?"

"It's probably an hour's walk, and if traffic starts moving again, you'll be in danger of being run down."

Stone got out his cell phone to call Leo Goldman and explain his absence. "I can't get a connection," he said. "Zero bars."

"Sounds like we're in a dead zone," the driver said.

Stone got out of the car and stood on the door sill for a little elevation. "I can't see a damned thing but parked cars."

"This is L.A.," the driver said.

Stone got back in and started on the crossword. Since it was a Monday, the easiest day, that took eleven minutes by his watch. He put his head back on the headrest and closed his eyes for a moment.

W e're moving," the driver said suddenly. "That's the longest tie-up I've ever had on the freeway."

"How long have we been stopped?"

The driver checked his watch. "An hour and thirty-five minutes. The radio said eleven vehicles had to be cleared away."

They arrived at the executive building at Centurion in time to see Leo Goldman Jr. and the remainder of the board getting into golf carts for the short trip to the studio canteen for lunch.

"Where the hell have you been?" Leo asked.

"Stuck on the freeway for an hour and thirty-five minutes—an eleven-car pileup."

"That's not even near a record," Leo said. "Hop in. I'll bring you up to date."

Stone got in beside him. "I hope you didn't need my vote for anything important."

"Nah, it was pretty routine, except for the Boris Tirov thing."

"What happened?"

"We had a hell of a fight among ourselves. He had a couple of advocates on the board, but the rest of us were pissed off about the ass he made of himself on TV and in the *Times.*"

"I'm not surprised," Stone said.

"Boris is sure going to be. His buddies on the board will have already hit him with the news."

"He actually left Sony for the deal at Centurion?"

"There never was a deal here. He was assisted out of Sony with a pat on the back and a kick in the ass, and he was trying to save face and pressure us to let him move onto the lot. I don't think we'd even rent him office space at this point. The guy's a moneymaker, but he's an asshole. Everybody who's worked with him says so. I expect Gala has told you about that."

"Gala doesn't like to talk about him, so I've heard only the bare minimum, and I couldn't find anything to like in that."

They pulled up at the canteen, and everybody got out of the carts and went into the dining room, where a large table had been reserved for the board. Two of them hung back at the door, their cell phones glued to their heads.

"I'm glad I'm not a part of those conversations," Leo said.

They took their seats, Stone next to Leo.

"Oh, and Ben Bacchetti was confirmed as senior VP in charge of production."

"I'm delighted to hear it," Stone said.

"The kid is going to be great. There hasn't been any-body that smart at the studio since me. Not that your kid isn't smart—he just doesn't have the ambition to run things, the way Ben does. All he wants to do is write and direct movies, and that's just fine with me—he keeps go-ing like he is, and he'll be one of the greats."

"Thank you, Leo. I'm glad to hear that."

Leo's cell phone went off. "Goldman. He's where? I don't care what he says, I don't want to see him. And revoke his gate pass right now. I don't want him on the lot again." Leo hung up. "That was our head of security. Boris Tirov showed up at the main gate, demanding to see me. The guard didn't like the way he sounded and called his boss, who called me. You heard my response."

"Everybody at the table heard it, Leo," Stone said.

"I wanted his buddies to hear it. Now no one will so much as mention his name to me again. Nothing like a little yelling to make a point."

Stone laughed. "That works, does it?"

"You bet your sweet ass it works. I'm not going to spend my last couple of years here dealing with assholes. Life is too short, especially mine."

"Are you unwell, Leo?"

"Let's just say I've been better. My doctor says I'll have a good year or two, then one day I'll clutch my chest and turn blue."

"How about a transplant?"

"I'm not a candidate for that, and anyway, who wants to spend months in bed getting over it? I mean, Bob Altman got himself a new ticker on the quiet, and nobody was the wiser, not even the insurance companies, and he worked like a dervish for another ten, eleven years after his transplant. Tell you the truth, I'm not anxious to live all that long. I've had a great ride, I'll leave the studio in great shape, and if he's as good as I think he'll be, Ben will have a shot at succeeding me. Anyway, my wife would put me in the Motion Picture Home the minute I got to be a pain in the ass, and I don't want to sit around there in a wheelchair listening to old actors tell me how they were screwed out of the Oscar that time."

"I don't blame you, Leo," Stone said.

Stone got back to the house at the Arrington in time for a swim and a drink by the pool with the Bacchettis, the Eagles, and Gala. And Bob, who was soaking wet.

"Boris didn't get his deal at Centurion," Stone said to her in a quiet moment.

"I heard from him about it. He takes the view that you screwed him because of me."

"I wasn't even at the meeting," Stone said. He related his freeway experience. "I got there in time for lunch."

"I don't think Boris will ever buy that," Gala said.

"Not for a minute. He's always liked having a bête noire in his life, somebody to blame for his failures, and now, it looks like you're it. I'm sorry."

"Don't worry about it," Stone said. "Anyway, what could he do to me?"

6

Stone's son, Peter, arrived for pre-party drinks with Ben Bacchetti, and Stone sat them down in the library with his houseguests.

"Congratulations, Ben," Stone said. "I missed the board meeting today, but I heard about it from Leo Goldman."

"Thank you, Stone," Ben said. "I signed my first production order today." He raised his glass to Gala. "It's a wonderful script," he said. "I'm not going to mess with it, and I'll see that nobody else does, either."

"That's the nicest thing anybody has ever said to me, Ben," Gala replied.

"From now on, you have your agent send your ideas directly to me, and we'll cut some red tape."

"I like having the ear of God," she said.

"Peter," Stone said, "Leo told me today that if you keep going like you have, you're going to be one of the greats."

Peter laughed. "Hyperbole is Leo Goldman's native

tongue," he said. Peter took a sip of his drink. "Dad, there's something you should know."

Ben broke in. "This one is my fault—let me tell him."

"Okay, tell me," Stone said.

"I invited Boris Tirov to the party tonight, at a time when I thought he would be the new guy on the lot."

"Uh-oh," Gala said quietly.

"I've tried to reach him, but he's not at home, and he's not answering his cell."

"He must be smart enough not to show up tonight," Dino said.

"Don't count on it," Gala threw in.

"Well," Dino said, "if he does show, Stone, as host, can just explain to him that he's no longer welcome."

"Gee, thanks, Dino," Stone said.

"I don't want to be anywhere nearby when that happens," Gala said.

"Is he likely to make a fuss?" Stone asked.

Gala just rolled her eyes.

Stone excused himself for a moment and went into the living room, where he picked up a phone and called the head of hotel security.

"Yes, Mr. Barrington?"

"I'm having a party tonight at the house, and I've had word that there may be an unruly guest."

"We can take care of that. I'll send a couple of men over."

"Plainclothes, please, and ask them to handle it as discreetly as possible."

"Of course. Our people are good at that. May I have the gentleman's name?"

"Boris Tirov."

"Ah, yes, we had to remove that gentleman from the bar a couple of weeks ago. He took a swing at the film critic of the *L.A. Times*. Apparently, the man didn't like his movies enough. I'll have the main gate warn me when he arrives."

Stone thanked the man and returned to his guests.

By seven o'clock most of the guest list had arrived, and servers were bringing platters from the kitchen to the buffet tables set up by the pool. Stone was in a conversation with Billy Barnett, who had become an important part of Peter and Ben's production company, when he glanced toward the hedge separating the pool from a guesthouse beyond and saw Boris Tirov step past the hedge, a drink already in his hand. "Oh, shit," he said.

"What's wrong?" Billy asked.

"A disinvited guest has just snuck into the party." He looked around for the security men and saw them on the opposite side of the group, where one would expect guests to arrive.

"Would you like me to speak to the gentleman?" Billy asked.

"No, I'll handle it myself." Stone set his drink on a table and walked around the pool, meeting Tirov before he could reach the crowd. "Good evening, Mr. Tirov," he said, offering his hand. "I'm Stone Barrington."

Tirov brushed the hand aside. "Ah," he said, "the guy who torpedoed my deal at Centurion today."

"You've been misinformed," Stone replied. "I wasn't at the board meeting this morning."

"You lying piece of shit," Tirov said, swaying slightly. "I know who you are and why you killed my deal."

Stone realized that the man was already drunk. "You never had a deal at Centurion," he said, "but if I had been at the meeting, I would have done what I could to see that it didn't happen."

Tirov threw his drink in Stone's face, momentarily blinding him, and swung with a wide left at his head.

Stone barely had time to see it coming, but he took a step backward toward the pool, coming close to stepping into the water. Tirov's momentum took him straight into the pool, making a huge splash.

Stone looked up to see Billy Barnett moving toward him, followed closely by the two hotel security guards. He looked back toward Tirov, who was flailing in the water. Stone wondered if the man could swim. He saw a life ring with a length of rope hanging on a post a few feet away, and he retrieved it and tossed it to Tirov. He certainly wasn't going in after him.

"Let security take care of it," he said to Billy, taking his arm and steering him back toward the party.

"We've got this, Mr. Barrington," one of the guards said.

"Take him out past the guesthouse and around to wherever he parked his car," Stone said, handing the man the end of the rope. "If you think he's too drunk, drive him home."

"Yes, sir. We'll take care of it."

Stone took a handkerchief from his pocket and dabbed

at his face and clothes. It wasn't bad enough to require a change.

"Oh," he said, turning to the guards. "Tell the front gate not to admit him to the grounds again, on my authority, and tell the restaurant manager not to take any further reservations from him."

"Yes, sir."

Stone and Billy returned to the party. Ben approached. "I saw that," he said. "I'm going to bar the guy from the studio."

"Leo's already taken care of that," Stone replied, "and he won't be welcome at the Arrington, either. Did you include any press for the party?"

"A couple of film critics."

"Then they will already have phoned their papers. You'd better get studio publicity to make some calls, and if they can't kill the story, at least be sure they have the facts straight."

"Good idea." Ben reached for his cell.

Stone grabbed a new drink from a passing waiter.

"I've heard some nasty things about that guy," Billy Barnett said. "You'd better watch yourself for a while."

"I don't think he'll be a problem. He's going to come off badly in the press over his lost Centurion deal, and I think he'll want to lie low for a while."

"The rumor is, he's connected to the Russian mob," Billy said.

"Oh, God, not those people again," Stone said, groaning.

"Don't go anywhere alone while you're out here," Billy said. "I can arrange for studio security to hang with you, until you're ready to go back to New York."

"Thanks, Billy, but I don't think that'll be necessary." Stone went to find Gala.

Ben put away his phone and approached Billy. "I heard that, Billy," he said. "Good idea—put a couple of people on Stone, but not too closely. Keep them in the background."

"Got it," Billy said.

7

S tone woke the following morning as the butler brought the breakfast cart into his bedroom. He woke Gala gently, and they had the breakfast. Stone began to read the *New York Times*, and Gala started on the L.A. papers.

"Uh-oh," she said.

"What's wrong?"

"Last night's incident made the papers, both the *Times* and the *Hollywood Reporter*."

"Are the pieces accurate?"

"Entirely."

"We can thank the Centurion press office for that."

"The problem is, any factual account of last night's events will humiliate Boris."

"Fine with me."

"Not that he doesn't deserve the humiliation, it's just that he will react badly."

"He seems to react badly to everything," Stone observed.

"Everything but unqualified praise," she admitted.

"Well, I don't see what I can do about that, except ignore him."

"Good luck with that."

"Do you have a suggestion for handling this?"

"That's the problem—there's no way to handle it. I mean, I don't think that Centurion is going to reverse its decision, do you?"

"Certainly not."

"Then we'll just have to sit it out and hope he doesn't show his face around the hotel again."

"Sounds like a plan."

"The *L. A. Times* piece refers to his being escorted out of the bar last week, after he insulted their film critic."

"The head of security mentioned that. Did I tell you that I ordered him banned from the hotel grounds?"

"No, but what a good idea!"

"And Leo Goldman has banned him from Centurion, canceled his gate pass."

The phone at bedside rang.

"Yes?"

"Mr. Barrington, there's a lady on the phone from an entertainment television show, *Hollywood Tonight*, who wishes to speak with you."

"All right, put her through." There was a click. "Mr. Barrington?"

"Yes?"

"This is Helen Carr at *Hollywood Tonight*."

"Good morning, Ms. Carr."

"I wonder if I could ask you a few questions about last night's incident at your home at the Arrington?"

"I'd rather not discuss it," Stone said, "but the piece in the *Times* this morning was substantially accurate."

"Mr. Tirov is saying that you pushed him into the swimming pool when he wasn't looking. Is that correct?"

"It is not. Mr. Tirov found his way into the pool without my assistance or that of anyone else, and there were numerous witnesses."

"May I quote you on that?"

"Please do, and now I'd like to finish my breakfast."

"Of course. Goodbye."

"Goodbye." He hung up the phone. "Now Tirov is saying I pushed him into the pool."

"He would say that."

Stone pushed away his tray. "I've got to get into the shower. Dino and I are playing golf at the Bel-Air Country Club, and we've got a ten o'clock tee time. What are your plans for the day?"

"I believe I'll stick close to home today. I'm sure Boris has found a way to blame me for last night, and I don't want to run into him."

"I don't blame you a bit."

S hortly before ten o'clock that morning, Stone and Dino stood, waiting for a foursome to tee off ahead of them at the Bel-Air Country Club, when they were approached by a man wearing a suit.

"Mr. Barrington?"

"Yes?"

"My name is Martin Glock. I'm the chairman of the membership committee at the club."

This didn't sound good, but Stone extended his hand. "How do you do, Mr. Glock?"

"Very well, thank you. We're aware that you've been playing here for a year or so as a guest of Leo Goldman at Centurion Studios."

"That's correct." I'm about to be kicked out of here, he thought. I smell Boris Tirov.

"Well, the membership committee met earlier this morning and elected three new members—yourself, your son, Peter, and his business partner, Ben Bacchetti. You'll be notified by mail, of course, but I wanted to take the opportunity to meet you and give you the news personally."

Stone heaved a sigh of relief. "Thank you so much, Mr. Glock, I'm delighted to hear it. May I introduce my guest? This is Dino Bacchetti, New York's police commissioner."

The two men shook hands. "Welcome, Commissioner. We'd be delighted to have you at the club anytime."

"Thank you, Mr. Glock."

"Please call me Martin. I'm afraid I have other news that isn't so good," Glock said.

"Oh?" Now what?

"The committee also considered the application of Mr. Boris Tirov, and he was declined, not least because of what we all read in the papers this morning. That, of course, is entirely confidential."

"Of course," Stone said. "I hope Mr. Tirov won't be given the impression that I had anything to do with his being declined."

"Certainly not. In cases like this we never give a reason for declining. You gentlemen appear to be up for teeing off. I hope you have a pleasant round."

"Thank you," Stone said. He teed his shot, took a couple of practice swings, and sliced his drive a good ten yards into the rough.

"Ah, your maiden drive as a new member," Dino said, teeing his ball. He took a practice swing and drove his shot even with Stone's but right down the center of the fairway.

They played the first nine and were making the turn when two large men made an appearance, apparently leaving their car in Stone Canyon Drive and coming through the high hedge.

"More members of the committee, come to congratulate you?" Dino asked.

"I doubt it," Stone said, picking a club from his bag and leaning on it. "I expect them to have Russian accents. Are you armed?"

Dino took his driver from his bag. "I am now."

"You Barrington?" the larger of the two asked. His accent was, indeed, Russian.

"Yes, I am, and this is my dear friend, the police commissioner."

The man looked at Dino and blinked. "That don't look like him."

"I get that all the time," Dino said.

"We got a message for you, Barrington," the man said, unbuttoning his jacket, "from Boris Tirov." He put his hand under his jacket.

"If that hand comes out with anything in it," Stone said, "you're going to get a message from the edge of a steel sand wedge, in your teeth." He displayed the implement for emphasis.

"And a driver, too," Dino said, waggling his club.

The man's hand stopped, then came out empty. "Dis is de message from Boris—he gonna kick your ass."

"Tell him," Stone said, "that I wish him a continued lack of success in that effort. Oh, and you might tell him there's news from the membership committee of this golf club—he has been rejected as a member." Stone smiled. "We just heard."

"He ain't gonna like that message," the man said.

"I hope not," Stone replied. "Now get your ass back through that hedge and out of here." He took a step toward the man, sand wedge at the ready.

The two men fumbled their way through the hedge and, a moment later, were heard to drive away.

"I think," Dino said, "you'd better start arming yourself with something more threatening than a sand wedge."

8

Stone and Dino finished their round and adjourned to the clubhouse bar for a sandwich.

Martin Glock was there and introduced them to a few other members, then he placed a key on the table. "Here's your locker key, Stone. I think you'll find it commodious enough for the commissioner's clubs, as well."

"Thank you, Martin."

"Oddly enough, I had a visit from Mr. Tirov while you were playing. Apparently, he had got wind of his rejection by the committee. I can't imagine how."

"Bad news travels fast, I suppose."

"Ah, yes. Mr. Tirov had to be assisted from the grounds—for the last time, I hope."

"I hope so, too."

"We've since heard that he's been barred from Centurion Studios and from the Arrington, as well."

"I can confirm that," Stone said.

"It seems the committee made the right decision. Good day, gentlemen." He strolled away.

"Well," Dino said, "if Boris was angry last night, imagine how he must be feeling right about now."

"I've given enough thought to Mr. Tirov," Stone said. "He is now officially barred from my mind."

They returned to the Arrington after lunch, and Stone excused himself for a swim. He got into his suit, grabbed a towel, and walked out to the pool, where he encountered the President of the United States happily swimming laps. He sat on the edge of the pool and waited for her to finish, while two Secret Service agents, a man and a woman, kept an eye on him.

Kate Lee pulled herself out of the pool and sat next to him. "I hope you don't mind my borrowing your pool. Mine was occupied. How are you, Stone?"

"I'm very well, thank you," he replied, putting a towel around her shoulders. "To what do I owe the honor?"

"Only a whim. Once in a while, I like to forget I'm a fairly new mother."

"And how is the heir?"

"Having his afternoon nap," she replied, "under the watchful eyes of a nanny and two Secret Service agents."

"Can I get you anything? Lunch? Other refreshment?"

"No, I'm perfectly fine. Though, from what I read in this morning's papers, you are not. Who is this fellow Tirov?"

"A nuisance who used to be married to a friend of mine."

"Those are the worst kind of nuisances, aren't they?"

"They are. And it's hard to meet a woman of a suitable age who doesn't have one lingering somewhere in the background."

"I suppose it is. Still, you seem to manage in that arena. Seems I have a couple of trusted aides who used to help out."

"You do. I suppose their country needed them more than I did."

"That's a healthy way to look at it."

"Why mope? It doesn't do any good."

"By the way, I haven't thanked you personally for meeting with three of my candidates for the high court."

"I was happy to do so, and I quite liked two of them."

"Yes, well, nobody liked the third very much. I've made my choice, which will be announced in a few days, and I don't think you'll be disappointed."

"I'm sure I won't."

"The court's first gay member."

"That we know about."

She laughed. "Quite right." She got to her feet, toweling her hair. "Well, I've got a meeting with an important Japanese gentleman in a couple of hours. I suppose I'd better go let somebody do something with my hair."

Stone got to his feet and gave her a peck on the cheek. "You'll knock him dead."

"From your lips to God's ear," she said, and strolled back toward her cottage.

*   *   *

Before Stone could get into the water, Gala arrived in a robe. "Who was that woman I saw you with?" she asked, shedding the robe.

"You wouldn't believe me if I told you," he said.

"Was that really she?"

"It was. Seems somebody was using her pool."

"I'll add her name to the list of people I've almost met."

"We'll arrange a proper introduction on some other occasion."

She dove into the pool, and Stone followed her, keeping pace with her laps. Soon they tired and got out.

"I'd like some lunch," Gala said. "Join me?"

"Dino and I lunched at the Bel-Air." He picked up a phone and handed it to her, and she ordered a club sandwich.

"By the way, I ran into the chairman of the membership committee while we were waiting to tee off and learned that Peter, Ben, and I have been elected to membership there."

"Congratulations."

"Thank you. We also learned that the committee had rejected Boris."

"Oh, God, another blow to his ego. Can we all survive it?"

"We had a visit, in the middle of our round, from two Russian gentlemen bearing greetings from him."

"Did anybody get hurt?"

"I threatened them with a sand wedge, and they went away."

"Good."

"And the membership chairman had a personal visit from Boris, which resulted in his being thrown out of the place."

"Boris isn't having a very good week, is he?"

"No, he's not, and it's going to get worse, unless he learns to contain himself."

"I wouldn't count on that," she said. "Maybe today would be a good time to go back to Santa Fe."

"Are you serious?"

"I am. Distance has always been the best tool when dealing with Boris."

"I'm unaccustomed to running from my enemies."

"You can put that on me. I can fly commercial, if you're not ready to leave."

"If you'll go and pack now, we can be there for cocktails."

She held his head in her hands and kissed him. "Thank you, my dear. I will feel ever so much better with every mile I can put between Boris and me."

Stone dispatched her to get ready, then he called the airport and ordered fuel, got a weather briefing, and filed a flight plan.

Dino came out of the house. "I hear you're flying back to Santa Fe."

"We are. Gala would like some distance between her and her ex."

"Good idea."

"Why don't you come with us? Spend a couple of days?"

"I think we will. When are we leaving?"

"In an hour?"

"Good."

9

The four of them, plus Bob, arrived in Santa Fe and piled into Gala's Range Rover, which her housekeeper had left for her, driving away the Aston Martin.

They arrived at Gala's house, and she installed the Bacchettis in the guesthouse, then headed toward the kitchen.

Stone was toting in their bags when he heard a crash, followed by a scream. He rushed into the kitchen, ready for a fight. Gala was cowering by the pantry door, and the place was a mess.

"It was a bear!" Gala shouted. "I saw him rush around the corner when I screamed."

Dino ran into the kitchen, his gun drawn. "What is it?"

"A visit from Papa Bear," Stone said. "He stayed for lunch." He waved a hand.

"Jesus," Dino said. "He wasn't very neat, was he?"

"Can you take a look outside and see if he's gone? You're the one with the weapon."

"Sure." Dino trod carefully through the mess and had a look outside. "Gone," he said, holstering his gun.

Stone hung up the phone. "I talked with Ed Eagle. He's calling somebody from the state wildlife service, and he gave me the name of a commercial cleaning business."

Finally, they were able to sit down for a drink, while the cleaners did their work. One of them came in, carrying a bucket. "Here's the problem," he said, holding up a broken bottle bearing a label. "A quart of honey."

"I buy honey in little jars," Gala said. "I like a spoonful in my tea, but I've never bought a quart."

"It was smeared on your back door," the cleaner said, "then the jar was broken outside. That brought the bear."

Gala put her face in her hands. "It's Boris," she said.

Later, an official of the wildlife service arrived and took a report. Stone showed him the remains of the broken honey jar.

"That would do it," he said. "She loves her honey."

"She?"

"And two cubs," the man said. "I found their tracks outside. We're going to have to organize a hunt. She's got a den somewhere up in the hills, and we'll have to anesthetize her and the cubs and take them up into the Sangre de Cristo Mountains for resettlement."

"She won't come back?"

"There's no telling," the man said. "We do the best we can. She'll remember where she found the honey, though." He gave Stone his card and left.

"I didn't hear you volunteering for the hunt," Dino said.

"I'm a city boy. What do I know about bear hunting? I'd just be in the way."

"Problem is, nobody's hunting Boris," Gala said.

"Once we get the house secured, you come back to New York with us," Stone said. "You deserve a rest from that guy."

"Invitation gratefully accepted," she replied.

They spent the following day getting the kitchen door replaced and the alarm system repaired, then took off for New York.

At Stone's house Gala seemed to relax for the first time since leaving L.A. Then she got a phone call; she listened for a moment, thanked the caller, and hung up in tears. "That was a friend of mine who's a real estate agent in Santa Fe. She heard that Boris is house hunting."

"In Santa Fe?"

"In Tesuque," she replied. "He wants to move into my neighborhood."

"I'll call Ed Eagle and ask him to get a temporary restraining order against Boris," Stone said.

"Will that work?"

"I'll find out." Stone called Ed and had a long conversation with him, then hung up. "Ed's going to try for an order that will keep him out of a two-mile radius from your home. If he can get it, and he thinks he can, that will keep him out of Tesuque."

"For now."

"Now is what we have to deal with."

"I can't impose on your hospitality forever."

"You're not imposing." Stone had a thought. "You expressed an interest in seeing my house in England. Still interested?"

"Oh, yes! Boris would never figure that out."

"You can bring your computer and work there."

"Perfect!"

"Let me make some calls and see if we can catch a ride on a bigger jet. It's kind of a trek in mine—we'd have to spend a night in Newfoundland or Ireland to break up the trip."

"However you want to do it is fine with me."

It took two calls before he found that the Strategic Services jet was flying to Paris the following day and could drop them in the south of England. Gala was thrilled with the news.

Stone had another thought. "Gala, do you know what kind of cell phone Boris uses?"

"He always gets the latest iPhone."

"Do you have the number?"

She recited it from memory.

Stone called his tech guy, Bob Cantor.

"Hello."

"Bob, it's Stone. You told me once that you had been working on some kind of tracer software for cell phones."

"I did, and it's up and running."

Stone gave him Tirov's number. "Can you arrange for me to get warnings if that phone is anywhere near me, like in England?"

"Sure. I'll send the guy an irresistible e-mail, and if he opens it, it will plant the software on his phone. At what range do you want the warning to be effective?"

"Couple of hundred miles?"

"Consider it done."

"Thanks, Bob." He hung up.

"What was that about?" she asked.

"Bob will arrange for us to get a warning if Boris gets within two hundred miles of us."

"How can he do that?"

"Don't ask."

"I won't."

"You might want to do a little shopping for England while you're in New York. It'll be pleasant this time of year, but it's not L.A. or Santa Fe."

"You mean I'll need a raincoat?"

"That's what I mean. A sweater or two, as well. The weather is, well, changeable."

Gala grabbed her purse. "Bloomingdale's, here I come." She kissed him goodbye and fled the house.

Stone thought he might take a few extra things, as well.

10

Gala finished her shopping at Bloomingdale's, then got a cab to the Ralph Lauren store at Madison and Seventy-second Street, thinking she would buy Stone a gift for his kindness to her. She looked around the antique jewelry department on the ground floor and found a handsome silver flask that looked big enough to hold a bottle of Knob Creek. She was waiting for it to be gift wrapped when she looked up and saw her ex-husband walk through the front door. She froze and tried to keep her face expressionless.

"Well, hello there," Boris said, striding toward her.

She held up an arm to fend him off. "Please," she said.

"Please, what? Aren't you glad to see me?"

"I am not."

"I'm sorry I wasn't there to help you with your encounter with the bear," he said. "Those things can be a real nuisance, I'm told. Once they associate your place with food, they come back over and over. I'd keep a shot-gun handy, if I were you."

"A shotgun might be a very good idea," she said.

"I hope you weren't thinking of me when you said that."

"What I think is no longer your business."

"What brings you to New York? Not running from me, I hope, because you can't. I'll always know where you are, and I'll always be there, if I like."

"I'm afraid Tesuque is no longer welcoming to you."

"What?"

"Just don't try buying in the village."

"Why, Gala, do you think you can stop me from living where I like?"

"Wait and see."

"That sounds a very interesting threat."

"Not a threat, a promise."

"We'll see. I keep track of you, you know. It's easy in this electronic age."

The salesclerk brought her package, and she signed for it and left Boris standing there.

"You'll be hearing from me!" he called after her as the door closed behind her.

She got into a cab, thinking. "Fifth Avenue and Fifty-ninth Street," she said to the driver.

He dropped her and she took the elevator downstairs to the Apple store. Half an hour later she left with a new number in her cell phone, and on the way home she com-posed an e-mail to a list of dear friends, giving them the new number and asking that they keep the number con-fidential.

*   *   *

S tone was at his desk when she got back.

"A productive shopping trip?" he asked.

"Yes and no."

"How's that?"

"I found the things I need for the trip, but I also ran into guess who at Ralph Lauren."

"I have to guess?"

"It won't be hard."

Stone's face fell. "Not what's-his-name!"

"One and the same."

"How did . . . Never mind, I think I know how he tracked you."

"How?"

"My airplane. There's an app that will allow you to follow any aircraft's track across the country. He would have tracked us to Santa Fe, then here."

"He has an airplane, too—a Learjet."

"What's his tail number?"

She told him.

Stone got on his iPhone and tracked the number. "It's at Teterboro, at Jet Aviation, where I park."

"He usually goes somewhere else on the field—Atlantic Aviation, I think."

"Not this time. He thinks he has us in his crosshairs, but he doesn't."

"Why not?"

"Because we're leaving tomorrow on the Strategic Services jet, a Gulfstream 650, and he won't be expecting that. He'll end up just watching their hangar, where I keep my airplane, until he gets tired of it. We'll be in England before he figures it out." He picked up the phone and called Mike Freeman at Strategic Services.

"You ready for your flight tomorrow, Stone?"

"I am, Mike. Would you let your pilot know that we'd like to board in the hangar, before the airplane is towed out?"

"Sure. Somebody tailing you?"

"Probably a couple of Russian gentlemen."

"I'll see what I can do about that."

"Thanks, I appreciate that. Will you be flying with us tomorrow?"

"Me and Viv Bacchetti. We have business in Paris and Rome."

"Why don't you stop by my place for a couple of days, since we're landing there anyway."

"Wish I could, but duty calls. Maybe on the way back, if you're there long enough. We'll be on the continent for a week to ten days. One of our stops is attending the opening of the new Arrington, in Rome. Will you be coming down for that?"

"It's a thought. Let's see how it goes."

"Okay, see you tomorrow." He hung up.

"We'll board tomorrow in the hangar, protecting us from prying eyes. My friend Mike Freeman is coming with us, and so is Viv Bacchetti, who works for him."

"How nice. Oh, and here's a little something for you." She handed him a gift-wrapped package.

Stone untied the ribbon and opened it. "Wow! That will hold a whole bottle!" He walked to the bar, opened a new bottle of Knob Creek, found a little silver funnel and filled the flask. "Perfect!" He gave her a big kiss.

"I thought it was *you*."

"And you were right." He set the flask in his briefcase. "Come on, you haven't had the tour yet."

He showed her the living room, dining room, and his study, then took her up to the master suite, where Fred had already deposited her luggage in her dressing room.

"What are we doing for dinner tonight?"

"I think we'll have it here, in my study, just the two of us."

"Then I don't have to dress?"

"You may wear as little as you like."

"Well, no, not if someone is serving us."

"A dressing gown will do."

"I think that's called 'slipping into something more comfortable.'"

"I believe so."

"What time are we departing tomorrow?"

"We taxi at eight AM sharp, which means we'll have to leave the house at six-thirty, to allow for rush-hour traffic between here and Teterboro. Breakfast at five?"

"If you can wake me."

"I'll find a way."

11

F red drove them to Teterboro the following morning in the Bentley, and they used the back entrance
to the Strategic Services hangar to avoid walking to
the airplane through Jet Aviation.

The crew welcomed them and took their luggage, and
shortly, Mike and Viv were aboard, along with some
other Strategic employees. A tractor towed the big business jet out of the hangar and onto the ramp, and the
crew, having already run through their initial checklists,
immediately started the engines. Moments later they
were taxiing.

Mike came and sat down next to Stone. "You were
right about having a tail. Two large Russian gentlemen.
My people discouraged them, and they have no idea that
you're on this aircraft."

"Thank you, Mike, that's a relief."

"The crew has requested an expedited departure.

There's not a lot of traffic this morning, so we'll be wheels-up shortly." As he spoke the airplane made a turn and began its takeoff roll; a moment later the nose lifted, and they heard the sound of the landing gear coming up.

"We're off," Stone said to Gala.

"What a relief!"

"He won't know we're on this airplane, so he won't know where we're going."

"Wonderful. I think he's been tracking me with my cell phone, so I went to the Apple store yesterday and had the number changed. Only a few people have the new number."

"Good move."

Half an hour later they were at flight level 510—fifty thousand feet—and headed toward the Atlantic. As they leveled off, the captain turned off the seat belt sign, and Mike excused himself. "Gotta go to work," he said. "We're having a planning meeting for the opening of the Rome Arrington."

Stone opened his briefcase and dug into the envelope of paperwork that his secretary, Joan Robertson, had put there for him, next to his new flask. He looked up at Gala, who was already asleep, a light cashmere blanket tucked around her. He checked the moving map display for their routing, which took them over Newfoundland, south of Greenland and Iceland, making landfall in Scotland. From there they would be cleared to the old World War II bomber strip on Stone's property, near Beaulicu (pronounced "Bewley"), seven thousand feet of well-kept concrete runway. They were flying higher and faster than the airlines, and with a tailwind of more than a hundred knots, their time en route would be only another five hours and change. Stone settled down to work, e-mailing his responses to letters, with a copy to Joan, all handled by the on-board Wi-Fi.

They were off the southern tip of Greenland, in severe clear weather, when the flight attendant brought him a cordless phone. "Satphone for you," she said.

"Hello?"

"It's Joan." She sounded breathless.

"Are you all right?"

"I think so. We just had a . . . disturbance here."

"What kind of disturbance?"

"A man walked through the street door—I hadn't locked it—and demanded to see you."

"Who was he?"

"I don't know—fiftyish, thick gray hair, some sort of accent."

"Boris Tirov."

"If you say so. Who is he?"

"Gala's ex-husband."

"Not another one of those. You have a collection."

"What happened?"

"I told him you were not available, and before I could stop him, he barged into your office. I went after him with my .45." Joan kept the pistol in a desk drawer. "He was trying to take it away from me when Fred walked in from the garage and saw what was going on. He kicked the guy in a knee, bringing him down, and I got in a lick to his head with the .45. Fred got him in some sort of armlock and hustled him out onto the street, where the guy made a run for a car, as best he could with a sore knee. I called Dino and left it with him."

"That was exactly the right thing to do," Stone said. "You and Fred handled yourselves perfectly. I doubt if he'll come around again, but he does have some muscle at his disposal, so keep the street door locked, and don't let anyone in you don't know."

"I already figured out that part."

"I hope you didn't mention where I was."

"Nope, just that you were unavailable."

"He'll probably have somebody keep an eye on the house. If you see anybody suspicious, call Dino. Tirov's people tend to be big Russian guys with bald heads, though some of them I've seen have hair."

"I'll keep that in mind."

"Joan?"

"Yes?"

"Try not to shoot anybody, if you can help it. The paperwork would be awful to deal with."

"And I'd be the one dealing with it?"

"There is that, too."

"Next time, a heads-up would be nice, if you're expecting rough visitors."

"I wasn't expecting it, and that's my fault. You and Fred handled it beautifully."

"Thank you so much. That makes me feel almost human again. That guy scared the shit out of me."

"I know how that must have been. Tell you what, I'll

get Mike Freeman to station a couple of men over there for a few days."

"I would really appreciate that. Otherwise, I'd have to make Fred sit in my office all day."

"Consider it done. You okay now?"

"Much better," she said. "I might have a little of your bourbon."

"Feel free—you've earned it. Bye."

"Bye." They both hung up.

He looked at Gala and found her staring at him. "I think I got the gist of that from your end of the conversation."

"Good, then I won't have to repeat myself. You didn't hear Joan's description of how she and Fred dealt with Boris. Fred kicked him in the knee, and Joan clipped him with her .45."

"Clipped him?"

"Hit him in the head. Then Fred threw him into the street."

"Oh, good."

"Excuse me a minute, I need to talk with Mike." He got up and went forward to where the Strategic people were holding their meeting, whispered his request to Mike, and got a quick nod. Mike picked up a telephone and dialed a number.

Stone returned to his seat and found Gala asleep again. Soon, he was asleep himself.

12

The G650 set down on the Windward Hall landing strip in the long English twilight. The crew shut down one engine while Stone, Gala, Bob, and their luggage were taken off, then as they got into the estate's Range Rover, the engine was restarted and the aircraft took off on its short flight to Le Bourget, Paris.

"Oh, look!" Gala said as the house hove into view. Bob seemed to have pretty much the same reaction, putting his head out the window and barking at the house. All the lights were on, and the place glowed. "It's so beautiful!" Gala said.

They were settled into the master suite, then went down to the library, where a table had been set for their dinner. They had had only a sandwich on the airplane.

Stone phoned home and got Joan. "Everything all right there?"

"No further disturbance," Joan said, "and Mike's people are camped out in my office. We're happy as clams here."

"Good. We're just sitting down to dinner, so I'll say goodbye."

Geoffrey, the butler, had left a selection of wines for their dinner; Stone chose one and uncorked it, then decanted it to rid the wine of its sediment. They had a drink before the fire while the wine took a breath.

"It's another world," Gala said, looking around, "and one without Boris in it."

"The best kind."

Dinner was served, and they enjoyed themselves.

The following morning, after a perfect night's sleep, Stone decided that they should attend the grand opening of the Rome Arrington, a few days hence. At noon he called Pat Frank, who ran the aircraft management service that took care of his airplane, and asked her to have his Citation CJ3 Plus flown to his home in England.

"I can arrange that," Pat said. "How soon do you need it?"

"A couple of days will be okay, but do something else for me, please."

"Sure."

"Have my tail number blocked from the various flight-tracking services."

"Is someone too interested in your movements?"

"That is the case."

"I'd better get on that now, then, it takes a day or two to get it done."

"Tell your pilot he'll be driven to Heathrow for his flight home."

"Will do. Anything else?"

"Not at the moment." They both hung up.

"That was easy," Gala said.

"Everything is easier when you're organized."

Stone looked out the window at the sky. "The forecast is good for today. How would you like a ride and a picnic lunch?"

"Sounds perfect."

T he horses were brought from the stables, and they cantered across the estate, jumped a stone wall, and were on the property next door. "That's our Arrington country hotel," Stone said, pointing at the larger house as they rode past. "The two properties together run to something over five hundred acres."

"What a nice neighbor to have."

They rode along the Beaulieu River, which was at flood tide, and found a spot for lunch in the shade of some trees. The horses nibbled at the grass while they spread a blanket and unpacked their lunch. Stone opened a bottle of cold Chardonnay, and they lunched on smoked salmon sandwiches and a salad.

"Two days ago we were in the high desert of Santa Fe," she said, "and suddenly, we're in England, picnicking."

"A miracle of modern-day air travel."

"A miracle of some sort. I feel safe for the first time since my divorce was final. I don't think I had realized the extent to which Boris was eating at my sense of well-being. I confess to you that I considered shooting him once. My sister, Susannah, dealt with an ex-husband that way."

"Do you remember what a hassle that was for her, and especially for Ed, who had to deal with the legal consequences?"

"I remember, and she told me it was worth it to be rid of him."

"Self-defense is an effective motive for a shooting, but killing someone, for whatever reason, is a pain in the ass. That will haunt Susannah for her whole life."

"At least she *has* a life."

"You have a point. Just remember that killing somebody is never an easy solution to your problems. Between Ed and me, we can sue Boris into submission. It will take a while, and it will be expensive, but it can be done."

"The problem is, Boris doesn't understand your logic. He considers revenge a reasonable motive for anything, and between his money and his connections with the Russian mob, he has the means to carry it out. I can tell you from experience that right now, he's very angry, and he's plotting."

"He's also on the other side of a very large ocean, and he will have plenty of time to cool off before we cross it again."

"You don't understand, Stone. Boris doesn't cool off, he just simmers until the next time he comes to a boil."

"How has he managed to succeed in Hollywood if he's that kind of person? He's going to have a very hard time finding another studio deal, after what's happened over the past ten days."

"Hollywood doesn't much care what kind of person he is, as long as he makes money for them, and his series of thrillers have brought in something like a billion and a half dollars in worldwide ticket sales over the past four years. That kind of cash flow can cause the community to look the other way. I'll bet you that within a week, in spite of all that happened with Centurion and the Arrington and the Bel-Air Country Club, Boris will have a deal with another studio."

"I won't take that bet, because you could be right," Stone said. "Come on, let's ride down to the mouth of the river, and I'll show you the Solent."

"What's the Solent?"

"It's the body of water that separates England from the Isle of Wight. It's only a couple of miles wide, but it's the capital of yachting in England, maybe in Europe."

"Do you have a boat?"

"I have one on order that's due for delivery here any day, now."

"What sort of boat?"

"A Hinckley 43, a very nice little motor yacht. It will be good for pottering around the Solent and up and down the English Channel, and it's easily managed by one or two people, so it doesn't require a professional crew."

"Is it American-made?"

"Yes. I didn't know enough about British boats to be comfortable ordering one, but I know Hinckley very well. Their factory is an hour's drive from my house in Maine."

"Can we go out on it when it comes?"

"That's what it's for." Stone's cell phone vibrated in his pocket, and he glanced at the phone. A message appeared on-screen: Tracking Tirov. Stone pressed a button, and a map of the British Isles appeared on the screen. A green ball appeared over Ireland, and it was moving toward England.

"What is it?" Gala asked

"Just a text message," Stone replied, and put away the phone.

13

They rode back to the house, gave the horses to the groom, and went upstairs for a jet lag–defeating nap. Gala was sleeping soundly in minutes. Stone switched on his phone and chose the tracking app. The green dot was at Heathrow.

She woke him from his nap in the late afternoon with a gentle touch, followed by more caresses. He rose to the occasion, and soon they were entwined. Recovery required another, shorter nap, afterward they showered together, then dressed for dinner.

While Gala did her makeup, Stone checked his phone again. The green dot was in the West End of London, and by zooming in, he could place it at Claridge's Hotel.

They were having drinks when Geoffrey came in with

a telephone. "Dame Felicity Devonshire for you, Mr. Barrington."

Stone took the phone from him. "Good evening," he said.

"My spies told me you were back."

"An unexpected trip. I've brought a friend. Where are you?"

"I just got to my Beaulieu River house."

"We're just having a drink. Why don't you join us for dinner?"

"Sold. I'm assuming your friend is female?"

"Quite right."

"No matter. I'll be at your dock in half an hour."

"You'll be met." He hung up and rang for Geoffrey.

"Yes, sir?"

"Dame Felicity will be at our dock in half an hour. Will you have her met, please? And we'll need another place set for dinner."

"And who is Dame Felicity Devonshire?" Gala asked.

"An old acquaintance. You'll enjoy her."

"And why does her name sound familiar?"

"She is the director of MI6, the British foreign intelligence service, the equivalent of our CIA."

"Ah, I expect I've read that name in the papers."

"Her name used to be a deep dark secret, but things have loosened up a bit."

"And how did you come to know her?"

Stone thought about that. "Let's see. . . . Ah yes, MI6 retained me once to help them locate a former operative of theirs in the States."

"And did you locate the operative?"

"I did, but I didn't know it for a while. He had changed his identity."

"It all sounds very mysterious."

"Mysterious and confidential. I had to sign the Official Secrets Act, which means I could be jailed if I blabbed."

"So you won't tell me more?"

"What, do you want to see me in Wormwood Scrubs prison?"

"You make it sound ghastly."

"All British prisons are ghastly. Hardly any of them have proper plumbing, last time I heard."

"How do they . . . ?"

"Slop buckets."

"Ugh."

"Yes, I think they haven't updated because they consider the conditions to be a deterrent to criminals."

"It's enough of a deterrent for me."

"And for me, too, so don't wheedle me into compromising myself."

"Was I wheedling?"

"You were about to, weren't you?"

"Well, yes, though I like to think I would have wheedled charmingly."

"I don't doubt it for a moment."

"I should have wheedled when we were in bed, then I would have had more leverage."

"So to speak."

She laughed. "So to speak."

*   *   *

Felicity bustled in on schedule, introductions were made, and a stiff whiskey and soda placed in her hand by Geoffrey, who had not had to ask her pleasure.

"I feel so at home in this house," she said, and behind her, Gala rolled her eyes.

"You've known it far longer than I," Stone said, letting himself off her hook. He turned to Gala. "It was Felicity who insisted I fly here from Rome. She made me buy the house."

"What happened to the previous owner?"

"He was ill at the time and died a few weeks later."

"It all looks so fresh," she said.

"Yes, a well-known London designer completely redid it for the previous owner. It was nearly done when I first saw it."

"She is a very good designer," Gala said, casting an eye around the room.

"She is, indeed," Felicity said. "Stone and his French partner had her do the big house next door, too. It's now an Arrington."

"We saw it this afternoon while riding," Gala said.

"Stone, has your new boat arrived?"

"It's due any day. Hinckley is sending over a team to launch it and to educate me in its operation."

"Wasn't your last boat a Hinckley?"

"Yes, but the layout and equipment are all new to me. I'll need to know how to handle light maintenance."

"And who will do the heavy maintenance?"

"Hinckley has arranged that with a Southampton yard."

"How convenient."

"Do you live nearby, Dame Felicity?" Gala asked.

"Oh, yes, just across the river."

"How convenient."

Stone cringed a little.

"Yes, it is, isn't it? And you must drop the Dame—I'm just plain Felicity."

"Thank you."

"You are most welcome, Gala."

Geoffrey called them to table, and they polished off their drinks. They were given a pâté of smoked mackerel to start, with a glass of very dry sherry, and a crown roast of lamb to follow, with potatoes au gratin and haricots verts.

"The lamb is from the estate next door," Stone said, "and the vegetables are from our own garden."

"And the wine?" Gala asked.

"A Chateau Palmer 1978," Stone replied, swirling some in his glass and tasting it. "I think we'll drink it."

Both women made appreciative noises about the wine.

"Felicity," Gala said, "Stone tells me you are in the intelligence business."

"I hope that's all he told you," she said, "or I'll have to have him clapped in irons."

"He was very discreet," Gala said. "But I'm a screen-writer by trade, and I sometimes write about your sort of derring-do. Perhaps if Stone gives you enough wine, you'll tell me some trade secrets that I can put into a film."

"If Stone gives me enough wine, he knows I'll tell all," Felicity replied. "So I'd better be very careful."

Stone poured her another glass of the Palmer, and they all had a good laugh.

14

In bed after dinner Gala threw a leg over Stone's and stuck her tongue in his ear.

Stone responded.

"Now that I have your attention," she said.

"You have it. Now what?"

"I wanted to bring up a subject that I have not broached before."

"Why haven't you broached it?"

"Because the occasion had not arisen."

"The occasion for what?"

"A potential threesome."

Now she had his attention. "When did that occasion arise?"

"At dinner."

"Somehow I missed that."

"Men can be *so* obtuse."

"I suppose so."

"It was obvious that you and Dame Felicity have, in the past, been an item. Perhaps you still are."

"Not at the moment."

She laughed. "Well, right now, I'm taking up all the space."

"Are you saying you'd like to share the space with Felicity?"

"The thought crossed my mind. It crossed hers, too."

"Somehow I missed that."

"Of course you did. She made it perfectly clear to me, though."

"How, exactly, did she do that?"

"I'm not sure I should tell you. I don't know how you would react."

"Try me."

"All right, she ran a fingernail up the inside of my thigh, under the dinner table."

"You're kidding."

"Nope."

"And how did you respond to that?"

"With pleasure. I told her I'd get back to her."

"I didn't hear that, and I was there all the time."

"Oh, not in so many words. I just gave her to understand that the matter was under consideration."

"How, exactly, did you convey that?"

"Let's just say that I was discreetly receptive."

"Oh."

"And, need I point out that since the subject arose, you have responded in your own particular way?" She held him in her hand and squeezed.

"I think I must be responding to you."

"Well, I hope so, but the subject under discussion produced a pronounced indication of interest. Have you and Felicity ever entertained another woman in bed?"

"Not that I recall."

"Well, if that had occurred, I'm sure you would recall it."

"I expect so."

"What experience have you had with threesomes?"

"That's a very direct question," he said.

"I'm a very direct woman."

"I've noticed that and found it attractive."

"So, answer the question."

"A couple of times."

"With what success?"

"Well, it happened—I guess that's success."

"And how did you respond?"

"How do you think I responded?"

"Let me put it another way—on each occasion, who seemed to enjoy it most?"

"On both occasions, the women seemed to enjoy it most."

"Enjoyed each other, you mean?"

"Well, yes."

"At your expense?"

"You might put it that way."

"That's unfortunate. It shows a lack of courtesy on their part. You were, after all, the host."

"I suppose so."

"Well, let me make you a promise. Should we, you and

I, decide, both of us together, to invite another woman into our bed, you will not go unattended. By either of us."

"How can you speak for the other woman?"

"It's a matter of judgment. Felicity, for example, is more interested in you than in me—although she is certainly interested in me. She demonstrated that to my satisfaction tonight."

"You amaze me."

"I assure you, should we decide to extend the invitation, Felicity and I will both amaze you."

"How does one extend such an invitation?"

"You leave that to me."

"Now that I've answered your questions, how much experience have you had in this area?"

"Five or six times, starting in college."

"With what result?"

"After some initial fumbling, very satisfactory."

At that point, the phone rang, and Stone picked it up. "Hello?"

"It's Felicity."

"Hello, there." He held the phone away from his ear, so that Gala could listen in.

"I'm down at your dock, and my boat won't start. Neither Geoffrey nor I can make it work."

Stone looked at Gala, who was smiling and nodding. "In that case, I think Geoffrey should return you to the house, and Gala and I will make you comfortable here. The boat can wait until tomorrow."

"What a lovely invitation."

Gala leaned in. "We will both look forward to receiving you. Just come up to the master suite."

"How delightful. See you shortly." She hung up, and so did Stone.

"See how easy that was?" Gala said.

"I am astonished," Stone replied.

"Now, you move over to the center of the bed, and leave room for her on the other side of you."

Stone complied.

Shortly, there was a soft knock on the door.

"Come in," Gala called.

Felicity entered the room, came over to the bed, and kissed, first Stone, then Gala.

"Use my dressing room," Gala said, pointing. "There's a dressing gown, if you need one."

"I don't think I will need it," Felicity said, heading for the dressing room. She emerged shortly and got into bed next to Stone. Everyone kissed, then, as if by plan, the two women concentrated on Stone, who received the attention with alacrity.

Then they turned their attention to each other, while Stone watched and offered the occasional caress.

When they had satisfied each other and given Stone time to recover, they received him in turn, while the other watched and helped.

Then, exhausted, they all fell asleep.

The following morning, they repeated the experience, with variations. Then, while the two women showered together, Stone ordered breakfast and joined them, until the food arrived.

*   *   *

Following breakfast, they returned custody of Felicity to Geoffrey, who returned her to the dock.

"Oh, I'd better go and have a look at her boat," Stone said.

"Don't bother," Felicity replied. "I'm sure it will start immediately."

They both laughed.

"Now," Gala said when Felicity had departed, "was that a satisfactory experience?"

"Entirely satisfactory," Stone said, kissing her.

"It could happen again," Gala said, "with Felicity or some other suitable woman."

"How will I know when?"

"I'll be sure and let you know. Just place yourself in my hands, so to speak."

"I rather enjoy being in your hands, so to speak."

15

S tone was settling into the study to get some work done when Gala came in. "Would you mind terribly if I missed lunch with you today? I'd like to run up to London and get some shopping done."

"Of course, go right ahead. I'll give you a car."

"I'd rather take the train, if someone will give me a lift to Southampton station."

Stone lifted a phone and spoke to Geoffrey, then hung up. "The car will be out front in five minutes. Get Geoffrey's number and let him know on what train you're returning, and he'll meet you at the station."

She kissed him and departed.

Stone worked until early afternoon, having a sandwich in the library for lunch, then, as New York began its day, began receiving calls. Joan was first.

"We're still alive and well here," she said.

"Good. I think you can dismiss Mike's men. I have reason to believe that Tirov has left the city."

"Will do."

Bob Cantor called next. "I've made some refinements to my tracking software," he said. He gave Stone instructions on reloading the software. "There," he said. "Would you like to add any other numbers to be tracked?"

Stone thought about it, then gave Bob Gala's new number.

"Great, you're all set. I've assigned the color yellow to her phone, to make it easier to distinguish it. If you want to add any other phones, you'll be given a choice of colors."

"Thanks, Bob." He hung up, then switched on the phone and checked for Gala. He picked up a yellow dot in the Savile Row area of London, and by zooming in, he was able to identify the location of Cecconi's, a restaurant. Then, to his surprise, a green dot appeared on the screen at the same location, but slightly apart from the yellow. He called Gala's number.

"Hello?"

"Hi, where are you?"

"I'm at Cecconi's, having a bite at the bar," she said.

"Then you should know that Tirov appears to be in the same restaurant."

"Oh, my God! How did you know?"

"I neglected to tell you that Bob Cantor's app had tracked him to London. My advice is just to pay your check and sneak out, so as to avoid a confrontation."

"I certainly will. Goodbye."

Stone watched as the yellow dot left the location and

moved down to Burlington Arcade, while the green dot remained. Relieved, he closed his phone.

Geoffrey came into the room. "Dame Felicity is on the phone for you, Mr. Barrington. Line one."

"Thank you, Geoffrey. Any trouble getting her boat started this morning?"

"None whatever, sir. I think it must have been flooded."

Stone picked up the phone. "Good morning again."

"And good morning to you."

"No trouble getting your boat started this morning?"

"None. I expect the engine was flooded. Did we surprise you last night?"

"Yes, but very pleasantly. I can't think when I've enjoyed being surprised so much."

"You certainly rose to the occasion, and you acquitted yourself very nicely."

"I had a lot of inspiration."

"Perhaps we'll do it again sometime."

"I wouldn't be surprised."

"She's a lovely girl. I can see why you're so attracted to her."

"She said much the same about you."

"I'm so glad. Oh, has your post arrived yet?"

"Not yet."

"When it does, you may expect to receive some interesting news."

"Is that meant to be a surprise, too?"

"It is."

At that moment, Geoffrey entered with some letters on a silver tray.

"Ah, here's the post now. Which one is the surprise?"

"The one posted from the Isle of Wight."

Stone found the postmark and opened the letter. It was from the secretary of the famous old yacht club across the Solent, informing him that he had been elected to membership. "Good God!" he said. "How did this happen?"

"Secretly," she said. "You made a very good impression at the club, and if you'll remember, you had several flag officers as guests at your dinner party last year."

"Yes, I remember."

"It was not difficult to gather the requisite number of proposers for your application, all of them prominent in the club. Those things can't be rushed, but nearly a year has passed, and the wheels ground steadily in your absence."

"I can't thank you enough, Felicity," he said earnestly. "It's a wonderful club, and I shall enjoy using it."

"Let me give you a phone number," she said.

He wrote it down.

"That's the club tailor, in Southampton. Ring him and he'll come over and measure you for a reefer suit and a mess kit, and he'll sell you a cap, as well. You'll need both."

"I shall certainly do so."

"You'll also need a stickpin for your necktie. That's part of the regalia. Benzie's, the jewelry store on the Parade in Cowes, will provide that."

"I'll stop in on my next trip over."

"I can't wait to see your new boat."

"I'll ring you as soon as I get my hands on it."

"Goodbye then, and congratulations."

"Thank you."

"And *au revoir*."

"Indeed." He hung up, called the tailor to make an appointment.

"You're at Windward Hall, on the Beaulieu, is that right, Mr. Barrington?"

"That's correct."

"I have another call to make near you today. I could visit you at, say, four?"

"Perfect."

"And may I ask, sir, what size hat do you wear?"

"Seven and a half."

"I'll bring a couple."

"Good. See you then." He hung up.

He had been working for an hour when a call came in on his cell phone. "Hello?"

"Stone, it's Phil Bennett, at Hinckley." Bennett was the sales director.

"How are you, Phil?"

"Very well, thanks. I have good news. Your boat arrived at Southampton the day before yesterday and cleared customs yesterday. Our team is working on unpacking and cleaning it now, and they tell me they can deliver her to your dock tomorrow around noon."

"Excellent news!"

"Their names are Chris and Dustin. I'll give you their cell numbers."

Stone wrote them down.

"They've arranged lodging at an inn near your house, so your training can begin tomorrow, if that's all right."

Three days of training were included in the price. "It could not be more perfect."

"Is your dock well marked?"

"There's a sign saying 'Windward Hall.'"

"They'll call when they're a few minutes out."

"I'll look forward to seeing them." He hung up and Geoffrey reappeared.

"Ms. Wilde has rung from London. She'll be on the five-ten from Waterloo Station. Shall I meet her, sir?"

"No, just bring the Porsche around, and I'll meet her myself."

"You know the route to the station, sir?"

"I do."

Geoffrey handed him the keys to the Porsche. "The car is already out front, sir. I'd allow twenty minutes to drive to the station."

"That's good. I'm expecting a tailor at four o'clock. You may show him in here when he arrives."

"Very good, sir." And Geoffrey left him to his work.

The tailor arrived on time, and Stone selected fabric for the two suits, then tried on a hat. He had never worn a club yachting cap, and, in the mirror, he thought he looked ridiculous. Nevertheless, he bought two.

16

Stone met Gala and several shopping bags at Southampton station and drove her back to the house. "How did your day go?"

"Just fine. I enjoyed myself."

"Did you encounter Boris at Cecconi?"

"I was sitting on the back side of the bar, and I saw him come in and take a table on the other side of the room. I got out without being seen, I think."

"That's a relief. What do you suppose he's doing in London?"

"Business, I expect. He often shoots at Pinewood Studios."

"So, he's not stalking you in England?"

"I don't think so."

"Good. Oh, more good news—my new boat is being delivered to the dock at around noon tomorrow. Part of my deal with Hinckley is that I get three days' training. Would you enjoy that?"

"I would. Will it be hard, do you think?"

"Hinckleys are very easy to handle. Do you mind if I ask Felicity to join us?"

"Not at all."

"She called this morning. She got me elected to the yacht club at Cowes while I was away."

"Congratulations."

"I'll take you to dinner there. You'll enjoy it."

They arrived back at Windward Hall, and Gala went to put away her things and take a nap. Stone called Felicity, told her about the boat, and arranged to pick her up at her dock.

"I'll need to leave for London around five," she said. "Early meeting Monday morning."

"We'll have you back by then."

T he following day, they took a box of sandwiches down to the dock, just in time to see the new boat coming up the river. She pulled alongside, and Stone and Gala took her lines.

Half an hour later, they had been through the drill of checking fluids, locating the major systems. They picked up Felicity, and she and Gala were introduced to the Jet-Stick, which controlled the boat.

"All Hinckley motorboats have jet drives," Chris told her. "There's no propeller and no rudder. The JetStick controls a computer that controls both jet drives and a bow thruster, so if you want to go ahead, you push the stick forward. If you want to go aft, you push it backward, and if you want to go sideways, you push it sideways, which is very handy for docking."

They both tried docking the boat and found it easy.

"And you can spin the boat on her own axis, by twisting the JetStick." Chris demonstrated.

They took the boat down the river and Chris demonstrated the electric anchoring process, then they had lunch.

At five, they returned Felicity to her dock, then practiced more docking at Windward. Then Stone had the two Hinckley men driven to their inn, and arranged a pickup time for the following day.

"I think one more day of training will do it for me," Stone said. "It's similar enough to my old Hinckley Picnic Boat."

"Good, then we'll have a day or two to see some of England," Chris said.

Stone and Gala returned to Windward Hall for dinner.

They were having drinks in the library when Geoffrey entered the room. "There's a call for Ms. Wilde," he said.

"That's odd," Gala said. "Who's calling?"

"He wouldn't say, but the gentleman did have a foreign accent."

Stone and Gala exchanged a glance. "Geoffrey, tell the gentleman that there is no Ms. Wilde here, nor will there be, and ask him not to phone again."

Geoffrey left to deliver the message. "Thank you, Stone. I can't imagine how he got this number."

"The house is listed in the phone book. What I can't imagine is how he learned where I live."

"Boris has been known to employ private detectives to get information on the people he does business with. It would not shock me to learn that he uses them in London, as well."

Geoffrey returned to refresh their drinks.

"How did the gentleman take it, Geoffrey?" Stone asked.

"Poorly, sir. I had finally to hang up on him."

"If he calls back, just tell him to go away."

"With pleasure, sir. Dinner will be served in about twenty minutes."

"If Boris persists, I'm going to have to find a way to deal with him," Stone said.

"I hope it doesn't come to that."

"He seems to be pathological about you."

"I don't think that's too strong a term, but I don't think you can have him committed."

"And it would be a lot of trouble to kill him. Still . . ."

Gala laughed. "Don't be tempted."

"I'll try to restrain myself."

Stone's cell phone rang. "Hello?"

"Mr. Barrington?"

"Yes?"

"This is Jefferson Bramble. I'm the delivery pilot for your airplane."

"Where are you?"

"I've made landfall, and I'm about an hour out of your airfield."

"Fly the published approach into my strip, and I'll

have customs meet you, and someone to drive you wherever you need to go."

"Just to the nearest railroad station. I'll get a train to London. I have a hotel reservation there."

"Thank you, Jefferson." They hung up as Geoffrey entered with dinner.

"Geoffrey, my airplane is landing in an hour. Will you phone the customs people and inform them, then have the pilot driven to the station after he's cleared with the local officials?"

"Certainly, sir. Customs are getting accustomed to visiting your airfield."

"Good." They sat down to dinner.

An hour later, as they were on coffee, the door to the library opened, and Dino walked in.

"Good evening," he said.

"Good God! You didn't tell me you were coming."

"I hitched a ride on your airplane—Joan arranged it for me. I'll fly down to Rome with you for the opening of the Arrington."

"Sit down and have some dinner." Geoffrey was ready for him.

"You must be tired," Stone said.

"Well, it wasn't the same as traveling on a G650." He sat down, and Stone poured him a glass of wine. When he was finished, Geoffrey took him upstairs and got him quartered.

Stone and Gala soon followed.

17

The following morning they met downstairs for breakfast. "We have a choice for you," Stone said to Dino. "You can come out with us on my new boat—I'm still in training—or you can sit on your ass all day."

"I did enough of that yesterday," Dino said. "I'll take the boat."

Chris and Dustin were waiting for them, and they did a quick review of checking fluids and the starting procedure, then they cast off and started downriver with Gala at the helm and Dino watching her like a hawk. As they neared the mouth of the river another boat passed them, going in the opposite direction. Gala ducked and asked Dino to take the helm, and they exchanged seats.

"Something wrong?" Stone asked.

"That other boat—there were two men on it, and I know one of them."

"Who is he?"

"His name is Kharzy, big fellow with a bald head. He sometimes works for Boris."

"Did you see Boris aboard?"

"I saw the back of one other man, but I don't think it was Boris. If he's aboard, he must be below."

Stone moved her to a cabin seat then took the seat next to Dino. "Are you armed?" he asked.

"Always," Dino replied. "Shall I stand by to repel boarders?"

"I don't know if they saw Gala. Let's see if they turn around." Stone watched as the boat continued up the river. He got out his cell phone.

"Good morning, Windward Hall."

"Geoffrey, it's Mr. Barrington. There is a boat headed upriver that may contain the gentleman who called last night. Please go down to the dock and refuse them permission to land. If they attempt to land, call the police and tell them we have intruders who are making a nuisance of themselves."

"Right away, sir."

"Please keep me posted on the outcome."

"Certainly, sir." They both hung up.

"Now, let's get out of here, so that when they come back we'll already be in Cowes." He shoved the throttles forward, and they were soon doing thirty knots up the Solent. When they were out of sight of the Beaulieu River, Stone got out his phone and called the yacht club.

"Good morning, Royal Yacht Squadron."

"Good morning, this is Stone Barrington. I'm a new member."

"Of course, Mr. Barrington, we're looking forward to seeing you at the Castle."

"I'm motoring on the Solent at the moment, headed your way. May I book lunch for five people, dressed in sailing clothes?"

"Of course, sir. We'll be serving in the pavilion, behind the Castle."

"Half an hour?"

"Very good, sir."

"May we dock at the Squadron Marina?"

"Of course, sir. I'll let the dockmaster know. What size yacht are you?"

"A forty-three-foot motor yacht, beam is fourteen feet six inches, and we draw twenty-eight inches. Her name is *Indian Summer*."

"Very good, sir. We'll see you soon."

Stone slowed as they approached the Castle and pulled into the marina. A boatman was waiting to take their lines, and they were soon made fast.

"Now I see why you're wearing that ridiculous cap," Dino said, as they walked ashore, through the gates, and up to the pavilion at the top of the lawn.

They had a good lunch, then Stone, Dino, and Gala walked over to the Squadron jeweler, Benzie's, while the Hinckley men made the boat ready for departure. Once there, Stone bought a Squadron tie pin, and he bought Gala a ladies' burgee pin.

Back on the boat, Stone tried a few maneuvers inside

the small marina for practice, then they departed the harbor and headed back down the Solent toward the mouth of the Beaulieu River. Stone's phone rang.

"Yes?"

"It's Geoffrey, sir. Your call was very timely. The boat attempted a landing, but I refused their lines and waved them off. A police car arrived at that moment, and an officer explained to them that the dock was private property and did not welcome uninvited guests."

"How many were aboard?"

"Three, sir. One of them sounded very much like the gentleman on the phone last evening."

"What happened then?"

"They crossed the river and attempted to tie up at Dame Felicity's dock. They were greeted there by two of her security staff bearing automatic weapons and were rebuffed. They then continued upriver a bit too far and ran aground on a falling tide. The harbormaster pulled them off the mud, and they headed back downriver."

"That's all fine, Geoffrey. Thank you for handling it so well."

Shortly they turned into the Beaulieu and were careful to follow the channel upriver. Halfway to the Windward dock, Stone asked Gala to go below. She did so, and they passed the boat they had seen earlier, now headed back to the Solent, with two men in sight. Boris had apparently gone below. Stone ignored the waves of the big bald man and his cohort, and he recognized the bald man as one of those who had accosted him at the Bel-Air Country Club.

When the boat was out of sight, Stone called Gala

back to the cockpit. "The coast is now clear, and so is the river."

"Did you get a good look at them?"

"Two of them. I knew one. I believe Boris may have been below. Geoffrey said that the third man sounded like the man on the phone last night. They got a somewhat hotter reception at Felicity's dock. Clearly, they didn't know on whose property they were about to trespass, and they were greeted by armed guards." He explained to Chris and Dustin, "The property across the river is owned by the head of MI6, the British foreign intelligence agency, whose members do not suffer fools gladly."

They tied up at the Windward dock, and tidied up the boat. Then Chris and Dustin presented the paperwork for British registration of the yacht and an acceptance document for the boat. "All the safety equipment required by the British is aboard, and the boat is fully legal here," Dustin said, handing him a card. "Should you need parts or service of any kind, call these people, who are aware of your boat."

Geoffrey came down to drive them back to the house and gave Stone a package. "Dame Felicity sent this to you by messenger," he said.

Stone opened it to find a Squadron white burgee and a British white ensign, which could be flown only by Royal Navy vessels and members of the Royal Yacht Squadron.

"But I'm an American," he said to Geoffrey. "I can't fly this ensign."

"Dame Felicity says that if the yacht is British-registered, an American member may fly the white ensign."

Stone rigged both flags on their staffs and left them below for future use.

A cheerful fire awaited them in the library, and they had drinks before dressing for dinner.

18

Over dinner, Stone brought Dino up to date on the problems with Boris Tirov.

"What do you suggest?" Stone asked.

"Suggest? I'm out of my jurisdiction. What's the name of that police inspector you dealt with last year after the murder? Sherlock something?"

"Deputy Chief Inspector Holmes," Stone replied. "No Sherlock."

"Why don't you give him a call?"

"Good idea," Stone replied. "I'll ring him in the morning."

"When do we head for Rome?"

"Tomorrow afternoon. The celebration isn't until the day after."

"Are we staying at the Arrington?"

"Yep."

"What do the celebrations consist of?"

"A big cocktail party, followed by a dinner for as many people as can be squeezed into the dining room."

"Who are the guests?"

"I've left that up to Marcel duBois, so I have no idea. I imagine they'll be pretty, though."

"It's a good thing I went shopping in London," Gala said. "I found the perfect dress at Harvey Nicks."

"Perfect is good enough for me," Stone said.

After dinner, Geoffrey announced a phone call from Dame Felicity for Stone.

"Good evening."

"Good evening. What the hell is going on down there? I've heard there was a disturbance at my dock today."

"I didn't witness the event, but Geoffrey tells me that weapons were brandished by your people, but no shots were fired by anyone."

"Who were the would-be intruders?"

"One of them we believe to be Gala's ex-husband."

"Is he mad?"

"Very possibly. He's certainly unbalanced, and he has some unsavory Russian connections."

"What a delightful combination of personal traits. If there's a next time, I'll tell my people to fire at will."

"Please wait until I'm in Rome, which will occur to-morrow evening."

"How long will you be away?"

"A couple of days, I guess. It's the grand opening of the new Arrington."

"Ah."

"Yes. Would you like to come along?"

"Love to, but events in the Muddle East demand my attention. I expect to have all that solved by the weekend, though, so perhaps I'll come down and see you and Gala?"

Stone felt a stirring at the thought. "Hold on." He covered the phone. "Gala, would you like to see Felicity this weekend?"

Gala managed a warm smile. "Of course."

"Saturday is good, Felicity."

"Your place or mine?"

"Windward Hall."

"Sevenish?"

"Perfect. I'll be sure and let you know if we're detained in Rome."

"You'd better. Bye-bye." They hung up.

"How is the old girl?" Dino asked.

"As ever. Sorry, I forgot to send your regards."

"What's keeping her busy?"

"What she calls the Muddle East, but she plans to solve all that by the weekend."

"Good luck to her."

"I'll tell her you said so."

They adjourned to the fireplace for brandy.

"You know," Dino said, "this is my favorite house of yours."

"Then you must come more often. There's nothing like an English summer."

"I've heard that."

"Perhaps you should just toss in the New York towel and retire here."

"That's a damned fine idea, but I'm not sure Viv is ready for retirement. She's up for chief operating officer of Strategic Services soon, and she'll be making a ton of money."

"Maybe she could do the job out of London, or even out of here. We've still got the offices downstairs that the kids used when they were shooting their movie here last year."

"I like the way you think. All she needs is a video and Internet connection. You can run anything from anywhere these days."

"Take it up with her."

"I'll do that."

"Would you like me to nudge Mike in that direction? I sometimes think he'd rather not spend all that much time in New York."

"Not yet. Let me broach the subject with my better half, see how it flies."

"You do that."

"How about you? Are you ready to spend more time here and less in New York?"

"I'm not sure how I'd like an English winter. I'm told it rains."

"Can't be any worse than a New York winter. It snows."

"You have a point."

"Let's both cogitate."

"Agreed."

*   *   *

L ater that night, Stone and Gala were canoodling in bed.

"Are you ready for another encounter with Felicity?" he asked.

"I will be by Saturday," she said. "Right now I'm more content with you."

"How much of your sex life have you spent in bed with other women?"

"That sounds like a polite way of asking if I'm a lesbian."

"I don't think that, you're too happy in bed with me."

"Well, the answer to your question is a tiny percentage, perhaps half a dozen occasions, starting in college. I'm very particular about whom I sleep with, regardless of gender, and generally speaking, I've found a great many more qualified males than females. Does my occasional attraction to women disturb you?"

"No, I can perfectly understand how someone could be attracted to women."

She laughed. "But not to men?"

"That's much more difficult to understand."

"I'll grant you that," she replied, then returned her attention to arousing him.

19

The following morning Stone rang Hampshire police headquarters and asked for Deputy Chief Inspector Holmes. He was first informed that the gentleman was now chief inspector, then connected. He invited Holmes to lunch that day, and his invitation was accepted.

Stone recalled that Holmes appreciated old sherry, and he found a very good example of a dry Oloroso in Windward's cellar and asked the cook to order Dover sole. When Holmes arrived he was plied first with the sherry, then with the sole and a bread pudding.

Having sufficiently relaxed his guest, Stone got to the point. "Chief Inspector, I have a problem to which I hope you can suggest a solution."

"I would be pleased to offer my advice, Mr. Barrington. What seems to be the problem?"

"I have a houseguest at the moment, a Ms. Gala Wilde,

who is a Hollywood screenwriter and a person of some substance. She has, since her divorce a year ago, been troubled by the unwanted attentions of her former husband, a man of Russian birth named Boris Tirov."

"The film producer?"

Stone was surprised that Holmes had heard of him. "Yes."

"I thought the most recent in his series of thrillers was disappointing."

"Perhaps you are right," Stone said, "and that could, in fact, be a contributing factor in his attentions to his former wife—an ego thing, perhaps." This didn't make any sense to Stone, but Holmes apparently thought it did.

"Ah, yes," he said. "And what form are his attentions taking?"

"He has pursued her relentlessly, even though they live in different cities—he in Los Angeles, she in Santa Fe, New Mexico—and he has even followed her to England, on the pretense of doing business here."

"I am aware that Mr. Tirov sometimes films at Pinewood Studios," Holmes said.

"He has followed her to this house by boat," Stone said, "and has even intruded upon the dock of Dame Felicity Devonshire, where he was repelled by her armed security people. Dame Felicity was alarmed to hear that he has connections to the Russian mob."

"Ah, yes, I had heard that. I am astonished to hear that he would intrude upon your privacy here, and especially upon that of Dame Felicity. Do you think he understands who she is?"

"I've no way of knowing that," Stone admitted, "but

I was surprised to hear that he had to be repelled by her guards."

"I suppose Americans—and Russians—might be less aware of her identity than Englishmen."

"Perhaps so."

"I take it you wish to have your property protected by the Hampshire police?"

"I am reluctant to make such a request, but I would be grateful for your advice on how to proceed."

"I should think that a uniformed officer at your gate and another on your dock for a few days might achieve the desired result," Holmes said.

"That would be extremely generous of you."

"I'll see to it upon my return to my office."

"I wonder if there is a suitable police charity to which I might contribute by way of thanks?"

"There is." Holmes told him its name, and Stone instructed Geoffrey to ask the estate manager, Major Bugg, to produce a check, which Holmes found to be very generous. He was also able to persuade the policeman to depart with a bottle of the Oloroso.

On his way out, the chief inspector was also glad to reacquaint himself with the commissioner of New York City Police, whom he had met on an earlier visit to Windward Hall.

As he departed, Stone felt glad that Holmes now rated his own car and driver, since he would have not wished the gentleman to attempt the roads with so much Oloroso on board.

"How much did the man have to drink?" Dino asked as the car drove away.

"About half a bottle of very potent sherry," Stone replied.

"Any luck with police help?"

"A uniformed officer at the gate and another at the dock."

"I would call that sherry well spent," Dino said.

"I would call it expensive police protection," Stone replied, "given the rarity of the Oloroso."

"How rare was it?"

"Probably obtainable only at auction, after spirited bidding."

"You may have a point," Dino agreed.

"Would you like to try a glass?"

"I would."

"Come with me," Stone said, and they repaired to the library to conduct a tasting.

20

Before departing for Rome, Stone called the cell number of the CIA station chief in Rome.

"How are you, Jim?"

"As well as can be expected, Stone. Are you coming to Rome for the opening of the Arrington?"

"I am, and I hope you got your invitation."

"I did, and my wife is going nuts. We'll be there. Tell me, would you like some hangar space in our facility at Ciampino?"

Ciampino was Rome's principal general aviation airport.

"Thank you, yes."

"When do you expect to arrive there?"

"Between four and five this afternoon."

"A line cart will be waiting to escort you to our hangar there. Are you being met by a car and driver?"

"I expect Marcel to provide that transportation."

"I will leave word at the gate, and the vehicle will be escorted into the hangar. Please wait for your airplane to be towed inside before deplaning—it's more secure that way. I assume your tail number is unchanged?"

"That is correct."

"Then I'll look forward to seeing you at the festivities tomorrow night." They both hung up.

Stone called Marcel duBois's office and asked for a large Mercedes van to meet them at Ciampino.

Stone hung up the phone and found Dino watching him. "You never cease to amaze me," he said.

"How's that?"

"You are probably the only American civilian who would have the balls to make that phone call."

"You will have noticed that I didn't ask for anything."

"No, you waited for him to offer."

"It seemed the polite way to handle it, and as a result, your tender body will be protected from attempts by terroristic opportunists."

"As will yours and Gala's."

"I can find nothing to object to in that."

Dino laughed. "Come to think of it, neither can I."

They lifted off Stone's airfield at mid-afternoon and followed their filed flight plan across Europe, thence to Rome, where they were vectored for landing at Ciampino. As promised, a golf cart bearing a large sign, FOLLOW ME, led them to a large hangar, and the door opened to admit them. A lineman waved them to a stop just outside, then a tug attached itself to the airplane's nosewheel and towed them into the hangar, where a large black Mercedes van awaited.

The driver loaded their luggage into the van, then drove them out of the hangar and off the airport to the autostrada for Rome. They drove into the very heart of the city to the hill overlooking the Spanish Steps, past the Hassler Villa Medici hotel and the Trinità dei Monti church to the new Arrington.

Though the hotel was not yet officially open, they were greeted inside the front door by the general manager, the head bellman, and the director of housekeeping and whisked to the penthouse floor and into one of three presidential suites with a spectacular view of St. Peter's Basilica in the distance, plus a view of the Medici Gardens from another terrace.

Vivian Bacchetti awaited them in the living room, and Dino's bags were whisked into their bedroom, while Stone and Gala were ushered into the presidential bedroom. They left the staff to unpack for them and returned to the large living room, where a waiter was uncorking a bottle of Veuve Clicquot Grande Dame champagne.

"Ladies and gentlemen," the general manager said, "welcome to the Arrington. Your garments will be pressed and returned to your rooms shortly by way of the service entrance, so that you will not be disturbed."

Stone thanked the man, then returned to the champagne, which had been poured into Baccarat flutes. They all drank thirstily.

"A good flight?" Viv asked.

"The best kind—an uneventful one," Stone replied. "And are your security arrangements for the hotel complete?"

"Didn't you see all the guards downstairs?"

"Not a one."

"And that's the way we at Strategic Services prefer it. It does not reassure guests to have men in black uniforms and body armor waving around automatic weapons. That would cause them to wonder what they are being protected from."

"Good point," Stone said. "What opposition, if any, do you anticipate?"

"None from the local Mafia. Yours and Dino's actions of last year have both thinned their ranks and cooled their ardor. We look for generic opposition—protesters and deluded Middle Eastern terrorists wishing to make a name for themselves."

"Is that last one a possibility?"

"Both Italian and American intelligence sources, plus our own people, consider that possibility remote in the extreme. Nevertheless, we have done everything possible to anticipate it. Should anyone have anything to protest— political, environmental, or whatever—we will leave them to the Italian police, who have cleared sufficient cell space to accommodate a large crowd."

"I feel safer already," Stone said. Then the doorbell rang, and Stone's partner in the Arrington and the company's CEO, Marcel duBois, swept into the room, hugging, kissing, and shaking hands, and inquiring of their health, their happiness, and any possible desires they might dream up.

Stone introduced Gala. "We are all well, happy, and most comfortably accommodated, Marcel," Stone said. "You have outdone yourself."

"Thank you, Stone, and let me mention two things. If there is any object or item in this suite that you desire, please steal it and take it home with you. I refer, especially, to the cashmere dressing gowns and slippers, custom-made by the house of Loro Piana, to the measurements you provided."

The women oohed and aahed.

"Does that mean I can take the Bechstein grand piano home with me?" Dino asked.

"Should you wish it, my good friend, Dino. I will have it airfreighted to your New York apartment, and it will arrive before you do."

"Only joking, Marcel," Dino replied. "I did not doubt your hospitality."

"Thank you for the Mercedes van that met us at the airport, Marcel," Stone said.

"It will be at your disposal for your entire stay," Marcel replied, "and it will return you to Ciampino when you really must go."

"Marcel, I know how hard you've worked to bring off this opening, and I want to thank you sincerely for leaving nothing for me to do."

"Stone, your presence, and that of your friends, is all you need provide on this occasion. Now, if there is nothing else I can do for you here, I beg to leave you, for others are more demanding." He shook their hands again and left.

"What a charming and generous man," Gala said when he had gone.

"And that," Stone said, "is only your first impression. There is much more to come."

21

They had dinner in their suite that evening, and the following day the women took the van and went shopping, while Stone talked with Joan and a few clients on the phone and Dino administered the NYPD from afar.

The following morning the new hotel began to fill with its first guests, all of whom had booked months ahead for the occasion. Because so many Los Angeleans had experienced the Bel-Air Arrington, there was a particularly large contingent from the film business, with many faces that Stone recognized but could not necessarily name.

One fact, though, registered with Stone instantly as he entered the grand ballroom, where dinner was being served: Boris Tirov was sitting at an all-Hollywood table, his eyes locked with Stone's.

Stone immediately found Marcel. "At table number

eight there is a man to whose presence I object," he whispered in the Frenchman's ear. "His name is Boris Tirov."

Marcel whipped out a sheaf of papers from an inside pocket and consulted it. "Yes, it is here. Cine International Studios, an Italian company, bought the table months ago, to entertain Hollywood people, and Tirov is their guest. Why do you object to his presence?"

"He is Gala's ex-husband, and he has been harassing her since their divorce. Is there any way to get him thrown out of here?"

"Not without insulting the studio," Marcel replied. "Instead, I will assign a couple of security people to keep an eye on Tirov and see that he does not disturb you or your lady."

"Thank you, Marcel." Stone returned to table number one and his group. Only Marcel's seat was empty, and he would join them when he could. From his seat, Stone had a good view of Tirov's table. He seemed to be trying to attract Gala's attention.

"Don't look at Boris," Stone said to her. "I'm sorry he's here, but there's nothing I can do about that. Security will keep an eye on him, though."

"I would not give him the satisfaction of looking that way," she replied.

Then the orchestra stopped playing, and the leader came to the microphone. "A very special request to honor a very special lady," he said, and gave the orchestra a downbeat.

"Oh, God," Gala said, keeping her smile fixed. "That's the theme from Boris's first film. He always referred to it as 'our song.'"

"Just keep looking at me," Stone said, "and ignore it."

"Looking at you is always comforting," she said.

Dinner was served, and everyone at table one relaxed, seemingly unaware of Tirov's presence in the room. Then, as dessert was served, Stone's eye was caught by movement at the Cine International table. Boris Tirov had got to his feet, and he left the table and began to cross the ballroom, stopping along the way to greet acquaintances. As he neared table number one, Stone got to his feet, then Tirov veered away and headed toward a hallway where the restrooms were. Stone followed him, ignoring Gala's tugging at his sleeve. It was the first time he and Tirov had been in the same place since the incident at his pool at the Bel-Air Arrington.

He saw Tirov enter the men's room and two plainclothes security men take up station outside. Stone walked through the door and found Tirov alone there, zipping his fly and heading for a sink to wash his hands.

"Fancy meeting you here, Barrington," he said, glancing at him in the mirror.

Stone checked his tie in the mirror. "I thought I'd give you an opportunity to take another swing at me while you're still sober," he said.

"And have your security goons all over me?"

"I'll see that they don't interfere."

"How did Gala enjoy her visit from the Three Bears?" Tirov asked.

"How did you enjoy being banned from Centurion Studios, the Bel-Air Country Club, and the Arrington, all on the same day?"

"I suppose you had a hand in all that?"

"Actually, I had nothing to do with Centurion and the country club, but I did have the pleasure of seeing you banned from the Bel-Air Arrington, just as you will be banned from this hotel and any other the company should ever open. If you enjoy that sort of thing, I'll see what other indignities I might be able to inflict on you."

Tirov swung around to face him, and suddenly, there was a switchblade in his hand. "I think it's time to see how you operate without a liver," he said.

As Stone squared away to face him he heard the men's room door open, and a voice called out, "Everything all right in here, Mr. Barrington?"

Stone thought about that for a moment before answering and decided that he had no wish to bloody a brand-new men's room, especially with his own blood. "Not quite," he replied. "There's a man in here with a knife."

Two men with guns entered the room, and Tirov tossed the knife into the hole in the sinktop that led to a trash bin.

"Gentlemen," Stone said, "please place this man in handcuffs, then recover the knife and turn both over to the Rome police, as quietly as possible. I think a night or two in a Roman jail would do him a lot of good."

The two guards began carrying out Stone's instructions.

Tirov managed a sardonic smile. "You and I will discuss this on another occasion," he said. "Perhaps in the company of Gala."

"Gentlemen," Stone said to the guards, "on second thought, remove the handcuffs and stand away from him, between him and the knife. Oh, and you might frisk him for other weapons."

"Are you sure, Mr. Barrington?"

"Yes, and the two of you can wait outside and make sure no one enters until we're done here."

They patted down Tirov and removed the handcuffs, then left the room.

"Now," Stone said, "what would you like to discuss?"

Tirov came straight at him with a big swing, and Stone managed to catch his wrist and use his momentum against him, throwing him against a urinal. Tirov tried again, and Stone hit him once with a straight left to the nose, then struck him once, hard, under the heart. The man went to his knees, a hand to his face, where blood was flowing.

"Is there anything else you'd like to talk about?" Stone asked.

Tirov said nothing but stayed on his knees.

Stone went to the door and opened it. "Give him a chance to clean himself up, then throw him out the back door and radio your colleagues at the entrances to see that he doesn't reenter the premises."

Stone walked back to his table and sat down. Dino handed him a napkin. "There's a little blood on your knuckles," he said.

Stone took the napkin and wiped his hand.

"Anybody I know?" Dino asked.

"Nope," Stone replied.

"How badly did you hurt him?" Gala asked quietly.

"Not badly enough," Stone replied. He had a feeling that he was going to have to do it again.

22

Stone attended a board meeting of the Arrington corporation the following morning, and it dragged on through lunch.

Afterward, Marcel took him aside for a moment.

"I understand there was an altercation in the men's room during dinner last night."

"I'm afraid that's correct. I didn't go in there to start a fight. I just wanted to tell him to leave Gala alone."

"But a fight started anyway?"

"Tirov produced a knife and made remarks about what he was going to do to my liver. At that point, the security people entered, and he threw away the knife. After they had searched him for other weapons, I asked them to leave us alone."

"Dear God, like schoolboys."

"It was going to come to this, and there was nothing I could do about it. I thought that, alone in the men's room, with guards at the door, might be the best place to resolve the issue."

"And how did you resolve it?"

"He attacked me, and I hit him twice, gave him a bloody nose. He had no more fight left in him, so I asked the security people to allow him to clean up, then escort him from the building and not allow him to return."

"Well, I suppose that's better than having him arrested."

"That was my first thought."

"I'm glad you didn't act on it. We'd have been all over the yellow press this morning. As it was, they didn't get wind of what happened. Security found Tirov's car and driver and put him in it. Presumably, he went home."

"I should think so. He was a mess, and he wouldn't have wanted his friends at the table to see him. I think his nose may be broken. By the way, Marcel, I've already barred him from our Bel-Air hotel. I'd like him barred from all our hotels, present and future."

"Agreed. I'll send out an e-mail to the managers."

"Especially the one next door to me in England. It would be like him to try to check in there."

"All right, especially that one." He sat down at his computer and wrote the e-mail. "Uh-oh," he said. "I got an immediate reply from the Beaulieu hotel. Tirov has a reservation for a week, checking in tonight. I'll have them get in touch with Tirov and cancel."

"Thank you, Marcel."

"When are you returning to England?"

"This afternoon. I'll release the van at the airport."

*   *   *

S tone went back to the Arrington and found his party lounging in their suite.

"Everybody ready to go back to England?"

"We're flying back to New York with Mike Freeman," Dino said.

"I can be ready in an hour," Gala said. "I'll get started now." Viv went with her to help.

"Sit down," Dino said, "I have some news."

Stone sat down. "Hit me with it."

"You'll recall our conversation in England about my retiring from the NYPD?"

"I recall that, and I'd be happy to have you at Windward Hall for as much of the year as you'd like."

"Well, out of the blue, Mike Freeman approached me and suggested that I come to work for Strategic Services as a board member and consultant."

"Now that's interesting."

"You're damned right it is. The money is three times my city salary, and I'd have the freedom to spend time in England or wherever else I'd like. The only problem I can see is that when Viv gets moved up to chief operating officer, I'd be working for my wife."

Stone laughed. "She'd probably be a pretty good boss."

"She'd just be the boss. Would you want to work for your wife?"

"Well, I'm staying out of that conversation. It's one

that only you and Viv should be involved in. Maybe Mike could have you report only to him."

"Now *that's* a good idea! I'll talk with him about it on the plane home."

"I expect you're going to need to have a conversation with the mayor, too."

"Right. I want to make sure he picks the right successor. I don't want some ass in the job, rolling back everything I've done, and I don't want my going to affect his plans for running for reelection."

"Let me sweeten the deal for you," Stone said.

"You go right ahead and do that."

"You and Viv are welcome for as long as you like in *all* my houses—L.A., Maine, Paris, and Windward."

"That is, indeed, very sweet."

In due course, Gala appeared, they said their goodbyes and left for the airport. They drove into the CIA hangar and were met by the manager.

"We had some people snooping around this morning," the man said.

"What people and what kind of snooping?"

"Two men tried to talk their way into the hangar. They got nowhere, of course, but they were asking about you. You know anything about that?"

"Was one of them a big bald guy?"

"Yes."

"I know what's behind it—it's personal, nothing to do with you folks. The problem will be resolved with my departure, and we're ready to go, as soon as I get a preflight inspection done. I've already filed a flight plan."

"Just let me know when you're ready to taxi."

"Will do." Stone loaded their luggage and began his preflight. Half an hour later they were being towed from the big hangar onto the ramp. Stone looked around for signs of Tirov's minions: there were various vehicles parked nearby but none that looked particularly threatening. I hope, he thought, that nobody's lurking in the weeds with a shoulder-fired missile. He consoled himself with the idea that not even Tirov could be that stupid.

Stone got his clearance and was cleared to taxi to the runway. That took ten minutes, and he kept a sharp eye out for threats of any sort. He was cleared for takeoff as they reached the runway, so he did a rolling start, advancing the throttles and starting his takeoff roll as he turned onto the centerline. Half a minute later they were climbing out of Ciampino, unmolested. Stone breathed a sigh of relief.

England came into view an hour and a half later, green and pleasant in the clear air and sunshine, as they descended over the Channel. They set down and taxied toward the hangar, and Stone saw Bob jump down from the Range Rover and run toward them. He cut the engines immediately to avoid accidents. As soon as Stone had the door open, Bob ran up the stairs to greet them. "Home again," Stone said.

"I've come to think of it that way, too," Gala replied.

23

S tone had hardly reached the house when Geoffrey told him he had a call from the manager of the Arrington property next door.

"Yes?"

"Mr. Barrington, this is Mr. Scott, at the Arrington."

"Yes, Mr. Scott."

"Earlier today we received an e-mail from Mr. duBois in Rome, asking us to deny registration to a Mr. Boris Tirov."

"Yes, I'm aware of that."

"Our desk clerk replied that Mr. Tirov had a reservation for a week, beginning today."

"I know all that."

"What the desk clerk failed to make clear was that Mr. Tirov had already checked in. We met his flight from Rome this morning and drove him to the hotel. He is in his suite now, and so are his traveling companions, in theirs."

"Can you get him out?"

"I'm afraid that, under law, once a guest is in possession of his rooms we cannot oust him unless he fails to pay upon presentation of his bill."

Stone thought for a moment. "Can you shut down the hotel on some pretense? A power failure, something like that?"

"Sir, the hotel is full, and all the guests with bookings have checked in. If we shut down the hotel we would greatly inconvenience guests with whom we are trying to build loyalty, and incidentally, we would lose a great deal of money. Also, we would be obliged to furnish them with other accommodation at our expense."

"All right, I understand. Don't shut down the hotel. What are our alternatives?"

"We have none, sir. Unless Mr. Tirov and his guests conduct themselves in a manner that would tread upon the rights of the other guests, we are, well, stuck with them."

"How many security personnel are typically on duty?"

"Four in the daytime, two after midnight."

"Can you summon other security staff?"

"Yes, sir, in an emergency."

"Please add another man, and should Tirov or his guests leave the building, have them followed. Should they trespass on my property, please call the police, in the person of Detective Chief Superintendent Holmes, of the Hampshire police, and tell him. Bill my account for the extra personnel."

"As you wish, Mr. Barrington. May I inquire, with respect, what the difficulty is with Mr. Tirov?"

"He is an obstreperous person who may be a danger to a guest of mine. He had to be ejected from the Rome Arrington last night after he attacked me with a knife."

"I hope you are all right, sir."

"I am. Please have Tirov followed."

"I quite understand, sir, and I will follow your instructions to the letter."

"Thank you, Mr. Scott." Stone hung up and found Gala watching him.

"I heard most of that," she said. "Boris is next door?"

"I'm afraid so, and there's nothing I can do about it except have him followed."

Gala collapsed onto a sofa. "Then I should go back to Santa Fe," she said. "My presence here is causing too much trouble."

"Nonsense. I won't allow him to bother us. Hotel security will follow him, if he leaves the building, and the local police have already been warned about him. You will be perfectly safe here, and no trouble at all. I would be very unhappy if you were back in Santa Fe and I here."

"Well, if you're sure."

"And anyway, we've already invited Felicity Devonshire for dinner tomorrow night . . . and she'll be staying over."

"Well," Gala said, smiling, "there is that, isn't there?"

"There certainly is."

Gala patted the seat next to her, and Stone sat down. "Are you sure you want Felicity to stay over? I mean, it's all very well for me, but . . ."

"It's all very well for me, too," he replied.

"It was last time, wasn't it?"

"I enjoyed myself—and both of you."

"It was the first time I've been in a threesome that worked for everybody," she said. "I mean, jealousies do arise sometimes—usually, in fact."

"I didn't feel that at all."

"Neither did I, and I don't believe Felicity did."

"Then we should be fine."

"You'll tell me, if it's not?"

"I'm sure that, if we encounter difficulties, we'll work them out in a civilized manner."

"Are you aroused, talking about this?"

"I am."

"So am I."

"Then let's go upstairs right now."

She got up and led him out of the room and up the stairs. Once in the master bedroom, it took them only seconds to undress.

24

After dinner and after the making of love, Gala elected to have a Jacuzzi in the master bath, while Stone and Felicity enjoyed a cognac in bed.

"Such a nice evening," Felicity said.

"I am entirely in agreement," Stone sighed.

"Funny how easy it is with the three of us."

"Gala and I said pretty much the same thing to each other."

"I know I shouldn't have to mention this," Felicity said, "but I do."

"Mention what?"

"This can never go any further than this room and the three of us."

"You're right, you shouldn't have to mention it."

"The tabloids have taken an interest in my sex life in the past," she said, "but helpful people managed to quiet them."

"I'm glad."

"If they knew that you and I were doing the horizontal bunny hop, they'd love it, but they wouldn't print it. But if they knew that the three of us were doing it, all at the same time, nothing would stop them from publishing."

"I'm sure."

"I've got some good years left in my job, and I want to serve them out without a scandal. After that . . ."

"You mean a scandal would be all right after you've retired?"

"Oh, I'd be asked everywhere by everybody!"

Stone laughed, then turned serious. "Felicity, I want to ask you a favor. I know I shouldn't, but . . ."

"Ask away—the worst I can do is tell you to go fuck yourself."

Stone laughed. "I've no need to do that."

"I suppose not."

"The favor is, I need some foreign intelligence, and you're in that business."

"Indeed I am. What sort of intelligence?"

"Gala was once married to a Russian named Boris Tirov."

"Sounds familiar. Isn't he in the movie business?"

"He is, as is Gala—that's how they met. They were divorced a year or so ago, and since then he's made her life hell—making demands outside their settlement agreement, following her around, taking too much of an interest in whom she sees socially."

"Taking too much of an interest in you, you mean?"

"Yes. It wouldn't bother me so much if it didn't bother her so much."

"I see. Would you like me to have someone shoot him?"

"Gosh, I hadn't thought of that. Could you, please?"

"I'm sure you've thought of that, but I couldn't have him assassinated unless he were *my* ex-husband."

"I'd be very grateful if you could have him looked into. He's been in the States for only a few years. Before that he was an actor, then a producer in Russia."

"Do you know anything about his existence there?"

"There are rumors that he's connected to the Russian mob, and he employs some people who give credence to that."

"A nasty lot."

"Indeed."

"What is it you want to know?"

"I'd like to know anything that would help me deal with the man, get him off our backs."

"Dirt?"

"I'd love some dirt, but it would have to be bad enough so that I could threaten him with it."

"I've got a man headed back to Moscow next week after some home leave. I could ask him to put his shell-like ear to the ground, I suppose. He's the sort who would be amused by the request. Do you think this Tirov might have government connections in Russia?"

"I've no idea. He must be famous there, though, because he's had a string of movies that have been worldwide hits and made him a ton of money. I should think the folks in Moscow would be very proud of their expat."

"That should make it easier to investigate him. What will happen if I can't find something you can use against him?"

"I'll just have to strangle him, I guess. Did I mention that he's staying next door?"

"At your new Arrington? No, you didn't."

"I had him banned from all the Arringtons, but before the word got to the management next door, Tirov had already checked in for a week, and apparently the law gives him some rights of possession. As long as he pays his bill they can't kick him out, unless he disturbs the other guests."

"You don't suppose he's the Peeping Tom type, do you?"

"I wouldn't put it past him."

"Good God! Do you think he's got a telescope trained on us at this moment?" She pulled the sheets over her very fine breasts.

"No, nothing like that. I've got hotel security tailing him."

"Is this the scoundrel who tried to come ashore from his boat at my dock?"

"Yes."

"So, he's already been snooping around here. I'm going to have to be very careful."

"You're already very careful. Your native caution operates at a high level."

"Quite true. If he tries anything like that again, I'll have him dealt with harshly."

"May I watch?"

"I doubt if there'll be time to invite you over, but you may hear small-arms fire from across the river."

"Then I'll let my imagination run riot."

Gala came out of the bathroom wearing only a large

towel. She dropped it and got back into bed. "What have you two been talking about?"

"Why, you, of course," Stone said. "What else?"

"It's true, darling," Felicity said, kissing her on the shoulder. "We've been discussing your technique in bed."

"I hope neither of you had any complaints."

"Certainly not. You received high marks on all counts."

"All counts," Stone echoed, nodding enthusiastically.

"Well, I'm happy to give satisfaction."

"Oh, more than satisfaction," Felicity said.

"Much more," Stone added.

"What rises above satisfaction?"

"Exultation," Stone said.

"Ecstasy," Felicity added.

"Well, that makes me feel very good," Gala said.

"Makes us feel pretty good, too," Stone replied.

Gala took him in her hand. "There is evidence that you are not lying," she said.

"Oh, good," Felicity said. "I like evidence."

25

At breakfast the following morning, Gala said, "Would you like to go riding this morning?"

"I'd love to," Stone replied, "but I have two video conference calls this morning."

"Do you mind if I go alone?"

"Not at all. You know the drill." He picked up the phone and arranged a horse for her, and she went to get dressed, then passed through the bedroom on her way out.

"Have I mentioned to you how good your ass looks in riding pants?"

"Everybody's ass looks good in riding pants—yours, too."

"Enjoy your morning."

"I will, don't worry."

Stone went down to the lower-level office and made his first conference call. When he had finished it occurred to him that Tirov might be abroad in the land, and he called Gala's cell number. No reply. He made his second call, which didn't take long, then he tried her phone again. Still no answer.

He tapped on the app that allowed him to track Tirov, and he got a green dot inside the hotel. Then, as he watched, the green dot moved outdoors. Shortly, it began to move faster. Tirov must be in a car, he thought.

As he watched, the yellow dot that was Gala's phone approached the house along the river, then made a turn toward the wood on the property. Tirov's green dot also headed in that direction.

Stone tried Gala's number again, but still got no reply. Then the two dots both approached the wood and a moment later, stopped. They had converged. Stone watched, horrified. The two dots remained together. He picked up the phone and ordered his horse. "Now," he said.

He changed hurriedly and ran down the stairs and out the front door, where the groom awaited, holding his usual gelding. He mounted quickly and galloped off toward the neighboring property. He took the stone wall at a dead run and headed for the wood. As he approached, a golf cart drove out of the wood toward the house, moving fast. There was one man aboard, and Stone couldn't make out who at that distance. He slowed and rode into the wood.

Shortly, he came to a clearing and found Gala mounting her horse from a large rock. She started at the sight of him.

"Is everything all right?"

"Yes," she said. "Did you finish your work?"

"I did, and as I approached, I saw someone ride away from the wood in a golf cart. Anybody we know?"

"It was Boris," she said. "He saw me from a window at the hotel and gave chase, I guess you'd say."

"And did he catch you?"

"He did. I stopped to pee in the woods, and when I came back he was there."

"What was the tenor of your meeting?"

"Uncomfortable. He wanted to engage in conversation, but I wouldn't talk to him. I led my horse away, looking for something to stand on to mount, and I heard his golf cart drive away. Then you turned up."

"I tried to phone you, but you didn't answer."

She took her phone from her jacket pocket and looked at it. "It's on mute," she said. "I'm sorry about that."

"No harm done. Are you ready to go back to the house?"

"I think I've had enough for one morning," she said.

"Then I'll ride back with you."

"I'll race you," she said, and spurred her mount to a run.

They took the wall flying and were neck and neck when they reached the stables. The groom took the horses.

"Cool them down for a bit before you stable them," Stone told the man, and they walked back to the house.

They lunched in the library, and Gala was uncharacteristically quiet.

"What would you like to do this afternoon?" Stone asked.

"I think I'll work for a while. I had an idea for a couple

of scenes this morning, and I want to get them on paper. You?"

"There's a book I want to start," he replied. "I think I'd like an afternoon of reading. Take the office next to mine downstairs. There's a printer there, if you need it."

"All right."

"Gala, you've been very quiet. Anything on your mind?"

"Nothing in particular," she said. "I think I'll go up to London tomorrow. The Chelsea Flower Show is on, and I have a friend who can get me a ticket. I'll take the train up."

"It should be a good day for it, no rain in the forecast. That means you should take an umbrella. You never know in this country."

"That's probably good advice," she said.

Stone repaired to a wing chair with his book, and Gala went to work.

26

S tone had Gala driven to the station early the following morning. "Call me, and I'll pick you up on the return trip," he said to her. She kissed him and left.

A little later, Stone's phone rang. "Hello?"

"Mr. Barrington, it's Mr. Scott at the Beaulieu Arrington."

"Good morning, Mr. Scott. Have you found an excuse to throw Boris Tirov out of your hotel?"

"I'm pleased to say that it wasn't necessary. Mr. Tirov checked out five minutes ago of his own volition. A car came to get him. I thought you'd like to know."

"I'm very pleased to hear it. Did you have any problems with him?"

"He sent a steak back to the kitchen, saying it was overcooked. Otherwise, he was just the usual guest."

"Thank you for letting me know."

*   *   *

S tone lunched alone in the library, which had become his favorite room. Geoffrey came in: "Mr. Barrington, Dame Felicity is on the phone for you."

Stone picked it up. "Hello, there."

"And a happy noon to you. My request for information on Mr. Tirov has produced unexpectedly rapid results."

"That was pretty quick."

"Turns out, it wasn't very hard to get."

"What did you find out?"

"There is a Viktor Petrov connection," Felicity replied. "Turns out Tirov and President Petrov were classmates at the KGB Academy in Minsk, so they go way back."

"I don't know if that's good news or bad."

"Neither do I. This is raw data, unprocessed."

"Go on."

"The two young men served together for some years, then Petrov went into politics, and Tirov got a lucky break."

"What sort of break?"

"He appeared in a documentary film about the KGB, and someone from the government film studio saw it and took an interest in him—offered him a significant part in a movie. He won some sort of acting award, and he appeared to have a career ahead as an actor. Acting, however, bored him, and he began writing and producing films. After some years of this he got an exit visa and left for Hollywood, taking a script with him that the Russian studio had paid him for. Word is, Petrov personally financed his move to the States and intervened to get him the necessary visas, both Russian and American. The rest, as they say in Hollywood, is history."

"Any dirt?"

"It's said that Petrov doesn't have any friends that aren't of use. While working in Russian films, Tirov arranged introductions for Petrov to beautiful and compliant young actresses, and the two did a lot of partying together. At the film studio, Tirov was known as Petrov's pimp, and Petrov rewarded him by pushing him for important assignments."

"Petrov's Pimp. I like the alliteration."

"It has a ring, doesn't it? There's more. On several occasions actresses at the studio who resisted Tirov's charms suffered truncated careers, so his advances took on an air of casting couch or else."

"Aha."

"And on one occasion, a young woman who had resisted, but whose considerable ability as an actress rose above his ability to thwart her career, was found, afloat, in the River Neva."

"That's nasty."

"Isn't it? It's interesting that her death was coincidental with Tirov's rather sudden craving for greener pastures in the USA."

"Do you know her name?"

"Elena Ivanov."

"I know that actress," Stone said. "Didn't she appear in a Russian film that got an Academy Award nomination for best foreign film?"

"Yes, she did. The film was called, ironically, *The River*, and she received much attention. It was her first big part and her last appearance in a film."

"What an interesting story," Stone said.

"And it's all verifiable from public sources should, say, a journalist take an interest in it. I have dispatched a written account to you by messenger. You'll have it before the day is out. Oh, and one other thing. Ms. Ivanov was so famous in Russia by that time that even the government could not suppress the investigation into her death. Boris Tirov was the chief and only suspect in her death, and the Moscow police had obtained a warrant for his arrest. He got out of the country in a private jet owned by another friend and former classmate of Petrov. Tirov flew to Paris and waited there a few days while Petrov secured the appropriate visas, then he flew commercial directly to Los Angeles."

"I don't suppose that warrant is still outstanding?"

"Suffice it to say that Tirov has not returned to Russia since. Apparently, Petrov made no move to void the warrant. Elena Ivanov was too beautiful and too famous, and given the hullabaloo attending her death, he may have been glad to see the back of his old friend Boris."

"My dear Felicity, I can't thank you enough."

"Of course you can. I'll see you both this weekend."

"Lovely idea."

"And if further dirt comes my way, I'll let you know." They both hung up.

An envelope arrived later in the afternoon, and Stone read the half-dozen pages inside. "I believe," he said aloud to himself, "this is what they call in Hollywood, 'dynamite.'"

S tone got into the Porsche, stuck Felicity's envelope between his seat and the transmission tunnel, and met the 6:10 from Waterloo Station. Gala got into the Porsche with a huge bouquet of calla lilies but managed a kiss anyway.

Stone pulled out of the station, trying to think of the best way to tell her what he had learned about Tirov. "How was the flower show?"

"Oh, it was just brilliant! I don't think I've ever had such a good time."

"By the way, speaking of a good time, I spoke to Felicity and invited her for dinner this weekend."

"Oh, that will be fun!"

"More fun than the flower show?"

She smiled. "After a fashion."

"Gala," he said, "changing the subject—do you think you know everything there is to know about Boris Tirov?"

"Probably, but if there's anything I don't know, I don't want to know it."

"Are you sure?"

"Yes, I'm sure. I'm very tired of the subject, and I hope you won't bring it up again."

"Well . . ."

"And, Stone, I know very well that you'd like to get back at Boris for the trouble he's caused us, but I hope you won't do that. I hope you won't even think of it."

"I can't promise I won't think of it—that's involuntary."

"Then, if you must think about it, don't tell me what you're thinking, and if you do something, don't tell me what you're doing. If you're planning to punch him in the nose again, I don't want to watch or even hear about it. I would prefer to remain ignorant of anything to do with Boris."

"So be it," Stone said.

27

Stone didn't sleep well. Boris Tirov occupied his mind and his imagination. Stone was not good at revenge, and he knew it, but this was different. Gala was no longer discussing the matter, so he had no one to argue with about it. He thought of calling Dino, but being of Sicilian descent, he would take the revenge option immediately.

Sometime after midnight his iPhone made the sound that indicated he was receiving an e-mail. He couldn't sleep anyway, so he opened the e-mail; it was from Bob, his tech advisor:

> Stone, I've made some enhancements to my tracking app. You *can* now replay up to 24 hours of the tracking of a subject. Useful to see where he went yesterday. Try it out.

Stone yawned and opened the app. He selected 24 hours from a menu and pressed the Play button. Boris's green dot appeared, and Stone zoomed in to get a street location, which turned out to be Claridge's Hotel. He scrolled through the hours as the green dot moved around the West End to several stops and came back to the hotel. Then an odd thing happened: Gala's yellow dot appeared on the screen and became superimposed on the green dot. It was one PM yesterday, and Gala was at Claridge's. The yellow dot remained there for more than an hour, then moved offscreen. Stone zoomed out and watched as the yellow dot traveled to the King's Road, in Chelsea, location of the Chelsea Flower Show. At about three-thirty, the dot moved across London to Waterloo Station, then moved south toward Southampton, arriving at the station a little after six.

Stone switched off the phone. That was twice in twenty-four hours that Gala had been at the same location as Tirov. Stone didn't like coincidences.

He got into a dressing gown and went down to the library, taking Felicity's report on Tirov with him. It was ten hours earlier in L.A. He called the Bel-Air Arrington and asked for the restaurant manager.

"Yes, Mr. Barrington?"

"Do you remember a while back you told me that you had had Boris Tirov ejected from the restaurant and the property, because he had slugged a movie critic?"

"Yes, Mr. Barrington?"

"Who was the critic?"

"James Towbin, of the *Los Angeles Times*."

"Do you happen to have a fax number for Mr. Towbin?"

"Let me check my computer. He has a charge account here, so I probably do. Ah, here it is. Would you like his home or office fax number?"

"Home, please."

The man gave him the number. "Anything else I can do for you, Mr. Barrington?"

"No. Thanks for your help." He hung up and went to the cupboard that housed the fax machine. He had set it up himself, and he remembered that he had not specified that his name or fax number appear on faxes sent, so a fax received would be anonymous. He faxed Felicity's report to James Towbin.

He thought a bit longer, then he looked up the home fax number of his close friend Holly Barker, who was currently serving as national security advisor to President Katharine Lee. He faxed her the report, adding a hand-written page: "I have been assured by my entirely reliable source that the information in this document is factual. Call me when you've read it."

He went back to his chair and dozed for a while, then his iPhone rang. The calling number was blocked. "Hello?"

"It's Holly. How are you?"

"Very well indeed, and you?"

"Working all the time, as usual. I think I can guess where this report came from. Well, all right, there's a cryptic watermark in the paper that I recognize."

"Would a newspaper journalist recognize the water-mark?"

"Not unless he had had dealings with MI6. Has a jour-nalist read it?"

"It has been faxed to one at the *L.A. Times*."

"Which one?"

"James Towbin, the film critic."

"Well, I expect that, if he has read it, he has passed it on to an editor for review."

"Seems logical."

"And why have I been gifted with this document?"

"It occurred to me that the Department of Immigration and Customs Enforcement might be interested to know that a person who had previously been issued a green card to live and work in the United States had an open warrant for his arrest on a charge of murder in his home country."

"Just as a journalist would be interested to know that the person in question was close to Viktor Petrov?"

"Quite so."

"The director of Immigration and Customs Enforcement was my dinner partner at a White House function last month. He gave me his card, which I have in my hand. It has half a dozen numbers on it, one of which is his home fax number. May I ask, what is your interest in Mr. Tirov?"

Stone gave her a rundown of his various encounters with the Russian over the past days.

"Well, I must say, the man sounds like an undesirable alien to me."

"I cannot but agree."

"I'll fire this off to the director of Immigration and Customs Enforcement, and incidentally, it occurs to me that the director of the FBI might find it interesting reading, as well. Shall I fax it to him?"

"What a good thought!"

"Do you have any other enemies I can destroy for you this evening?"

"Not this evening."

"Then I can only thank you for your noble and patriotic action in bringing this to the attention of your government."

"I do what I can," Stone said.

"When will you be headed this way?"

"Not in the foreseeable future. I'm in England. Do you have any plans for foreign travel?"

Holly sighed. "Would that I did. It would be good to see you."

"We'll manage that soon."

"Well, I have my work to do, so I'll say good night."

"And good night to you, too, Holly. Sweet dreams." They both hung up.

In the United States, in Los Angeles and Washington D.C., fax machines began to ring and be answered, followed shortly by an exchange of phone calls between high government officials. The national editor of a newspaper faxed a document to his editor in chief, who scrawled the words "Fact-check this to within an inch of its life" across the document and faxed it to another editor, who faxed it to his best fact-checker.

The following afternoon, at his desk, the editor looked up to see his fact-checker approaching. "This is good stuff," she said, handing him the document. "And it's supported by the public record. I had to pay a translator two hundred bucks to check the Moscow papers, though."

"I won't take it out of your pay," the editor said. He picked up the phone and called James Towbin. "Jim," he said, "your news item is pure gold. Would you like the deep personal satisfaction of publishing it under your byline?"

"Nothing would give me greater pleasure," Towbin said.

"I believe Mr. Tirov is about to sign with a major studio, is that correct?"

"According to my best information," Towbin replied.

"You might call a couple of people there for comment."

"Certainly."

"And when it goes to press, you can put it on the wire service, too."

28

Boris Tirov checked out of Claridge's at two PM the following day. While the porters loaded his nine pieces of luggage into the van that would follow his limousine, he stopped at the cashier's desk and checked every single item charged to his suite during his stay, questioning two of them that amounted to an aggregate of less than ten pounds. Satisfied, he signed the bill and left the hotel.

He was driven to Heathrow Airport, followed by the van containing his luggage and his two bodyguards, and thence to the VIP check-in for the new Emirates Air flight to Los Angeles. He showed his Russian passport to the agent at the desk and waved an arm at his pile of luggage and two companions. "All that is mine, including the two gentlemen, who are flying in the economy. You may divide the luggage among the three of us and charge the overage to my credit card, which you have on file."

"Certainly, Mr. Tirov," the young woman said. "Your cart is waiting."

Tirov got into an electric cart and was driven past the throngs directly leading to the tunnel to the giant A380 aircraft. There, he got out of the cart, showed his boarding pass, and walked past the crowd waiting to board, many of whom glowered at him. Once aboard the aircraft he was escorted to a door in the forward cabin and admitted to his private suite, which included a sitting room, bedroom, and toilet with a separate shower. A bottle of champagne was iced and waiting in a silver cooler.

"May I pour you a glass of champagne, Mr. Tirov?" the attendant asked.

"Yes, please."

She poured champagne. "Your phone and Internet service are up and running, sir," she said. "Is there anything else I can do for you?"

"What time is my scheduled massage?"

"About two hours after takeoff, sir. I will remind you fifteen minutes early, so that you will have time to get into your robe."

"Very good. And may I have something to read?"

"Of course, we have a variety of magazines on board. What would you prefer?"

"*Playboy?*"

"Of course, sir." She went to a compartment and retrieved the magazine. "It's on your reading list. We'll be taking off as soon as the other passengers are seated, about twenty-five minutes. Our arrival time in Los Angeles is seven PM Pacific time, and the time difference is eight hours. Would you like dinner?"

"Yes, thank you," Tirov said.

She hung up his jacket. "Dinner will be served shortly after takeoff. Just buzz, if you think of anything else," she said. She departed the suite, closing the door behind her.

Tirov got into his comfortable armchair, fastened his seat belt, and opened his magazine. Half an hour later, the gigantic airplane began to move, and shortly it rumbled down the runway and into the air. Ten minutes later, his dinner was served and a coffee poured for him. His tray was then collected, and he settled in for the flight. They were already at cruising altitude.

Tirov had expected to spend most of the trip taking phone calls and responding to e-mails, but none of either was received. He inquired of the flight attendant if his services were in working order and was told they were. He was unaccustomed to that silence. Soon, he undressed and lay down for a nap.

He was awakened for his hour's massage, then fell asleep again. He didn't wake until the flight attendant rang and informed him that landing was an hour away. He showered and changed his clothes and relaxed until the aircraft was docked at the gate. Another cart awaited him and drove him to immigration. He had a Global Entry card and a Known Traveler Number, so he checked in at a kiosk. Unusually, he was directed to entry lane number 10. Ordinarily, he did not have to speak to an immigration officer or clear customs.

He presented his passport to the officer in the booth,

who consulted his computer. "Ah, yes, Mr. Tirov," the man said. "Welcome back to the United States. We've been expecting you."

Expecting him? No one had ever said that to him before. "Thank you," he said, pleased.

The officer tucked a blank red card into his passport and returned it to him. "Please give this to the uniformed officer just there." He nodded toward a large man in a uniform.

Tirov approached the man and handed him the passport and card.

The officer didn't even glance at it. "Right this way, Mr. Tirov," he said, leading the way. They came to an unmarked door off the entry hall; the man opened it with a key and held it for him. "Please have a seat," he said. "Someone will be with you shortly." He handed Tirov his passport and closed the door behind him.

Tirov found himself in a small room with a table and three chairs, all of which were steel and bolted to the floor. The walls were gray and blank, and it seemed a good deal warmer than the air in the entry hall. Fifteen minutes passed, and Tirov took off his jacket and hung it on the back of his chair.

Another ten minutes passed, and Tirov was beginning to sweat. A door on the opposite side of the room from the one he had entered opened and a man in a dark suit with a briefcase entered and sat down. "Good evening, Mr. Tirov," he said. "I am Special Agent Martini of the Federal Bureau of Investigation. May I see your passport, please?"

Tirov retrieved the document from his jacket pocket and handed it over. "FBI? What is this about?"

"One moment, please." The agent inspected the passport carefully, opened it to a blank page, removed a large rubber stamp and an ink pad from his briefcase, and carefully stamped the page. He then took a red marking pen and drew a diagonal line across the page containing Tirov's name and photograph. Finally, he handed back the document.

Tirov opened it to the stamped page and read the message: *This passport is not valid for exit from any port of entry of the United States of America without the written permission of the Director of the Bureau of Immigration and Customs Enforcement or the Attorney General of the United States.*

"What the hell does this mean?" Tirov demanded.

The agent tucked his stamp and pen into his briefcase, removed an envelope and handed it to Tirov. "Read this, please, in my presence."

Tirov opened the envelope, removed a letter, and read it. It was on the letterhead of the director of Immigration and Customs Enforcement:

To: Boris Tirov

Dear Mr. Tirov:

When you applied for permanent residence in the United States some eight years ago, you completed and signed a form and made a sworn statement that you had never committed a crime in your country of origin, nor had you ever been arrested, nor had a warrant ever been issued for your arrest.

It has come to the attention of this Bureau that an arrest warrant on a charge of murder had been issued shortly before your departure from the Russian Republic, and that the warrant remains open and in force.

Therefore, your certificate of residency and work permit for the United States are hereby canceled, and you are ordered to depart the United States within thirty days of this date. When you leave the country you must depart from Los Angeles International Airport on a flight whose nonstop destination is Moscow.

You have the right to file an appeal of this order with a federal court during your thirty-day grace period.

The letter was signed by the director of Immigration and Customs Enforcement.

The FBI agent shoved another document across the table, along with a pen. "Sign this, indicating your receipt and understanding of the letter."

"But I don't understand it," Tirov said.

"The letter is clear and straightforward," the agent said. "Sign here. If you refuse to sign, you will be detained and shipped out on the next nonstop flight to Moscow."

Tirov signed the document. "My attorney is going to hear about this," he said.

The man returned the document to his briefcase. "You must also understand that, since you no longer have a valid work permit, you may not be employed or work in the United States, nor may you accept payment for any previous work in this country." He shoved another document across the table. "This is a list of your known financial accounts in the United States. Read it, and tell me if it is complete."

Tirov read the document, which contained the names and account numbers of a dozen of his personal and business bank and investment accounts. "Yes, it is complete."

"You have no other financial accounts in this country other than these?"

"I do not."

"Sign here."

Tirov signed.

"You may now continue to U.S. Customs, where your luggage and that of your two companions will be thoroughly examined. Any funds or financial documents found will be seized and held until your departure from this country." He handed Tirov a business card. "You must notify this office of your intended departure date and flight number twenty-four hours before departure. Good day." The man got up, unlocked the outer door, and held it open until Tirov could retrieve his jacket and briefcase.

Outside, his two companions awaited, in the custody of two uniformed officers, along with two large carts containing his luggage. They were marched into the customs hall, where four officers proceeded to open and search every piece of his luggage. The process took nearly four hours.

Tirov got into his limousine exhausted and livid. He called his attorney from the car.

29

S tone and Gala woke at the usual time, and their breakfast was brought to the master suite, along with the daily papers. Stone read the London *Times* first, while Gala read the *International New York Times*.

Gala gasped and showed her paper to Stone. In the lower left-hand corner of the front page was a headline: FILM PRODUCER CHARGED WITH MURDER. That gave him a little thrill. He read the article, which after two paragraphs was continued on the entertainment page.

The article reproduced all the allegations in Felicity's document, plus the writer, James Towbin, film critic of the *Los Angeles Times*, had sought comment from members of the management of the studio with which Tirov was about to sign a production deal. They professed themselves shocked and appalled at the news of the murder charge and said that any projected deal with Mr.

Tirov would be held in abeyance until the producer had had an opportunity to clear his name.

"Good God! Is this stuff true?" Gala asked.

"It is, according to the *Los Angeles Times*," he said. "And that is a credible newspaper."

"Boris never mentioned any of this to me. Now I understand why he never had any interest in returning to Russia, even for a visit. He was afraid of being arrested."

"It would appear so. It would also appear that he is going to have his hands full for the next month, trying not to get returned to Russia, where a trial and a long prison sentence might await him, so he will have little time to devote to harassing you."

"Well, that's a good thing," she said. "I don't think I understood until this moment how preoccupied I have been with his stalking of me. I feel an enormous weight has been lifted from my shoulders."

"I'm glad you feel that way," Stone said.

"Can the U.S. government really do this to him?"

"Certainly, if he lied on his application for a green card about his legal problems in Moscow. That's probably a felony, as well, and even if he manages to stay in the country, he might be prosecuted for that."

"Then he is either going to be in a U.S. jail or a Russian one?"

"Very likely," Stone said with some satisfaction.

Gala sat up in bed and looked Stone in the eye. "Tell me the truth, did you have anything to do with this?"

"Are you sure you want the truth?"

"Yes, I do."

"Yes, I did."

"How on earth did you manage it?"

"First, I asked a friend with connections in Moscow to research Boris's background. Then I sent the resulting report to James Towbin, the film critic of the *L.A. Times*, who, you may remember, had an unfortunate confrontation with Boris in the bar at the Arrington, resulting in a sore jaw for Mr. Towbin and the ejection of Boris from the hotel's grounds. The rest is journalism, and no doubt Mr. Towbin and his editors investigated the truth of the allegations and found them not wanting."

"Why didn't you tell me you were doing this?"

"Because you instructed me not to mention Tirov to you again, and I took you seriously."

S till in the back of his car in Los Angeles, Tirov reached his attorney, who had been sound asleep. "Kim, something terrible has happened."

"I know, I read the *Times* this morning. Do you have any idea what time it is, Boris?"

"I'm sorry, I'm just off a plane from London, and I have no idea."

"Well, as long as I'm awake, let me give you my best advice. You are going to be besieged by the press for days over this. Are you at home?"

"I'm on the way home in my car."

"Well, don't be surprised if you find them camped on your doorstep when you get there."

"Oh, shit! What am I going to say?"

"You are going to say that, on advice of your attorney, you have *nothing whatever* to say at this time. You may say that, after taking legal advice, you might be filing suit against a number of people over the propagation of these outrageous lies." He paused, waited for a reply, and got none. "Boris, these *are* outrageous lies, aren't they?"

Boris thought about that. "It's complicated," he said.

"*Complicated*? You had damned well better not say that to the media. You get some sleep, if you can, then you, your agent, and your publicist be in my office at, let's see, eleven o'clock, and together we'll figure out how to handle this. I should tell you that I had a call this afternoon from the head of your new studio saying that the signing of contracts is on hold, and that you are to say nothing to the press until you have talked with their counsel. Come to think of it, I'd better ask him to join us. Now, Boris, go home, get some rest, and I'll see you all at eleven o'clock." He hung up.

A s Tirov's car turned into his front drive, a swarm of a dozen people, some of them with lights and cameras, eddied around his car. "Get us inside!" Tirov yelled at his driver, and the gates were already swinging open. Once through the gates, they began to swing shut again and the crowd, being intimately acquainted with the laws of trespass, hurried to get outside before being trapped inside.

The car pulled to a halt at the front door, followed by the baggage van. Tirov got out, expecting his butler to be at the door, but then he remembered that he had not warned his staff that he was being detained at the airport. He fumbled for his house key, finally found it, and went into the house. His minions began taking luggage upstairs, while Tirov headed for his home office. There was one phone call he had to make, and right now.

He sat down at his desk and pressed a speed-dial button on the phone. Immediately, a male voice answered: *"Da?"*

Tirov switched to his native tongue. "This is Boris Tirov. I wish to speak to him."

"One moment."

It was a long moment. "Mr. Tirov, he is unable to take your call at this moment, having guests for breakfast."

"Please ask him to call me. He has the number."

"I shall do so. He did ask me to tell you that he has read the *International New York Times*."

"Good, that will save us both time."

"That is what he said." The man hung up.

Tirov went to the bar and poured himself a stiff brandy, then sat down at his desk again to wait for the call, if indeed it would ever come.

Another two hours passed before the phone rang.

30

Tirov picked up the phone with trepidation. "Hello?"

A male voice. "The president will speak to you now."

There was a loud click, followed by another male voice. "Boris? Are you there?"

"I am here. I hope you are well, Viktor."

"Better than you, I expect. I read the article in the *International New York Times*."

"That, of course, is why I am calling."

"Of course."

"Although I am very reluctant to ask for your help, I must do so."

"I see. And how would you like me to help you?"

"If the warrant against me is still open, that will put me in a very difficult position."

"I can see how it would. Make your request."

"Will you quash the warrant?"

"It would be illegal for me to do so. Do you wish me to commit a crime on your behalf?"

"No, Viktor, I do not."

"Then what is it, exactly, you wish me to do?"

"It is my hope that there might be a way to make the warrant go away without doing anything illegal." Silence. "Or improper."

"Perhaps."

"That is all I ask."

"If the warrant were . . . shall we say, withdrawn, that would make it possible for you to return to Mother Russia, would it not?"

"Yes, I suppose it would."

"And if I do this for you, what, Boris, will you do for me?"

"Whatever is in my power. You have only to ask."

"Perhaps there is something."

"Please name it."

"There are two things you can do for me, Boris."

"Gladly."

"There is an American actress called Nathalie Dumont."

"Yes, I know her."

"I read in the newspaper that she is arriving in Moscow soon in conjunction with the release of her new film."

"Yes." He had not read the newspaper, and he didn't know.

"I would like to invite her to dinner at my home.

When I issue the invitation I would like to know that she will accept. It would embarrass me if she did not."

"I will be very glad to speak with her."

"You will ensure that she will accept?"

Boris gulped. "I will. She will accept, without fail."

"Very good. Then, as I mentioned, there is one more thing."

"Please tell me."

"If the warrant is lifted, you will be free to return to Moscow."

"Yes."

"Do not do so. Ever again."

Tirov was about to reply, but the phone had already been hung up.

Tirov switched on his computer and looked up the phone number for Nathalie Dumont. He could not bring himself to dial the number, because he knew she would hang up the moment she heard his voice. There had been that encounter when he had bedded her, and it had not ended well.

He went online to the website for the *International New York Times* and moved to the entertainment section. He found the article about Dumont's visit to Moscow and found an attribution to her publicist, Howard Fine. Fine, Tirov reflected, despised him almost as much as Nathalie Dumont did. He thought about Howard Fine for a moment. He was old-school Hollywood, now in his seventies, on the last legs of his career. He needed a publicity coup.

Tirov looked up the number for Howard Fine and rang it.

"Hello," a voice said. Not sleepy, in spite of the hour. Howard would be accustomed to the late-night phone call and would be ready for anything.

"Howard, this is Boris Tirov, and I have very good news for you."

"You complete shit," Fine replied. "How do you have the nerve to call me at this hour? How do you have the nerve to call me at all?"

"Oh, I know what you think of me, Howard, but as I said, I have very good news for you—a coup that may allow you to hang on to a few of your clients for a while longer." There was a brief silence, and Tirov knew he had the man hooked.

"Go on," he said finally.

"I understand you are traveling to Moscow with Nathalie Dumont to promote her new film."

"Yes, that's right."

"Moscow can be a difficult place for a Western publicist to deal with. How would you like it if I were to arrange for Nathalie to be invited by the president to have dinner with him?"

"You can do that?"

"I can. He has already expressed an interest in meeting her."

"And I can publicize that?"

"You may do so."

"Without restriction?"

"You may announce that Nathalie has the invitation and that she has accepted. After the dinner, neither you nor Nathalie may make any comment about the occasion.

Is that perfectly clear? He is a very private person and does not wish his private meetings to be discussed."

"All right, I accept that condition."

"And so will Nathalie?"

"She will, you can count on it."

"Fine. Tomorrow either you or Nathalie may expect a phone call from the Kremlin, extending the invitation. You must accept immediately. If you have her booked for that time, you must cancel it. There can be no variation, clear?"

"I think that's reasonable."

"It is mandatory. He is not a person who wishes to negotiate his schedule."

"All right, agreed. Now, Boris, what do you want from me?"

"Only that you guarantee her appearance on schedule. He will, no doubt, send a car for her. For her, alone."

"All right, I guarantee her appearance."

"And you should not mention my name to Nathalie. You may take all the credit for this coup yourself."

"I have no problem with that," Fine replied with a chuckle.

"Oh, and there is one other thing, Howard."

"What's that?"

"Nathalie should be prepared to accommodate *all* of Viktor's wishes. I'm sure you take my meaning."

"*What?* I can't tell her that."

"I'm not suggesting that you tell her, merely that you prepare her for the eventuality. I think you can handle that, Howard—Nathalie is hardly a virgin, and you're an old pro. You know how these things work. After all, the dinner will be the most important event of her trip, the crown jewel of a junket that the studio has paid dearly for and that is crucial to the success of the film in that market, and if she does not accept the invitation, or if she does not perform as expected—and enjoy the experience—things could go terribly wrong for her and for you in Moscow. You understand."

Fine sighed deeply. "Yes."

Tirov hung up.

Tirov had just gotten into bed when his phone rang. "Hello?"

"I have him for you."

"Of course." His breathing quickened.

"Boris?"

"Yes, Viktor?"

"The prosecutor who filed the warrant against you is now an important judge, by my appointment. He has canceled the warrant, with a letter postdated twenty-four hours after the original filing, citing a lack of any supporting evidence. Anyone wishing confirmation of this may contact our ambassador in Washington, who is holding a regularly scheduled press conference tomorrow at two, Eastern time, at which a question will be asked about this and definitively answered."

"Thank you, Viktor. And Nathalie Dumont will be thrilled to accept your invitation to dinner at any time during her stay in Moscow that you may wish." He gave him Howard Fine's number. "He will arrange everything, and I am very sure that you will find her prepared to be excellent company."

"Thank you, Boris, and if that turns out to be true, perhaps you may visit Moscow sometime after all." He hung up.

Boris lay back in bed, taking deep breaths, trying to slow his heartbeat and his breathing.

31

Stone was having lunch alone, and Gala was out riding alone. Geoffrey entered the room. "A Ms. Holly Barker on the phone for you, Mr. Barrington."

Stone picked up the phone. "Good morning," he said. "I presume you are at breakfast."

"I'm having a cheese Danish at my desk, if that's what you call breakfast."

"You really must come here for a visit, and learn what breakfast is all about."

"I really must. I thought you might like to hear the fruits of your efforts."

"Oh, yes."

"Mr. Tirov arrived in Los Angeles last night aboard the luxurious new Emirates flight from London, having made the crossing in a private suite, only to be rumbled in immigration. He was taken to an interrogation room, where a letter from the director of Immigration and Customs Enforcement was read to him by an FBI agent, giving him thirty days' notice of deportation."

"That long? Why didn't they just bounce him?"

"There were only two other legal alternatives. They could arrest and imprison him immediately, until he made bail, or just deport him and allow him to go anywhere. Neither was warranted for a person who has held a green card for eight years. What they did do was stamp his passport with a notice that he must depart the country from LAX, within thirty days, with a nonstop destination of Moscow."

"Where he would be arrested on the murder warrant?"

"Exactly. Now, does that satisfy your definition of a pound of flesh?"

"I would rather have had his head on a pike, but I suppose a pound of flesh will have to do."

"Mustn't be greedy."

"Will he have any sort of appeal?"

"Yes, and I'm sure he will have a first-rate immigration lawyer to argue his case, but, since he has a murder warrant out for him, his case is unarguable, and he is, essentially, fucked."

"Which is no less than he deserves. The man has stuck his thumb in the eye of almost everybody he has come into contact with in the States, and was rapidly becoming persona non grata in the film business."

"What is it they say in the movie business? 'Be careful who you fuck on your way up the ladder of success, because you'll meet them again on the way down.' "

"I believe that's the gist of it."

"I'm going to give serious thought to busting out of this place and coming to see you. How long will you be there?"

"Awhile, maybe the summer."

"I expect there is a woman with you."

"Well, yes."

"Any chance of her abandoning you?"

"There's always that chance, if my personal history is any indication."

Holly laughed. "That's right, you do have a tendency to get dumped, don't you?"

"Let's just say that they often find it necessary to be somewhere else. I've become inured to it."

"If I come I would prefer not to share your company."

"Duly noted. Will you keep me up to date on the woes of Mr. Tirov?"

"I'll pass along whatever I hear. If he appeals, I'm sure his hearing will be well-attended by the entertainment press and TV shows."

"I'll set my DVR."

"Well, if you'll excuse me, I'll get back to saving the country from whatever the threat is today. Bye-bye." Holly hung up.

B oris Tirov awakened at nine and buzzed downstairs for his secretary.

"Yes, Mr. Tirov," the young man said.

"Telephone my agent and my publicist and tell them to be at Kim Kopchinsky's office at ten forty-five AM today, without fail, and to be on time. I will take them to lunch afterward. Then call Kim's secretary and tell her we'll be arriving at that hour instead of eleven o'clock and to invite him to lunch, as well. Then book me a table for four in the garden at Spago Beverly Hills at half past noon."

"Yes, sir. You have calls from the *Hollywood Reporter* and *People* magazine requesting interviews. What shall I tell them?"

"Tell them to call me back after lunch, and I'll have a statement for them. Also, suggest that they tune in to a press conference by the Russian ambassador at two PM, Eastern, today."

"Yes, sir."

H oward Fine was at his desk when his secretary buzzed. "Yes?"

"Howard, there's a man with an accent on the phone who says he's calling from the Kremlin. Is that a new restaurant?"

"No, my dear, it's a large building in Moscow."

"Idaho?"

"Russia."

"Oh!"

"Put him through." He waited for the buzz, then picked up the phone. "This is Howard Fine."

"Mr. Fine, I bring you greetings from President Viktor Petrov, of the Russian Federation."

"Please extend my greetings to the president."

"President Petrov wishes to extend, through you, an

invitation to Miss Nathalie Dumont for dinner on Thursday of this week at seven o'clock PM at his official residence in the Kremlin. Will Miss Dumont accept?"

"Miss Dumont will be delighted to accept," Fine replied. "I expect she would like to know how to dress."

"It will be black tie," the man replied. "I believe Miss Dumont is residing at the Hotel Baltschug Kempinski, across Red Square from the Kremlin."

"That is correct."

"The president's car will collect Miss Dumont at the main entrance of the hotel at a quarter to seven Thursday evening."

"She will be on time," Fine said.

"Excellent. Goodbye."

"Goodbye."

Fine buzzed his secretary. "Get me Nathalie Dumont."

"Yes, sir."

A moment later, she buzzed him. "Ms. Dumont on line one."

"Nathalie?"

"Hello, Howard," she replied, sounding bored.

"I have the most fabulous news!"

"The news is always fabulous from you, Howard."

"Then try this on for size. On Thursday evening in Moscow, you will be dining at the Kremlin, at the personal invitation of the president of the Russian Federation."

"Who?"

"Viktor Petrov, for Christ's sake!"

"Howard, if this is just some of your bullshit—"

"I assure you, my dear, no bullshit is involved. I have

just had the invitation from Petrov's personal secretary, in the Kremlin. This will be electrifying news in Moscow and will do wonders for our premiere on Friday. You and your movie will be the talk of Russia, and that will be reflected in the grosses!"

"Jesus! What do I wear?"

"It's black tie. Knowing the president's famous eye for beautiful women, I should think something revealing would be appropriate. The president is sending his car for you, and I will have photographers recording your departure from the hotel, which is within sight of the Kremlin."

"Well, thanks, Howard. How did you pull this off?"

"I have my contacts, my dear. I'll see you aboard the studio's jet tomorrow." He hung up feeling very much full of himself.

32

B oris Tirov arrived at the office of his attorney, Kim Kopchinsky, at five minutes before the hour to find his agent, Karl Muntz, and his publicist, Jean Jarman, sitting in the waiting room. He greeted them with a wave and proceeded directly to Kopchinsky's office without being announced.

"Good morning, Kim," Tirov said, taking a seat and indicating that the others should do so as well.

"Just make yourselves comfortable," Kopchinsky said wryly. "Anybody want a hot towel? A mani-pedi?"

"Kim, turn on the TV to CNN, and be quick about it. You won't want to miss any of this."

"What the fuck, Boris?"

"Just do it, it'll save billable hours."

Kopchinsky switched on the huge set on his wall and selected CNN.

The anchor gazed into the teleprompter and said,

"And now, we're going to go to the Russian embassy in Washington, where we're told an interesting question will be answered."

The TV switched to a small auditorium, where the ambassador was giving a boring answer to a question about the Ukraine.

"Boris," Kopchinsky said, "why are you putting us through this?"

"Shut up, Kim, and listen."

Then an off-camera voice shouted, "Mr. Ambassador, do you have any comment on the news that the film producer Boris Tirov was questioned on his arrival at LAX last night and is being shipped back to Moscow to answer a charge of murder in the death of Elena Ivanov eight years ago?"

"Yes, I do," the ambassador replied. "Earlier this morning I spoke to the chief prosecutor in Moscow. He informed me that the warrant for Mr. Tirov's arrest was withdrawn by the prosecutor only hours after first being filed, for lack of any evidence whatever. I spoke to the former prosecutor, now an important judge in the Russian Federation, and he told me that he remembered the incident well, that an assistant prosecutor in his office had filed the warrant with the wrong name on it, and when he discovered the error, the chief prosecutor ordered it withdrawn immediately, and he personally telephoned Mr. Tirov and apologized to him for any inconvenience. Accordingly, I spoke to the United States director of Immigration and Customs Enforcement this morning, and, as a result, he has now issued an order revoking the deportation order and has also apologized for the incorrect stamp entered into Mr. Tirov's passport. This embassy has issued a new passport to Mr. Tirov, which will be delivered to him by a consular official in Los Angeles today."

As Kopchinsky switched off the TV there was a knock at his door. His secretary stood there along with a tall man in a business suit. "A gentleman from the Russian consulate to see Mr. Tirov," she said. The man strode across the large office, shook Boris's hand, and handed him an envelope with a large wax seal. "Mr. Tirov, your new passport, with the compliments of the ambassador."

"Thank you," Boris replied, and the man left. Boris ripped open the envelope and held up the passport for all to see.

"Boris," Kopchinsky said, "how the fuck did you do that? I was ready to file the appeal."

"I made a phone call," Boris said. "Questions, anybody?"

The group stared at him dumbly. Finally Jean Jarman spoke. "Boris, this is a great relief. After all the fires I've had to put out for you lately at Centurion and the Bel-Air Country Club and the Arrington, I thought we were about at the end of our rope."

"Jean, I suggest you call the head of publicity at the studio and explain things to him. Kim, you call the head of the studio and explain what's happened, and, Karl, you call the head of production and tell him I want an immediate public announcement that our deal is still on, or I will be suing before sundown." He got to his feet. "I'll see you all at Spago Beverly Hills at twelve-thirty, and,

Jean, I want press there to cover the lunch, especially the *L.A. Times*."

"Right, Boris," she replied, producing a cell phone.

S tone and Gala were having a drink before dinner when Geoffrey announced a phone call from Holly Barker.

Stone picked up the phone. "Hi, there."

"Hi. It appears that we've had something of a reversal."

"What sort of reversal?"

"I've just e-mailed you a clip from a press conference with the Russian ambassador a few minutes ago." She hung up.

Stone got out his iPhone, found the e-mail, and he and Gala watched the press conference. They were dumbfounded. "How did he do that?" Stone asked.

"He sometimes brags about his friendship with Viktor Petrov," she said. "Maybe he wasn't lying."

Geoffrey announced that Dame Felicity was on the line.

"Hello?"

"I'm told the Russian ambassador to the United States has just held a rather unusual press conference."

"Gala and I have just watched it, and we are very nearly speechless."

"My people in Moscow actually went to the Russian prosecutor's office and viewed the arrest warrant. It had not been withdrawn."

"I wish I could explain it. Gala says Tirov has bragged about his friendship with Petrov."

"My information was that they were estranged. I will correct the record. See you at the weekend?"

"Of course." Stone hung up.

"I wonder what Tirov did for Petrov?" Gala asked. "There must have been something."

"I'd certainly like to know," Stone said.

In Los Angeles, Howard Fine watched a replay of the press conference in stunned silence. He was going to have to start cultivating Boris Tirov, he reckoned.

A meeting was convened at Stalwart Studios, which included the CEO, the head of production, and the head of publicity. They watched the tape in silence, then the CEO said, "Anybody have any doubt what our new position on Tirov's contract is?"

Heads were shaken.

"Let's find Boris a bigger bungalow than we promised," the CEO said, and the meeting broke up.

At Spago Beverly Hills, Boris Tirov held court at a center table in the garden. Photographs were taken by an *L.A. Times* photographer and those of the trade publications.

Across the garden, the film critic James Towbin switched seats with a companion so that his back was to Boris Tirov.

"I am so very glad that I sent the Tirov report to the editor before it ran," he said ruefully. "Otherwise, I'd be looking for a new job."

33

The studio's Boeing Business Jet, a corporate version of the 737, took off from Van Nuys Airport with nearly a full load, which included a digital film crew of three, two still photographers, the studio's CEO and head of publicity, three assistant publicists, a Russian translator, the stars of the film, Rod Rambeau and Nathalie Dumont, their personal assistants, her makeup artist and hairdresser, and her personal publicist, Howard Fine, in addition to the airplane's crew, a relief pilot, three flight attendants, and enough luggage to support a traveling circus. It would be a nonstop flight of some nine hours, with a stiff tailwind, to Moscow Ostafyevo Airport.

Over Wichita a three-course lunch with four wines was served, then everyone settled in for the long flight. Rambeau and Dumont each occupied a small suite of four facing luxurious chairs; Nathalie shared hers only with

Howard Fine, who dozed off almost immediately after dessert.

Shortly, the studio head of publicity, George Hammond, approached Nathalie. "Nathalie," he said, "Mr. Milestone would be very pleased if you would join him in his suite." Marvin Milestone, the studio's CEO, occupied an enclosed area that looked more like the living room in a small but luxurious apartment. As she rose from her seat, Nathalie wondered if a pass were in the offing. She was dressed in a Chanel suit and affected a cool, business-like mien for this invitation. To her relief, Hammond, after opening the door for her, followed her inside.

Marvin Milestone, a tall, elegantly dressed and barbered man with a face made florid by an unceasing flow of alcohol, rose to meet her and shook her hand. They had met half a dozen times socially, once at his home, but never at a business meeting.

"Come in, Nathalie, and make yourself comfortable," he said.

Nathalie chose a large chair facing his and sat down, demurely crossing her legs. "George," Milestone said to Hammond, "why don't you go and check on the film crew?"

Nathalie's heart sank; it was going to be a pass.

"Nathalie," Milestone said when Hammond had gone, "I saw the final cut of the film yesterday, and I want to tell you how delighted I am with the quality of the film and with your delightful performance."

"Thank you, Marvin," Nathalie replied with an appreciative smile.

"As you can tell by the load this airplane is carrying, we are taking Moscow and the Russian Federation very seriously as a future market for our films. This is the first time we have made a major effort in that country, with a gala premiere, followed by a large seated dinner and a ball, and an all-out publicity effort, akin to what we might do for a Radio City Music Hall opening."

"I'm delighted to be a part of it," Nathalie said.

"And I was delighted to hear that Howard Fine, through means I can only imagine, has arranged for you to be invited to dinner by President Viktor Petrov. That Howard is really something, isn't he?"

"He certainly is."

"Have you met Viktor Petrov before?"

"No, I haven't."

"I know him fairly well, and I thought it might be a good idea to prepare you a little for your dinner with him."

"Thank you," she said uncertainly. Prepare her?

"You'll find him—how shall I say?—gregarious. He can be quite warm-natured, especially after a few vodkas. My advice to you is, don't try to keep up with him in the drinks department—you'll want to keep your wits about you."

"I'll remember that."

"Viktor has quite a reputation with the ladies. I understand that many of them have found him to be a charmer."

"Oh, good."

"Nathalie, I recall from reading your contract that this is the first film in which you have had profits participation."

"Yes, it is."

"Two gross points, isn't it?"

"Yes, and I'm very pleased about that."

"I'm glad you're happy. My point is, if this junket goes the way we hope it will, we anticipate that ticket sales in the Russian Federation could add as much as twenty-five million dollars to this picture's gross, perhaps even more. That would mean a very large contribution to your bank account, in addition to other worldwide income, of course."

"That's certainly good news."

"Of course, that goal can only be achieved if we make a complete success of our publicity effort."

"I'll do whatever I can to help."

"I'm so happy to hear that. I just wanted you to understand that you have an important personal stake in making your dinner with Viktor Petrov a complete success."

Nathalie wondered what making the dinner a "complete success" would entail.

"I've no doubt that Viktor will find you extremely alluring."

Nathalie thought that she now knew where this was headed. Milestone did not leave her in doubt.

"If his reputation is to be believed, he will expect his attentions to be received warmly. Do you understand?"

"I think I'm beginning to."

"Not that this would have to be unpleasant. The man does have a reputation for pleasing women."

"Ah."

"I would never ask you to sleep with the man—unless

your heart were in it," Milestone said. "But I did want you to understand what is at stake for you, personally."

"You've made that very clear," Nathalie said.

"And I hope my candor has not offended you."

"I appreciate your frankness," she replied.

"One other thing. Petrov also has a reputation for making things difficult for those who disappoint him. I mean, we could suddenly find that the fire department has shut down our theater for the premiere, or there could be a catering disaster for our dinner afterward, or the print for our showing could be 'misplaced.' It could be very unpleasant for us and wreck our plans for making this film a hit in Russia."

"I see your point."

"I'm so glad." He rose. "Now, I expect you'd like to get some sleep, in order to arrive in Moscow fresh. I understand there will be photographers at the airport and at the hotel. The news of your dinner with the president has piqued the interest of the Moscow public." He shook her hand and opened the cabin door for her.

Nathalie fixed a smile on her face and returned to her seat. Howard Fine was snoring gently by now. She retrieved her handbag and fished out her iPhone.

"How did your meeting with Marvin go?"

She looked up to see George Hammond standing there, smiling.

"Very well, George," she replied.

"I'm delighted to hear it. Marvin just loved the movie, and he is a very perceptive man. It's good for you to know his thinking."

"I expect so," she replied.

"Well, I'll let you get a nap in. I'll ask your makeup girl to freshen you a bit before we disembark."

"Thank you, George." He went farther up the aisle.

Nathalie fired up her iPhone and tapped the calculator app. She wanted to know what two percent of twenty-five million dollars came to. She was pleasantly surprised.

34

Stone and Gala received Felicity Devonshire in the library on Friday evening. It was raining outside, and she entered shaking water from her luxuriant red hair.

"My goodness," Felicity said, "you'd think we were in England."

"I like England in the rain," Stone said.

"Ah, that's the secret for an American to feel at home in this country—he has to learn to enjoy the rainy days. Of course, it doesn't matter if a man's hair gets wet."

"Your hair looks lovely," Gala said. "Even wet."

Geoffrey brought her a brandy and soda, she raised it to her hosts, and they all drank. "Now," Felicity said, "more information has come my way about our recent lack of success in dealing with your Russian acquaintance."

Gala looked at Stone. "I knew you were mixed up in that business, but, Felicity, I had no idea you were."

"I was merely a supplier of commonly held information," she replied. "Nothing that might fall under the Official Secrets Act." She looked around. "Stone, are there any recording devices present in your home?"

"There are none," Stone said firmly. "Neither audio nor visual."

"Thank God for that," she said. "I really should have inquired earlier, but I trusted you."

"I hope you still do."

"I do, and you, too, Gala, that's why I can continue to speak about this without fear of disclosure. This information, if inference were taken to the extreme, would most certainly fall under the Act, and neither of you must ever say to anyone what I am about to say to you."

"Understood," Stone replied, and Gala nodded.

Geoffrey entered the room. "Dinner is ready to be served whenever you wish."

"Give us a few minutes, please, Geoffrey."

Geoffrey closed the door behind him.

Felicity waited a moment, then continued. "I now know how your Russian acquaintance wriggled out of his deportation order."

"I would certainly be interested in knowing that," Stone said.

"Information, from a source I cannot disclose, has made me aware that, earlier this week, a telephone conversation took place between himself and a very high Russian official."

"I thought there was supposed to be an estrangement between them," Stone said.

"Apparently, the relationship warmed just enough for your acquaintance to plead for the disappearance of the record of the charge against him."

"Ah."

"Which raises the question—what did the official require of him in return?"

"I have a feeling you are going to tell us," Stone said.

Felicity smiled a foxy smile. "I am. The official asked if his former friend were acquainted with a certain Hollywood actress, whose new film is premiering in Moscow tomorrow evening. When he replied in the affirmative, the official requested that he arrange for the actress to join him in his quarters for dinner. Apparently, your acquaintance was able to secure the woman for that purpose."

"I know who the actress is," Gala said. "I read in one of the trades online that the female star is Nathalie Dumont, who is a friend of mine."

"You are correct," Felicity replied. "Is she likely to accept such an obvious setup?"

"Not to help Boris, she isn't—she despises him."

"Then perhaps he worked through a third party—someone at her studio?" Stone suggested.

"That makes sense—it's the sort of thing Boris would think of."

"You didn't answer my question," Felicity pointed out. "And I'm dying to know. Would Ms. Dumont be agreeable to the assignation?"

Gala thought about that. "Not as a matter of course, I think, but if there were something important in it for her, then probably."

"Oh good!" Felicity cried, clapping her hands. "It's not often I get something this juicy crossing my desk."

"Suppose," Stone said, "that Ms. Dumont learned of the origin of the request?"

"She would not react well if she knew that it was Boris who desired it. In fact, I think she would take pleasure in refusing, if she thought it might cause him difficulties."

"Are you in touch with her?"

"I have her cell number," Gala replied. "Do you think it would work in Moscow?"

"They seem to work everywhere these days," Felicity said.

Gala reached into her bag for her phone. "What should I say to her?"

"Just that the dinner was arranged surreptitiously through Tirov, and that he's getting something important in return."

"All right." Gala went to her contacts and pressed the button. She turned on the speakerphone.

The number rang a few times, then a robovoice message played. Gala shrugged. "Nathalie, it's Gala. When you get this, please give me a call." She hung up and looked at her watch. "Felicity, did you say that the assignation was for tonight?"

"That was my information."

"It's an hour or two later in Moscow."

"Three hours later."

"Then she's probably at the Kremlin right now."

"Oh, well, there goes her virtue," Felicity said, "in a manner of speaking."

As they were going upstairs after dinner, Gala leaned close to Stone. "What was all that business about the Official Secrets Act?"

"It would seem," Stone said quietly, "that MI6 has somehow placed a recording device either in President Petrov's office or on his phone lines. Or both."

"Oh."

35

Nathalie Dumond stood in front of a three-way mirror in her hotel suite and gazed at herself in the dress she had chosen. He hair was piled high upon her head, and her dress was tight and strapless, exposing breasts of which she was proud, since they were her own and very beautiful. Her heels were high, bringing her total height to five feet, ten inches. Her only piece of jewelry was a choker of large diamonds, a relic of a former relationship with a billionaire boyfriend. She draped a black mink cape around her shoulders and secured it at the throat with a jeweled clasp. Perfection.

Her doorbell rang, and she opened it to find Howard Fine waiting for her. "I'll walk you down to the car," he said.

"Thank you, Howard."

They emerged from the elevator to find a brigade of TV cameramen and flash photographers lining a red carpet that had been laid from the lift to the curb outside, where awaited a large limousine of a type Nathalie had never seen before.

"It's a ZIL," Howard said to her. "No high-up Russian would be seen in anything else."

The hotel doorman held open the car door, and Nathalie got in and arranged herself on the plush velvet seat. Howard leaned in and said, "Knock 'im dead," and closed the door.

The car pulled smoothly away, and the cabin was nearly silent. The ZIL drove directly across Red Square, in a blatant contravention of the traffic rules, and drove up an ornate ramp and into the Kremlin itself, and thence to an entranceway guarded by two tightly uniformed soldiers. A man in a black suit emerged from the building, held open the car door, and assisted her. She took the proffered arm and was escorted into a marble hallway and after a short walk, into an elevator. The man pressed a button, then left the car. "You will be met," he said.

The elevator rose to the top floor, and when the doors opened, the president of the Russian Federation, Viktor Petrov, stood waiting for her, encased in a finely tailored tuxedo. He was an imposing man of about fifty, perhaps six-two or three, and more than two hundred pounds of firm muscle. His hair was iron gray, cut in a short military style. He made a good first impression.

"Good evening, and welcome to my home," Petrov said in lightly accented English. "I hope your drive here was not too tiring."

She laughed; the ride had been less than three minutes, and she had not expected him to be funny. "Hardly, and I'm very pleased to be here, Mr. President."

He offered her an arm and guided her into a large library of dark wood, gilt, and many leather-bound volumes. A small sofa awaited them, with a table set before it with vodka, other liquids, a mound of Beluga caviar, running to about a kilogram, she reckoned, with chopped onion and other condiments set beside it. He sat her down. "What do you wish to drink?"

"Vodka, please."

"He poured them both a glass from a frosty bottle and sat down beside her, thigh to thigh. "May I serve you caviar?"

"Thank you, yes."

He spooned a heap onto a crystal dish, added condiments and a small spoon, no blinis or biscuits. They raised their glasses and drained them, then dug into the caviar.

"And how is your visit to Moscow so far?" he asked.

"It's a beautiful city. I had hoped to see some of the countryside, but they have me on a tight schedule of interviews."

"Perhaps on another visit you may come to my dacha, in the country. It is quite beautiful and restful there."

She felt the first flush of the alcohol and resolved to sip from here on in. "Perhaps, who knows?"

"I have seen a number of your films," he said, "and I have always been much impressed with your performances."

"Thank you very much."

His eyes rested on her breasts. "That is a very lovely dress," he said. "It suits you."

She smiled broadly. "Thank you, that is a very nice compliment."

They lowered the level of the caviar and the vodka, as well, then a uniformed butler entered and announced dinner. They followed him to a small dining room with a terrace with a spectacular view of Red Square. They were served four courses of haute cuisine and three wines, chatting all the way. He was charming, witty, and sexy all at once, she thought. After dinner, she excused herself to freshen up, and when she returned, found that he had left the room as well.

She stood at the entrance to the terrace and let the night air play on her bare shoulders, very pleasantly tipsy. She heard a door open and close behind her, and felt him move toward her and kiss her on the back of the neck. She gave a little shiver, then felt the long zipper of her dress move down to the crack of her buttocks. The dress fell into a pool at her feet, exposing her only other clothing, a pair of black fishnet stockings, held up by a lace garter belt.

She felt him move back, and she turned around.

Petrov stood there, clad in only a pair of black socks, and sporting the largest penis she had ever seen outside a porno film.

Nathalie would later reflect that they were both appropriately dressed for the occasion.

36

Stone, Felicity, and Gala lay on his bed, spent, enjoying the afterglow. Gala's phone rang, and she reached for it on the bedside table. "It's Nathalie Dumont," she said.

"Oh," Felicity said, "put it on speaker."

Gala did so. "Hello?"

"Gala? It's Nathalie." She sounded breathless. "How did you find me in Moscow?"

"Apparently, cell phones work everywhere these days. I read online that you had quite a dinner date."

"Oh, God, did I!"

"And how did that go?"

"It was a combination of the best dinner and the best sex I've ever had!"

"Well, congratulations on both counts."

"That is the most amazing man! He's coming to the premiere of my movie tomorrow night as my date!"

"I'm sure the studio will be very happy about that."

"I thought Howard Fine was going to have a stroke when I told him, and I've already had an enormous bouquet of roses from Marvin Milestone. He says this is something new in the history of Hollywood."

"So, Howard Fine arranged your dinner?"

"He did. I don't know how the man does it, and he's what, seventy-five?"

"Could be. Howard has forgotten more than the young publicists know."

"Oh, and I'm staying over a few days after the premiere so that I can visit Viktor's dacha in the country."

"I hope you have the stamina for it."

"Don't you worry about that, Gala. Oh, I'm a little sore here and there, but after tonight, I'm up for anything! I don't want to go into much detail on a cell phone, but when I see you I'll give you a blow by blow. Are you in Santa Fe?"

"No, I'm in the south of England, visiting a friend who has a country house here."

"Oh, that sounds nice."

"It certainly is. I'd better let you go. I'm sure you're exhausted."

"Exhilarated," she replied. "Bye-bye." She hung up.

"You didn't tell her about Boris's involvement," Stone said.

"She was so excited, I didn't want to ruin it for her. Let's let Howard Fine take all the credit."

"Now we're back to square one, and Boris doesn't have a mark on him."

"You two will just have to think of something else,"

Felicity said. "Preferably something that doesn't involve me."

"You've been very kind, Felicity," Gala said.

"Yes, you have," Stone echoed. "I won't impose on your good nature any further."

"It's not that I didn't enjoy it, mind you. A tidbit for my memoirs when I'm a very old lady."

"What about the Official Secrets Act?"

"Then perhaps immediately after I die. I don't believe the Act survives death."

S tone was having breakfast in bed with Gala the following morning when his cell phone rang. "Hello?"

"It's Lance." Stone immediately tensed; a call from Lance was not always good news.

"Hello, Lance, how are you?"

"I'm quite well, thank you, considering the state of the world. That weighs heavily on my shoulders, but otherwise, I'm rather lighthearted."

"I'm so glad."

"I find I am going to be in your neighborhood today, and I'd love to see your house."

"Of course. I'll give you lunch."

"Is one o'clock all right? I have to make one other stop."

"That will be fine. Would you like to stay on a night or two?"

"What a nice invitation. Let me see what I can do with my schedule. See you at one."

Stone hung up.

"That was odd," Gala said.

"What was odd?"

"The tone of your voice—there was a wariness in it."

"I hadn't noticed, but I suppose I'm always a little wary where Lance Cabot is concerned."

"The CIA head?"

"One and the same. He's coming for lunch today and may stay the night."

"Why are you wary of him?"

"Lance always has an agenda, usually hidden, sometimes more than one. I expect he wants more than to see the house."

"Will I meet him?"

"Of course—you'll join us for lunch."

"I'll excuse myself if it seems he wants to be alone with you."

"That's very discreet of you, and don't worry, he'll find a way to let you know."

37

L ance's entourage was small: just two white SUVs. He dismounted from the front passenger seat, walked around the car and climbed the front steps, where Stone stood, waiting to meet him.

Stone offered his hand. "Welcome, Lance."

"Thank you, Stone," Lance replied, looking around at the house and the view. "You always have such good taste."

"Thank you. May I offer your people some lunch?" But the cars were already making a U-turn.

"Thank you, Stone, but they saw a nearby pub on our way here that they liked the look of."

"Come in."

"May I have a tour?" Lance asked.

"Of course." Stone started with the ground-floor offices, then they took the lift upstairs and saw some bedrooms, including the master suite, then they walked down to the main floor and saw the drawing room and the two dining rooms, large and small, before repairing to the library. Lance, who usually did not reveal much, seemed dazzled, especially by Gala. "I know your work on film," he said, "and I look forward to seeing much more of it."

"I'll do my best to keep you busy," Gala replied.

"It's not too early for a drink," Stone said.

"Have you a good single malt?"

Stone opened the liquor cabinet to display nearly a dozen.

"I'll try the Talisker," Lance said. "With a tiny bit of ice." He accepted the drink and the offer of a chair opposite the sofa, where Gala sat. He took a sip of the whiskey. "Ah, good! The Scots know their business, don't they?"

"They do," Stone agreed.

"How many houses have you these days, Stone? I lose count."

"Only five," Stone replied. "I sold Connecticut to Bill Eggers."

"This one was done by Susan Blackburn, from the look of it."

"It was. Susan had nearly finished a complete renovation for the previous owner when I bought the place."

"And why would the previous owner want to sell?"

"He was dying, and I think he wanted to leave his heirs cash instead of property."

"You're in business with Susan, aren't you?"

"No, my colleagues at Woodman & Weld helped her put together a business plan for expansion and found her some property and the money to buy it. The rest she has done herself."

"And done very well," Lance said.

"Do you have an interest in Susan's business, Lance?"

"Only in passing. I have a London property that I've owned for many years. It's rented at the moment, to a fellow from the embassy, but he's retiring, and I'm thinking of occupying it myself."

"Thinking of retiring yourself, are you?"

"Not a bit of it. But I seem to be spending more time in London these days—it's so close to everything in Europe. It would be nice to have something more than a hotel suite to work from."

"Would you like an introduction to Susan Blackburn?"

"Thank you, I met with her yesterday afternoon. We took a stroll through the house, and she made some notes. Your name came up."

"Not in vain, I hope."

"Certainly not! She's obviously very fond of you."

"I gave her another commission. She did the country house Arrington, next door."

"That was my other stop on the way here—very impressive. I understand you have a neighbor of my acquaintance, as well."

"Felicity? Yes, she's just across the river. It was she who brought this place to my attention and insisted I buy it."

"Ah, yes, I'm sure Felicity can be a helpful neighbor to have. In fact, I hear she's been helpful to you very recently."

"I expect you hear all sorts of things, Lance."

"What an astute observation!" Lance replied, laughing. "The latest thing I've heard is that Viktor Petrov is taking an interest in the American film business, and that you had something to do with that."

"The only people I know in the film business, apart from Gala, are in Hollywood, and I am not acquainted with Mr. Petrov."

"Well, I did not mean that you had a direct connection, but apparently you somehow spurred a Mr. Tirov to renew a connection with his old friend Viktor."

"Well, I may have helped make it necessary for Tirov to make that move. I was quite surprised by his dexterity, really."

"I can believe that! Just when you thought you had Tirov made permanently unwelcome in our country, bang! He plays the Petrov ace! An unfortunate twist in what I thought was a rather well-executed plot."

"Ah, well."

"Still, it's an ill wind that doesn't blow *somebody* some good, isn't it?"

"And who might that be?"

"I understand that the mere announcement that Petrov will attend the film's premiere tonight has caused a rush in advance ticket sales."

"Really?"

"I'm told the film may be grossing north of thirty million dollars in Russia, perhaps a great deal more."

"Well, I'm as happy for them as one can be who has no relationship with that studio."

"That's right, it's Centurion on whose board you serve, is it not?"

"You know very well it is, Lance."

"And, in an unusual arrangement, Centurion is co-financing the film with Stalwart Studios."

"I'm afraid I missed my first board meeting at Centurion because of a monumental traffic jam on I-405, so I was not aware of that arrangement."

"Ah, yes, that was the board meeting that nixed the production deal with Boris Tirov, wasn't it?"

"It was, and I regret missing it, because I would have liked to cast my vote against it. Still, Tirov *believes* I killed his deal, so I have all the fun of being his enemy while not having earned his enmity."

"On that count, at least," Lance said.

At that moment, Geoffrey called them to lunch, and Stone had to wait until halfway through the fish course before he could return to the subject of Tirov. "You were saying, Lance, that there are other reasons why Tirov should hate me?"

"Was I?" Lance munched on his turbot for a moment. "Oh, yes, well, there is the imbroglio with Tirov's near deportation, isn't there?"

"Tirov connects me with that?"

"It appears that his connections on the Russian side are nearly as good as your connections on our side. He certainly believes, rightly or wrongly, that you personally instigated that very embarrassing episode."

"Rightly," Stone said. "And I'm sorry it didn't work as planned."

Lance turned to Gala. "Ms. Wilde, given your personal experience of your former spouse, what effect would you think this knowledge would have upon Mr. Tirov's view of our mutual friend Stone?"

"I should think," Gala said, "that if he was annoyed before, he is *livid* now."

"How very well put!" Lance put down his fork, took

a large sip of his Bâtard-Montrachet, dabbed his lips with his napkin, and consulted his watch. "And now, Stone, having persuaded Ms. Wilde to deliver the bad news I had found so distasteful, I'm afraid I must hie myself back to a meeting at the embassy this afternoon. I hope you will forgive me for rushing away." He drew an envelope from his pocket. "Have you a pen?"

Stone offered him one.

"Having seen the new Arrington and your house, I am ready to sign the contract with Ms. Blackburn to design my property." He signed the document with a flourish, sealed it in the envelope, and handed it to Stone. "Would you be kind enough to send this out with your post?"

"Of course," Stone said, accepting the envelope.

Lance stood, kissed Gala's hand, shook Stone's, and made his way to the front door, where his entourage awaited.

Stone and Gala waved him off.

38

Stone walked Gala down to her office, next to his own.

"What was that business with Lance all about?" she asked.

"At least two things," Stone said. "He wanted to see some of Susan Blackburn's work, though he could have seen plenty of it in London, and he wanted to let me know that his spying is just as good as Felicity's, maybe better."

"How better?"

"The tap that Felicity has on Petrov's office and/or phone lines may actually be the CIA's, and she may be borrowing from it."

"Or the other way around."

"Yes, but Lance has made it possible for us to believe one or the other, instead of just the one. I guess that's good for his ego."

"You understand these things so much better than I."

"Not necessarily, I just know the two spies very well. I'm guessing, really."

"Your guesses are intriguing," she said. "You should have been a screenwriter." She logged onto a website. "Let's see how La Dumont's film is doing. Aha, Lance's information is good, but not good enough. The film is projected to do thirty-five million in Russia, and get this—Nathalie has two gross points! Lucky girl!"

"So she had business motives, as well as carnal ones, to spend a few days with Viktor Petrov."

"Her instincts are good all round."

"Did you and Ms. Dumont ever partake of each other?"

"Stone! One threesome, and you think I'm any-body's?"

Stone laughed.

"Actually, she did make a pass at me, once. We were sunbathing in the nude on the deck at her Malibu house. I dozed off, and she gave me a big kiss in an intimate place. I woke up, startled, not sure if I was dreaming, and she apologized profusely. If she had been a little more subtle, I might have been receptive—after all, she's very beautiful, especially when naked. She did find a way to say that it was a standing offer."

"The mind boggles!" He excused himself and went to his own office to check his e-mail.

Stone reflected that there had been another reason for Lance's visit, but he hadn't wanted to mention it to

Gala: Lance had thought it important to warn him that Boris Tirov remained a threat, probably more of a threat than before. Certainly, if the Russian had any inkling that Stone was behind the attempt to deport him, he would be, as Gala had put it, *livid*.

He called Mike Freeman at Strategic Services in New York. His secretary told Stone that Mike was traveling, but that she could connect him. There was a click.

"Michael Freeman."

"Mike, it's Stone."

"How are you?"

"Very well. Where are you?"

"On the Gulfstream, en route to Paris. What's up?"

"I think I may need a bit of security at Windward Hall."

"Gala's ex?"

"Exactly. Lance Cabot was here for lunch, and he went out of his way to tell me I should be worried. I was involved in a little chicanery, designed to get him deported from the U.S.A."

"Ah, yes, I read about that. Didn't work, did it?"

"No, he got Viktor Petrov to intervene on his behalf. The warrant vanished."

"And Tirov found out you were involved?"

"Lance seemed to think so."

"I should think that when Lance seems to think something, it might be time to be worried. How much coverage do you want?"

"A man on my dock and two at the house."

"Around the clock?"

"At least at first."

"Let's see, it's three o'clock U.K. time. I can have them there by, say, seven PM. We're talking a crew of nine."

"That's fine. I'd like them to be unobtrusive—Gala shouldn't know."

"Being guarded wouldn't make her feel better?"

"Maybe, but it might make her feel threatened."

"I see your point. I won't have them check in with you, then, they'll just materialize. I'll have them housed in the village, not on the estate."

"That might be better."

"Armed?"

"I don't want to cause you legal difficulties."

"We're licensed for that sort of thing."

"As you think best, then."

"Stone, did Dino tell you I've made him an offer to join us?"

"He did. Have you heard back from him?"

"We've had a couple of conversations. There are some political considerations, since the mayor is going to run for reelection, but I think his main concern is that he and Viv might get their wires crossed at work. I've told him that we'll call him a consultant, and he'll report directly to me. That seemed to satisfy him, so we'll see how the mayor reacts to news of his early departure. I take it this arose because of a conversation with you."

"I guess it did, at that."

"Then, if he joins us, I'll have you to thank."

"You can buy me a drink."

"Okay. I'd better make some calls and get your security set up. You won't notice them when they arrive, but I'll give you a number to call, if you want to speak to the team leader."

"Ready to copy."

"His name is Rob Poulter—ex–Special Air Service and MI5." He dictated the number.

"Got it. You can give him my cell number."

Stone looked up to find Gala standing in his doorway.

"I guess Lance had another motive for stopping by," she said.

"Yes, he did, and I thought it a good idea to have some eyes on the estate for a while."

"I think so, too."

Stone thanked Mike and hung up. "I'm glad you're okay with it. They will be unobtrusive, won't be in the house unless we require it."

"I'm glad they won't be in the bedroom," she said.

T hey had dinner and were getting undressed when Stone's cell phone rang. "Yes?"

"This is Rob Poulter. Is this Mr. Barrington?"

"It is."

"I just wanted you to know that we're on station."

"I asked the kitchen to leave a pot of coffee on and some sandwiches in the fridge. The back door will be unlocked."

"Thank you, that's very kind, but we have some packed food. The hot coffee will be good, though. If we have an alert, I'll ring your number once, then hang up."

"All right."

"And I'll do the same as an all-clear."

"Got it. I'm glad you're here, Rob."

"Good night, Mr. Barrington."

"Good night, Rob."

39

They made love for a while, then fell asleep in each other's arms. Stone was awakened by a noise, but he couldn't figure out what it was. He moved over in bed and discovered that his arm had grown numb from being under Gala's neck. He got up and went to the bathroom, massaging the arm, and gradually it came back to life. He was on his way back to bed when he figured out that the noise he had heard was his cell phone ringing. Once.

He found his pants and took the iPhone from the holster it lived in. There was one recent call. Then he remembered that one ring was an alert from Rob Poulter, and that another was cancellation of the alert. He had not heard the second ring. He took the phone into the bathroom, closed the door, and rang back Rob's number.

"Poulter."

"It's Barrington. What's up?"

"I have a man down on your dock."

"How bad?"

"Unconscious—apparent blow to the head."

"Did you bag anybody?"

"We've started a search. I've called for more men."

"Do you need transport for your man to a hospital?"

"He's being put into a vehicle now. We're six miles from the nearest casualty ward. He'll be there in ten minutes, and they've been advised of his arrival."

"Do you need any help from me?"

"Thank you, sir, but I don't want to deliver you into the wrong hands. You stay put. Are you armed?"

"I have a hunting rifle and a shotgun."

"I'd keep the shotgun handy. Would you like me to furnish you with a handgun?"

"Maybe later, and only if it can be done legally."

"I'll have that worked on. Ring you back when we're clear."

Stone hung up, put on a robe, and padded down to the study, where there was a gun rack hidden behind a panel. He loaded the shotgun, put a handful of shells in the pocket of his robe, and went back upstairs, the shotgun broken across his arm. He didn't want any accidents.

He sat in the shadows, in a chair by a window overlooking the front lawn. There was half a moon out, and he had a good view. He had been there perhaps fifteen minutes when the phone rang once: all clear. He went back into the bathroom, closed the door, and rang Poulter.

"Poulter."

"How's your man?"

"Conscious and talking. He came to in the van on the

way to the casualty ward. Mild concussion, he'll be fine after some sleep."

"How good is the opposition?"

"Anybody who could get over on my man would have to be either very good or very lucky. I'll assume very good."

"Did your search turn up anybody?"

"Not yet. I'm of the opinion that, having discovered a guard on the premises, the opposition thought better of an intrusion. They'd have no way of knowing how many of us there are."

"Do you have enough men?"

"I've doubled the guard. In a couple of hours more men will be arriving. I think we'll make ourselves more conspicuous, send a message to the opposition."

"Good. Do you need anything from me?"

"No, sir, we're very much self-contained. We may fetch some coffee from your kitchen so that any remaining watchers can see us doing it."

"Good night, then." Stone hung up, dropped his robe onto a chair, first having removed the shotgun shells from the pocket and setting them on his bedside table. He laid the shotgun on the floor within reach and got back into bed. It was some time before he could doze off.

He was wakened by Gala shaking him. Sunlight was streaming through the windows. Stone had not adopted the English custom of drawing the drapes, shutting out the night.

"What?" he managed to say.

"What is *that*?" Gala asked, pointing down. She was quite naked.

Stone looked over the edge of the bed. "That's a shotgun. Didn't you recognize it?"

"I know what it is—what's it doing there?"

"It's lying in readiness."

"Readiness for what?"

"You never know when a pheasant might disturb our sleep."

"I'll tell you what would disturb my sleep—the sound of a shotgun going off in my bedroom."

"I'll get a net for the pheasants—it's quieter."

"I'm going to get myself into a shower, if you're fairly certain I won't be disturbed by gunfire."

"I'm fairly certain."

She stalked off toward the bathroom. Stone picked up the phone and ordered breakfast, then he joined her in the shower.

"I hope you're unarmed," she said.

He pressed against her. "Not entirely."

"Is that a shotgun?"

"No, it's just glad to see you."

Stone had finished his breakfast and was on coffee when his cell rang. He glanced at it, but the call was blocked.

"Good morning, it's Mike. I understand there was a kerfuffle last night."

"How is your man?"

"He was released from the hospital this morning, and I gave him the day off for some rest. Another half a dozen men are already on the job."

"Did your man remember anything about last night?"

"Nothing. It's disturbing that anybody could get past him."

"Rob thought so, too. He thought that more men on the ground would send a message."

"I've taken steps to get a pistol permit issued to you by the Hampshire authorities. It should be delivered to you before the day is out. Chief Inspector Holmes was very helpful. The shotgun is legal, as long as it's not sawn off."

"I don't think Purdy's, the makers, would approve of that modification."

"Probably not. Are you feeling a little rattled?"

"No. Last night I was for a bit. Took me a while to get to sleep again."

"I'd like you a little rattled as long as this goes on," Mike said. "We view this as a serious matter."

"What's your advice?"

"You won't take it."

"Try me."

"Leave the country. Go back to the States, where you can shoot an intruder without bringing the world down on you. Pick your state with that in mind."

"My choices are New York, Maine, or California. Oh, and my girl has a place in Santa Fe."

"New Mexico fills the bill. Do you have your airplane in England?"

"Yes."

"Use it. I'd like you on American soil as soon as you can get there."

"Is tomorrow night soon enough?"

"What's wrong with tonight?"

"Am I in a hurry?"

"You should be."

"All right, we'll sleep tonight in the Azores and make New York tomorrow and Santa Fe soon after."

"Where in the Azores?"

"Santa Maria, for refueling."

"I'll arrange dinner, bed, and breakfast. Two people?"

"Yes."

"What time will you land?"

"I don't know, late afternoon, maybe."

"Does your airplane have a satphone?"

"Yes."

"Got a pen?"

"Yes."

Mike recited a number. "Call that when you're an hour out. You'll be met, and there'll be fuel, a weather forecast, and a flight plan filed for tomorrow morning. I'm assuming you'll be stopping in Newfoundland."

"Yes, St. John's."

"Shall I call Joan and have your man meet you at Teterboro?"

"Yes, thank you."

"I've just gotten a forecast. The Atlantic weather is gorgeous, you'll have severe clear all the way. Don't tarry in New York for long."

"Thanks, Mommy." Stone hung up.

Gala came out of the bathroom. "Anything new?"

"Yes, on advice of counsel, we're leaving for the States. You've got an hour to pack."

"Are things that bad here?"

"It's the best advice I can get."

"Where in the States?"

"We'll stop in New York for a day or so, then continue to Santa Fe and hunker down there, if that's all right with you."

"It's perfect for me. All this English greenery is getting on my nerves."

Bob came trotting in. "I think Bob will like it, too."

40

They took off from the Windward strip and made Santa Maria, Azores, in four hours. Stone spotted a man wearing an orange slicker and holding up two lighted plastic sticks and aimed for him. He shut down the engines and switched off power, while Gala got the cabin door open. Bob bounded down the stairs as if the lineman was an old friend to be greeted.

Another man in a leather jacket and a fedora stepped up. "Mr. Barrington? My name's Fernando. I'm a friend of Mike Freeman. Let's grab your bags and get moving."

They did so and got into an elderly Land Rover. "There'll be a man guarding your airplane all night, and you'll be ready to taxi at seven AM."

"Are you expecting any opposition?" Stone asked.

"Let's just say we'll be ready for it."

He drove them inland to a stone cottage on a hill. It

was well-furnished and comfortable. "My wife is in the kitchen preparing dinner," Fernando said.

They dined on local fish and fresh vegetables, with a bottle of Pico Branca served as well. By nine o'clock they were asleep.

They were wakened at five-thirty and told that breakfast would be ready in half an hour. After a quick shower, they sat down to omelets, orange juice, and strong coffee. At the airport, Stone signed for the fuel, looked over the forecast, and checked his fuel. Half an hour later they rotated and lifted off, headed northwest. Two hours later, Stone was startled by the ringing of his satphone.

"Hello?"

"It's Mike. Everything okay?"

"So far."

"I don't like the look of things at St. John's," he said. "We're diverting you to Gander." Gander was an old military base on the north of the island, half an hour from St. John's.

"What's going on at St. John's?"

"Unidentified people and vehicles on the ground. At Gander, stay in the airplane. You'll get a quick turn-around, and the fuel will be billed to us, later to you. At Teterboro, you'll taxi straight to the hangar. Stay aboard while you're towed in. Your car and driver will be inside."

"Whatever you say."

Stone called air traffic control on his high-frequency

radio and was cleared Direct Gander. Skies were still sunny at Gander, with its one, very long runway. A fuel truck was waiting. When the tanks were full, the fueler secured the caps and whirled a finger in the air for startup. Stone started the engines and got an immediate clearance to Teterboro from the tower. They were the only thing moving on the field, and five minutes later they were in the air.

At Teterboro, Stone followed Mike's instructions. Immediately after shutdown, the tractor towed them into the hangar, and the big door closed behind them. Bob went nuts when he saw Fred Flicker, who was waiting for them with all doors open. Luggage was loaded, Bob was emptied, and they were off for Manhattan. Once home, Fred drove into the garage, and they unloaded after the door was closed.

The sun was still up when they fell into bed.

The following morning Joan called while they were having breakfast in bed.

"How's the jet lag?" she asked.

"So far, so good."

"We had a visit from the phone company yesterday," she said. "Guy with a foreign accent said he needed to get into our main box to fix a problem in the neighborhood."

"How did you react to that?"

"I put my hand in my desk drawer and told him to bring me an authorization from his supervisor. We didn't see him again. I had Bob Cantor check out everything, and we're okay. How long are you staying?"

Stone thought about it. "We're leaving in an hour," he said, and hung up. "That okay with you?" he asked Gala, and she nodded. It was okay with Bob, too.

A t ten AM they lifted off for Santa Fe, and soon they were at flight level 400 and headed direct to their destination. It was a longer flight than Stone would have wished, with a big headwind, but they had the fuel for a nonstop flight, and with the two-hour favorable time change, they were landing in Santa Fe by early afternoon.

"Oh, my beautiful house!" Gala cried, looking around the immaculate place. "Marlene has cleaned so beautifully!"

Bob ran aimlessly around until he had located his dish, then demanded food and drink. Happily full, he went to his bed and fell sound asleep.

"Oh, I'm so happy to be home," Gala groaned as she settled into bed. "Not that I wasn't happy in England. It was the change I needed. I'm going to finish my screenplay in a couple of days, and then I can relax."

"Great," Stone said. She fell asleep immediately, but he could not relax until he and Bob had patrolled the perimeter of the property and made sure all the doors and windows were secured and the alarm turned on.

Stone read for a while, but it was nearly two AM before his mind relaxed enough for sleep.

Bob was way ahead of him.

S tone was awakened by a low growl from Bob, which quickly became a series of loud barks.

Gala stirred. "What's going on?"

"It's nothing, go back to sleep." He found Gala's pistol in the night table drawer, slipped on a robe and slippers, and let Bob lead the way. The dog trotted to the kitchen and stood by the back door. Stone put him on a leash and held it in his left hand, the pistol ready in the other. As soon as the door was open Bob practically dragged him outside and along the rear of the house. Then he stopped and sniffed the ground. There was enough light for Stone to see a large pile of animal scat, which Bob found fascinating.

They continued around the whole perimeter of the house and returned to the kitchen door from which they had gone out.

They went into the kitchen, where Stone gave Bob his breakfast, then poured a glass of orange juice for himself. He drank it at the kitchen table and let his heartbeat return to normal.

Finally, as dawn broke, Stone went back to bed and tried to get in another hour of sleep before Gala woke up. He managed half that before she turned up with scrambled eggs and bacon and set them on his belly.

"How did you sleep?" she asked.

"Got to sleep late, woke early, then got a few minutes more. I'm tired."

She took his tray away. "You go back to sleep," she said.

41

S tone slept soundly until mid-morning, when Bob
stuck a cold nose in his ear.

"What have you got against sleep?" he asked the
dog, and got his answer from a floor-thumping tail. "You
want to go out?"

Bob's response was affirmative.

"Go see Gala."

Bob did as he was told.

S tone was showered and shaved in time for lunch, then
he made a call to the ranger who had investigated the
bear earlier.

"I thought you were going to remove the bear," he
said to the man.

"We did. We anesthetized her, drove her up into the

Sangre de Cristo Mountains, and left her there to regain consciousness. She was already stirring when we left her."

"How about her cubs?"

"We never spotted them."

"Well, I think she must have come back for them, because the dog went off in the middle of the night, and I found a large pile of scat behind the house. Are the cubs old enough to survive on their own?"

"Either she's nursing them again, or they didn't make it."

"You want to have another shot at removing her?"

"I've got a new assignment that's taking all my time."

"Can I hire a private contractor to do the job?"

"If you know one, sure. All the guys I know would just kill her and the cubs, too."

"I don't want that."

"There's one other possibility that you should keep in mind."

"What's that?"

"This might not be the she-bear. It could be her mate, and he could be a lot harder to handle."

"Uh-oh. What's your best advice?"

"Two things. One, don't leave any food outside, and bring your garbage cans indoors. I've already told your neighbors to do that."

"What's number two?"

"Move out."

"For how long?"

"I wish I could tell you that—long enough for the bear to give up on finding food around the place, and who knows how long that is?"

Stone thanked the man and hung up, then he went into the bedroom, found Gala and reported his conversation with the ranger.

"So you want to go back to New York?"

"L.A. is closer. I've got an Arrington board meeting coming up out there in a few days—that might be long enough for the bear to forget about us."

"I guess I can finish my screenplay in L.A."

"I'll give you the study at the house—you can avoid interruption there."

She shrugged. "All right, but remember, Boris lives in L.A."

"We'll lie low—he won't know we're there."

B efore they took off, Stone called his son, Peter.
"Hi, Dad, you still in England?"

"No, I'm in Santa Fe, but I'll be in L.A. tonight. Can you and Ben and the girls come to dinner?"

"I can. I'll check with Ben."

"Ask Billy Barnett and his wife, too."

"All right."

"Leave me a voice mail about how many to expect."

"Will do. Seven o'clock all right?"

"Come at six for a drink."

"Okay."

They hung up.

* * *

Stone, Gala, and Bob landed at Santa Monica Airport at mid-afternoon and an Arrington car drove them to the hotel and home, to his house on the grounds. He got a message from Peter that there'd be six coming for dinner. He called his regular chef and gave her the news, then discussed a menu.

Everybody was there a little after six, and they had drinks beside the pool. When he had a chance, Stone sat down next to Billy Barnett, formerly Teddy Fay, in an earlier existence.

"I've been having some problems, Billy," he said.

"I've read about some of them."

"They're continuing. I tried to get him deported, but my plan backfired. I had a visit in England from Lance Cabot, who warned me that Tirov was still a threat. Mike Freeman put some people around my house, and one of them ended up in the hospital. Mike advised me to get back to the States. We went to Gala's place in Santa Fe, but we've had continuing bear problems there and we were advised to get out for a while. I've got a board meeting here in a couple of days, so this seemed like the best idea."

"Does Tirov know you're here?"

"Not that I'm aware of. It's my intention to stay holed up here until after the meeting."

"It sounds to me like Tirov is not going to be easy to discourage. Do you know what he wants?"

"Gala, I guess, but any sensible man would know that's not going to happen."

"Anything else?"

"Maybe me, dead."

"That's a serious problem and one that requires immediate attention."

"I'm doing all I can."

"Why don't I have a word with him?"

"A word? What does that mean?"

"It means I'll speak to him, see if he'll listen to reason."

"Why do you think that might work?"

"The man's a bully. He has that reputation, anyway. Bullies are accustomed to being the aggressor, the dominator. They're unaccustomed to being called on it."

"And how do you call him on it?"

"By invading his space."

"Do I want to know how this will happen?"

"No, you don't."

"I'm not sure I'm comfortable with that."

"Are you comfortable being the prey in this relationship?"

"Of course not."

"That won't change, unless Tirov is made to believe he should change his behavior."

"I don't want him dead, Billy."

"I would, in your circumstances, but I understand your qualms. Perhaps we can solve this and still leave him less than dead."

"What does 'less than dead' mean?"

"It's one of those expressions that offers a broad latitude in results. Perhaps we can just cause him to be less comfortable in his skin."

"I think I would be good with that."

"Then consider it done."

42

Back when Billy Barnett had been Teddy Fay, he had been a very careful man. He still was.

Teddy had spent twenty years working for the CIA, but not as an operative. He had risen to become head of the Agency's Technical Services division, where his work had been to supply and equip undercover agents with the tools that enabled them to carry out covert operations—weapons, clothing, poisons, burglars' tools, disguises—whatever they needed. In order for Teddy to do his job effectively he had to know the nature and details of each mission, and he had stored this information in his commodious memory. After his retirement he had begun carrying out missions of his own devising, which had not endeared him to the government and agency he had served so well for so many years.

Thus, he had become a fugitive, which had required a great many new skills. Finally, after acting to save the lives of two young men, Peter Barrington and Ben Bacchetti, the gratitude of Stone Barrington and his friendship with both the former and current presidents had resulted in a presidential pardon for Teddy's sins, for reasons of national security and sealed against any inquiry.

Teddy had become Billy Barnett and had gone to work for the two young men, who were beginning their careers as filmmakers, and eventually, after doing all sorts of jobs for them, he found himself serving in a production role, at which he was very good. When Ben had been promoted to head of production for the studio, there was more and better-paid work for Billy.

Billy had refrained from employing Teddy's methods, except on rare occasions, when the safety of his benefactors was in question, and it was clear to him now that the safety of Stone Barrington was in question.

Billy had developed a disaffinity for Russian mobsters. He had found them to be blunt instruments, without finesse and without much guile, either. From his earlier dealings with them he made some suppositions about Boris Tirov: he thought that Tirov would be guarded by two large men, partly out of a native paranoia, but also out of parsimony—he would be unwilling to pay more people, except under extreme duress. He thought that Tirov, who he knew to be very wealthy, would live in a well-fenced property, but not one so large as to require more security people. He knew there would be a dog, but probably just the one. There would also be a security system, but it would be little used, because Tirov would believe that two men and a dog were better, and because, with the three of them roaming the house and grounds, they would be continually setting off alarms, disturbing their master's sleep.

Billy took a day to scout Tirov's property and confirm all his suppositions, then he prepared. He visited the arsenal of Centurion Studios, where hundreds of weapons were housed, waiting to be used in shoot-'em-up films of all descriptions. There he found a dart gun, which he had designed and made for a film some years before. He paid a nighttime visit to the studio's pharmacy, part of the clinic the company maintained for its employees, and there chose a surgical tranquilizer, which allowed patients to remain conscious but immobilized and pain-free during minor procedures, so as to be able to answer the doctor's questions during surgery.

Thus armed, he stopped on the way home from work and purchased a Scotch egg, a snack preferred by the British members of the film community.

He went home, had dinner with his wife, and went to bed. He awoke at two AM, dressed in black clothing, and went to his car. He drove into the Hollywood Hills and found Tirov's house, then parked, facing downhill, two doors up the street. As he approached the target house, he heard a loud bark from the rear of the property. He leaned against the fence and gave a low whistle, then he heard the dog running toward him. He removed the wrapping from the Scotch egg, which was simply a boiled egg, packed in sausage and injected with a bit of tranquilizer, and tossed it over the fence. The dog, with its hypersensitive sense of smell, located it immediately, and Billy could hear him devouring it. Soon, he became quiet.

Billy chinned the fence and looked over. Perhaps

twenty feet away was the lump of a sleeping Alsatian. He placed both hands on the fence top, vaulted it, and knelt at the base of the hedge inside the fence. There he removed the dart gun from his bag and waited. Soon, a large bald man came out of the house, looked around and knelt by the dog, murmuring to it in Russian. Billy shot him with the dart and watched him crumple next to the sleeping dog. Two down, one to go.

He went to the sleeping man, found a semiautomatic pistol on his belt, removed it, and threw it into the hedge. He went to the rear of the house and peered into a kitchen, where another large man was making a sandwich. He sat down at a table, took a bite and chewed thoughtfully; then he put down the sandwich and came out the back door. "Sergei?" he called. "Sergei?"

Billy shot him with another dart. He fell to his knees, groping at his back to find what had bitten him. Billy walked over and struck him once at the back of the neck, and he fell forward, out.

Billy now knew that there were no motion detectors in the backyard, nor was the kitchen door armed as part of the alarm system. He walked into the kitchen, then stood for about a minute, listening for any footstep or hostile noise, while reloading the dart gun. From there, it was a simple matter to find the master bedroom, since someone there was snoring loudly.

Billy peered around the doorjamb and saw a sleeping male figure, who was doing the snoring. He also noted that the far side of the bed had been slept in and that there was a light on in the bathroom. Best to wait.

After five minutes or so Billy was surprised to see a

young woman, quite naked, emerge from the bathroom, dress, and gather her things, including some cash from a bedside table. Billy flattened against the wall. The bathroom light went out, and the woman left the bedroom and walked down the hall to the front door and out of the house. Outside, a car started and drove away. Billy had not seen a car parked out front, so he assumed that the woman had called for a pickup.

Now Billy stepped into the bedroom and fired a dart into the snoring figure on the bed. The man sat bolt upright for a moment, then fell back and began snoring again. Billy unscrewed the dart assembly from the end of the air pistol that held it, then walked to the bed and sat down on the edge. He pinched the man's nostrils closed, and his mouth fell open. Billy placed the barrel of the gun in his mouth and watched his eyes open in shock.

"Good evening, Boris," Billy said in a quiet voice. "Can you hear me?"

Tirov nodded.

"Good. I have an important message for you. I was asked by a friend to come here and either give you a message or kill you—my call. Do you understand?"

Tirov nodded and tried to speak. "Shut up, Boris," Billy said, and he did. "Good. I have decided to deliver the message, instead of killing you. Do you understand?"

Tirov nodded.

"Now, you have been misbehaving, making enemies everywhere. You have been thrown out of bars and clubhouses, you have been shunned by a major film studio, and you have come within an ace of being deported to your native country, where a murder charge awaited you.

I congratulate you on weaseling out of that one, but your weaseling days are over. Hereafter, you are going to become a charmer, warm and friendly to everyone. Do you understand?"

Boris nodded.

"If you harm or cause to be harmed any person, or insult or anger anyone at all, whether a studio executive, a waiter, or a car parker, I will hear about it, because I hear everything. Then I will come back into your home and kill you in your sleep. Do you understand?"

Boris nodded.

"Do you believe me?"

Boris nodded.

Billy removed the gun from his mouth. "Now you may go back to sleep."

"Who the fuck are you?" Boris managed to ask.

"Why, I thought you knew, Boris—I'm your worst nightmare. Sleep tight." Billy got up and went into the kitchen. He took a small electronic device from a pocket and laid it on the counter next to the phone. He unscrewed the mouthpiece of the instrument, then connected the device to two wires inside, then he replaced the mouthpiece and left by the front door. He walked up the street to his car, got in, released the brake, and let it roll downhill to the next corner. There he started the engine and drove home.

"That ought to do it," Billy said aloud to himself.

43

oris awoke well after dawn in a groggy state. He wriggled his fingers and toes, then sat up. He was a little thick-headed, but apparently unharmed; he thought he had had an especially vivid dream. The young woman who had fallen asleep next to him, after performing her duties, was gone.

He got up and went into the kitchen for coffee, which his men always prepared for him. There was no coffee, just a half-eaten sandwich on the table. Boris felt a little dizzy and sat down until the feeling passed. He noticed that the kitchen door to the back garden stood open, so he got up and closed it. As he did, he noticed a lump on the back lawn. He blinked a couple of times to clear his vision, then went back to the bedroom, got his glasses and put them on.

The lump on the back lawn moved a little, and Boris went outside to investigate. He prodded it with a toe, and it turned and looked at him. It was Ivan, one of his men.

He sat up and rubbed his face, then got to his feet unsteadily. "Good morning, boss," he said.

"What is this?" Tirov asked, plucking a dart from the man's back.

"I don't know, boss."

Tirov pointed the dart at another lump. "Is that Sergei? And Chichi?"

Ivan gazed at the lumps. "Yes, boss."

Tirov walked over to Sergei and plucked a dart from his neck. He examined the dog and could find no darts, but there was a lump of food on the ground. Both Sergei and the dog stirred.

"Get on your feet, Sergei!" he yelled. "You too, Chichi!"

Both of them struggled to stand. Chichi made it, but Sergei collapsed again. Tirov kicked him hard in the buttocks. "Get up, you ox!" he yelled in Russian. Sergei finally made it to his feet.

"What has happened here?" Tirov demanded. He got no answer from anybody, but as he thought about it, he realized that his vivid dream was no dream. He felt his own neck, found another dart, and yanked it out. "Invaded!" he shouted. "My house has been invaded! Where were you?"

"Unconscious, boss," Ivan said. "You too?"

"Go inside and make coffee," Tirov said. "We all need it, Chichi, too."

B illy Barnett arrived at work at the studio bungalow half an hour early, as usual, and made coffee in the kitchen. Twenty minutes later, all the staff were at their desks, most of them drinking his coffee. It was an Italian roast, espresso, and made very strong. Anyone who was not quite awake would be soon.

Billy's direct line rang. "Billy Barnett."

"Good morning, Billy, it's Stone Barrington."

"Good morning, Stone."

"I've had second thoughts about our conversation the other night, Billy, and I don't want you to take that chance."

"Please hold for a moment, Stone." He set down the phone, walked around his desk, and closed his office door, then came back and picked up the phone. "It's done," he said.

"What's done?"

"I visited the gentleman late last night and had a word with him."

"How did you do that?"

"I thought we decided it was better if you didn't know."

"Well, I didn't want to know before you did it, so I guess it's better if I don't know afterward."

"I think that's best, too. I believe I delivered the correct message. I don't think he will annoy you again. In fact, I don't think he will annoy anyone again. I couched my request in general terms—no names were mentioned."

"I see."

"Perhaps not really, but we've already agreed it's best if you don't."

"Yes, we have."

"Is there anything else I can do for you, Stone?"

Stone thought about that. "Do you have any experience dealing with bears, Billy?"

"Russians?"

"No, not Russians—real bears."

"None whatever, I'm afraid. Why do you ask?"

"Never mind, I'm just rambling. Thank you, Billy, hope to see you again soon."

"Same here, Stone." They both hung up.

B oris Tirov was tearing into a huge breakfast; he had never been so hungry. His two minions were hungry, too. Only Chichi seemed uninterested in food or drink. He had stared disconsolately at his bowl of strong coffee, which normally held water, then he had curled up in his kitchen bed and gone to sleep.

"What happened here last night?" Tirov demanded of nobody in particular.

"We were all shot with darts, drugged, and made unconscious," Ivan said.

"Obviously," Sergei agreed.

"I know that, you imbeciles, but who did this?"

"Probably someone hired for his expertise," Ivan said.

"But who hired him? Who would do this to me?"

"Boss," Ivan said, "the list is long."

"My ex-wife? Would Gala do this?"

"No, boss, not Gala," Ivan said. "She's too nice a person."

"She's not a nice person, she just doesn't have the guts."

"How about the lawyer?" Sergei posited.

"The lawyer? Barrington? He's just a lawyer—he doesn't know how to do this stuff, and he doesn't have the guts, either."

"Boss, who got you into trouble with the immigration?" Ivan asked.

"The lawyer," Sergei offered.

"The lawyer, the lawyer! Shut up about the lawyer!" Tirov shouted.

"It's the sort of thing a lawyer would do," Sergei replied.

"Our friends had trouble with the lawyer before, remember? The stories we heard? That stuff in Paris? That was the same guy, wasn't it? Barrington?"

"It wasn't Barrington in my house last night," Tirov said. "I heard his voice—it wasn't Barrington."

"Somebody he hired," Ivan said.

"That's right," Sergei offered.

"Who would he know, a lawyer like him?"

"Somebody very good," Ivan said. "I mean, he walked in here, put three men and a dog out of action, then . . ." Ivan stopped. "Then what did he do? You said you heard his voice?"

"He talked to me," Tirov said. "I was lying on the bed, and he talked to me."

"What did he say?"

"He said I should be nice to people."

"What people?"

"I don't know, he didn't mention anybody in particular. Just people in general, I guess. No, I take that back— he mentioned studio executives and waiters."

"And why did he think you would do that? Be nice to people?" Ivan asked.

"Because he said he would come back and kill me if I didn't do it."

The two men stared at him blankly. "Did you believe him?" Sergei asked finally.

"Yes," Tirov replied.

"So, what are you going to do?"

"I'm going to kill the lawyer."

"Didn't the guy last night say he would kill you if you weren't nice?"

"Yes."

"Killing the lawyer isn't nice."

"If I kill the lawyer, there's nobody to pay the guy from last night."

"Unless it's not the lawyer."

"What's not the lawyer?"

"Unless it's not the lawyer paying the guy."

Tirov thought about that. "The guy last night will never know it was me that killed the lawyer."

Ivan shrugged. "If you say so."

"I guess you want us to kill the lawyer," Sergei said.

"No, I want to do it myself."

Sergei brightened. "No kidding?"

"No kidding. Get me a pistol with a silencer."

"Okay," Sergei said.

44

Billy got home from the office; his wife drove herself, and she was still working, so he had the house to himself. He went into his workroom and picked up an electronic box that was connected to a phone line. The box was connected to a tape recorder, and it had a green light on its front, which was blinking. He opened the box and rewound the tape inside, and what he overheard was a conversation in the kitchen between Boris Tirov and his two minions, Ivan and Sergei. Billy did not like what he heard.

Tirov was in his home office when Sergei returned with the silenced gun and handed it to him. "This is a fucking .22!" Tirov yelled.

"Boss, it's the best thing for the job."

"A .22 is too light, it won't kill him outright."

"It will, if you shoot him twice in the head from close up."

"I could kill him with a baseball bat from close up. Why would I want to get close up?"

Sergei sighed. "Boss, I think we need to go do some target practice, okay?"

"Okay," Tirov said.

Sergei drove them through the hills to Mullholland Drive, then took a left and drove until the road became unpaved. They passed an illegal garbage dump, then he turned off the rough road onto something that was little more than a track. When he had put a hill between them and Mullholland, Sergei stopped the car and pressed the trunk button.

He came out with two plastic bags, one filled with small melons and one with guns. "Okay, boss," Sergei said, "what kind of gun you feel comfortable that will kill the guy?"

"A nine-millimeter or a .45," Tirov replied.

Sergei went and set up a row of half a dozen melons. He took a .45 from the plastic bag, checked to be sure it was loaded, then handed it to Tirov. "Okay, one in the chamber, safety is on. We're about twenty feet from the first melon, the one on the left. Put a round in that melon. Take your time."

"I haven't fired a pistol since I was in the KGB," Tirov said, adopting a combat stance and aiming the weapon. He fired, and the round kicked up the dirt well behind the melon, a foot high.

"Again," Sergei said. "Keep shooting until you hit it."

Tirov fired until the gun was empty. All the rounds missed, except the last one, which hit the melon next to the one he was aiming at.

Sergei handed him another gun. "Okay, try it with the nine-millimeter."

Tirov fired another magazine and missed every time.

"My point is, hardly anybody but an expert can hit anything the size of a head from twenty feet. I mean, I'm very good, and I might hit two out of three." He took the pistol from Tirov and handed him the .22. "Now walk over there to three feet and fire two into a melon, any melon."

Tirov walked over and fired two rounds into the melon.

"See? You either get close or you get yourself a rifle with a scope and practice a lot. The easy way is to get close."

"I get it," Tirov said. "I don't mind getting close. I'd like to look him in the eye while I'm killing him."

"If you look him in the eye, he'll duck or run or fight you. A pro doesn't look the mark in the eye—he walks up behind him and shoots the guy before he knows anybody's there."

"That may not be easy," Tirov said.

"This is why so few people are professional hit men for a living," Sergei explained. "It's hard. People don't want hard, they want easy. This is why they hire hit men. Handing over cash to a pro is easy. Do-it-yourself is hard."

Tirov handed the .22 to Sergei. "Reload this. I want to see how far away I can hit him."

Sergei popped in a loaded magazine and stood back.

Tirov began firing, getting closer and closer. He was at five feet before he hit a melon, and he missed the next two. "Okay, it looks like three feet," he said, half to himself.

"Good," Sergei said. "Now where do you see this happening?"

"Where do you suggest?" Tirov asked.

"I like parking garages," Sergei replied. "My favorite is a parking garage outside a movie theater, because everybody arrives and leaves at the same time."

"But I have to wait for him to go to the movies," Tirov complained.

"There is that. Okay, a parking garage anywhere except at a shopping mall. People are coming and going all the time in a shopping mall. A parking garage at an office building is good—people come to work, later they go home. And the acoustics are good—you can hear somebody coming fifty yards away."

"Forget about fucking parking garages, Sergei, I'm not going to sit around waiting for him to go to a parking garage."

"In that case, you gotta catch him going somewhere. You drive up beside him, shoot him through the window and scram. You need a good driver for that one."

"I can't wait for him to drive somewhere."

"Okay, then you invite him. Ask him to lunch, and shoot him when he's on the way."

"He's not going to accept an invitation to lunch from me."

"Because you haven't been nice to him?"

"Exactly."

"Then get somebody who's been nice to him to give him the invite."

"I'll think about it," Tirov said.

45

Gala was sitting at a desk in the study of Stone's Arrington house, her laptop on the desk. It was going well: she had her conclusion in mind now, and the dialogue in the final scenes was going well. Her cell phone rang. Without looking at it, she picked it up. "Hello?"

"Gala, it's Boris. Please don't hang up, I have something important to say."

"What is it, Boris, and make it quick—I'm working."

"First of all, I want to apologize to you for the trouble I've made. I'm very sorry, and I won't do it again."

"Thank you, I appreciate that."

"I want to apologize to Mr. Barrington, too. I'd like to take both of you to lunch at the Bel-Air."

"Boris, that's crazy. Why would Stone want to have lunch with you?"

"I've been seeing a therapist," Tirov said, "and she says

it's very important to my recovery that I personally apologize to everyone I've offended."

"Then either your therapist is insane, or she has no idea how many people you've offended. It would take years for you to personally apologize to all of them."

"I've got to start somewhere, haven't I? Please do this for me. Ask Mr. Barrington if he will bring you to lunch at the Bel-Air. After all, I have to apologize to you, too."

"All right, I'll ask him, but I won't recommend it."

"That's all I ask. I suggest tomorrow at one o'clock, in the Bel-Air garden restaurant. Later tomorrow afternoon, I have to leave for a location shoot. I'm starting a big Western, and I won't be back for weeks."

"I'll ask him. Goodbye." She hung up. He had broken her concentration; now she had to get her head back into the scene she was working on.

S tone stopped in. "Can you break for a bite?"

She closed the laptop. "Sure, I can use a break."

"I'll have lunch sent to the pool."

They settled down at a table there, and the food arrived.

"Stone," she said reluctantly, "I have to ask you a favor."

"Sure, how can I help?"

"I had a call from Boris this morning."

"Oh, no," Stone groaned.

"It's all right, it's nothing bad."

"What did he have to say?"

"He's begun to see a therapist, and as part of his treatment she has insisted that he see the people he's offended and apologize to them personally."

"That sounds like a twelve-step program."

"Maybe it is, I don't know, but he's begged me to bring you to lunch at the Bel-Air tomorrow, so that he can apologize to you."

"I don't want his apology," Stone said. "I just want him to be absent from our lives."

"I want that, too, and this may be the best way to accomplish it."

"I'm not sure I could have lunch with him without stabbing him with a fork."

"He was really very pathetic on the phone. I believe he's sincere. And I know him well enough that he won't let up until he's seen us."

"How about later in the week?"

"He's leaving tomorrow afternoon to go on location for several weeks."

Stone sighed. "I don't want to see him—not yet, anyway. I'm still too angry with him. Next time we're in L.A., maybe. When is he coming back from his location shoot?"

"He said several weeks."

"I'm sorry, I know you want this, but I don't really trust myself to see him, not even in a public place."

"All right, I'll tell him."

When they had finished lunch, Gala called Tirov.

"Gala?"

"Yes."

"Did you speak to him? Will the two of you join me?"

"I'm sorry, Boris, he has a business meeting tomorrow. He said perhaps next time we're in L.A."

"As you wish," Tirov said, and there was ice in his voice.

"I'll call you next time we're in L.A."

"My therapist says that if someone I've offended won't meet me, then I should send a gift."

"If you like, fine."

"I'll have it messengered to the Arrington tomorrow, before I leave for location. What suite number?"

"Just address it to Stone—the hotel will know. Have a good shoot." She hung up and went back to work. The lunch break helped; she got her scene finished.

The following morning Gala finished her script. She read through it once more, and was pleased with how well it flowed. She e-mailed it to her agent, who would print and messenger the hard copy to the studio.

She and Stone had lunch by the pool again, and they celebrated her completion of the script with champagne.

As they were finishing lunch, the butler approached. "Mr. Barrington, please excuse me. A delivery came for you, from Tiffany's. I put it on the table in the study."

"Thank you," Stone said. "I'm not expecting anything."

"I forgot to tell you," Gala said. "When I told Boris you couldn't have lunch, he said that his therapist had told him that if he couldn't see someone to whom he was apologizing, he should send a gift instead. He's always loved Tiffany's—it's probably a clock or a piece of crystal."

When they had finished lunch, they went into the house, and Stone found a large sky-blue box on the study table, tied with a white ribbon. There was no card. He was about to untie the ribbon when he stopped and looked at the box carefully. It looked like every other Tiffany's box he had ever seen: there were no marks or blemishes. He thought about it for a minute, then he sat down and got out his cell phone.

Gala came into the room. "Oh, is this the one from Boris?" She reached for the ribbon. "Shall I open it for you?"

"No!" Stone said, stopping her short. "Please don't touch it." He pressed a speed-dial button and waited.

"Billy Barnett," a man's voice said.

"Hi, it's Stone."

"What's up?"

"I had a lunch invitation from Boris Tirov yesterday. He told Gala his therapist wanted him to apologize to people he had offended."

"Really?"

"I declined, and he said he would send a gift instead. It arrived a few minutes ago. It's a large box from Tiffany's."

"Where is the box?"

"On a table in my study."

"Have you touched it?"

"No."

"Don't. I'll be there in twenty minutes. Please let the front gate know I'm coming."

Stone hung up, called the front gate and told them to let Billy in when he arrived.

B illy walked into the room without knocking, carrying a briefcase, and went straight to the box. He walked slowly around it, then lifted it carefully and peered at the bottom and set it down again. "Would you and Gala please leave the room?" he asked.

"Gala, please leave the room," Stone said.

She started for the door, then stopped. "What about you?"

"I'm going to stay with Billy."

She left the room and closed the door behind her.

"Are you sure?" Billy asked.

"If you're staying, I'm staying."

Billy set his briefcase on the table slowly, then opened it. He removed a small box cutter, placed his hand on top of the box, and pressed the box cutter against the side until it pierced the cardboard. Then he began sawing, until he had cut a circular hole about four inches in diameter. He then put the cut cardboard and the box cutter into the briefcase, bent over and sniffed at the hole. "Uh-oh," he said. He removed a small flashlight from his briefcase and shone its bright light into the box, then he turned it off and stepped back. "There's a piece of plastic explosive in there half the size of my hand—about four ounces, I estimate. Enough to destroy this room and kill anyone near it."

"I'm glad I didn't open it," Stone said.

"It's time to call the bomb squad," Billy said.

"What's the alternative?"

"I can disable it myself."

"Safely?"

"I wouldn't do it if I thought I'd get killed."

"Then let's leave the police out of it," Stone said. "It would take me days to deal with them."

Billy went back to his briefcase, removed a pair of wire cutters and the flashlight, and went to work. A minute later, he stood back. "All clear," he said. "What would you like me to do with the explosive?"

"I don't want it."

"Then I'll dispose of it, if that's all right."

"That's all right," Stone said.

Billy reached into the box through the hole he had made, removed a slab of what looked like modeling clay, put it into his briefcase, and closed it. He picked up the briefcase in one hand and the Tiffany's box in the other. "If you'll excuse me."

"Thank you, Billy," Stone said.

There was a knock on the door.

"Come in," Stone said.

Gala stuck her head in. "Everything all right?"

"Everything's fine," Stone said. "My board meeting is

tomorrow morning. Shall we go back to Santa Fe tomorrow afternoon?"

"Fine with me." She left.

Billy spoke up. "Don't you think it's about time you
dealt more positively with Tirov?"

"Perhaps it is. How would you advise handling it?"

"Let me give it some thought. I'll call you."

46

Teddy drove home, angry that Tirov had not taken him seriously. That night, he revisited his house and found the place deserted. Next day, he made some phone calls and learned that Tirov was shooting a Western at a place called the Bonanza Creek Movie Ranch, in New Mexico; the woman he talked to said the shoot was for five weeks. He didn't feel like going to New Mexico, so he decided to wait until Tirov returned.

Stone attended his board meeting in a hotel conference room; his friend Marcel duBois attended from Paris via video. He had lunch with the board, then he and Gala took off from Santa Monica at four o'clock. They picked up a big tailwind and were in Santa Fe in little more than an hour.

By the time they got to the house it was six o'clock and the sun was low in the sky. Stone stopped Gala's Range Rover out front. "Hang on here," he said, "and keep Bob with you. I want to have a look around the house before you come in. I'll call your cell when I'm done."

He carried their bags inside and set them by the front door, then as quietly as possible he checked out the master suite and the kitchen. All was in order; no visits from bears or ex-husbands. He called Gala. "The coast is clear. Come on in."

Stone fed Bob and built a fire in the kitchen hearth, and they had a drink before Gala fed him.

"You never told me what was in the box from Boris," she said.

"It was a homemade bomb," Stone replied.

"Are you serious?"

"Very serious. Billy disposed of it."

"Why didn't you call the police?"

"Because it would have kicked up a lot of dust, and nothing would have come of it. He would have denied everything, and we would have had no evidence that he sent it. He's not dumb enough to leave fingerprints or DNA on the box or the bomb."

"But why would he ask us to lunch one day, then send us a bomb the next?"

"I think that if we had left the Arrington, even for the short drive to the Bel-Air, something would have happened to us on the way. When we declined his invitation, he turned to other means. That's my best guess, anyway."

"Then what are you going to do?"

"I don't know yet. I know what I'd *like* to do, but you don't need to hear that."

"If I knew how to have him killed, I'd do it," Gala said.

"No, no, no, murder isn't the answer. I know someone who would do it, if I asked him, but I'm not going to."

"He deserves to die."

"Maybe he does, but I'm not going to make that decision. Quite apart from the moral considerations, which are daunting, murder is a very messy business, and there are too many ways to get caught. I know that all too well from my days as a homicide detective."

"Are there any circumstances under which you would kill him?"

Stone shrugged. "Self-defense. Tell me, when you were divorced, did you have the locks here changed?"

"Every one of them," she replied. "Were you thinking of luring him into the house?"

"No, that would make it murder."

"Tell you what, you lure him into the house, and I'll kill him."

Stone laughed. "Do you want to spend the rest of your life in the New Mexico State Prison?"

"Of course not."

"There's an old saying among criminals—'If you can't do the time, don't do the crime.' That's jailhouse wisdom."

She fixed them another drink, then started dinner. "I'm just going to make some pasta," she said.

"I'll be pitifully grateful for anything," he said.

Stone's cell phone rang. "Hello?"

"Hi, it's Billy Barnett."

"Hi, Billy."

"Did you leave L.A.?"

"Yes, we're in Santa Fe, at Gala's house."

"I'm sorry to hear that."

"Why, do you miss us already?"

"I had a look around Tirov's house last night, and he wasn't there. I made some calls and found out that he's at a place called Bonanza Creek Movie Ranch, making a Western."

"Yes, he told Gala that he was going on location."

"Do you know where the Bonanza Creek Movie Ranch is?"

"No idea."

"It's just outside Santa Fe. Gala's place is in Tesuque, right?"

"Right."

"Then you're about ten, fifteen miles from Bonanza Creek."

"Oh, shit."

"My sentiments exactly," Billy said. "I think it would be a good idea if you invited me out there?"

"Consider yourself invited."

"I'll borrow the Mustang from Peter and come tomorrow morning."

"We have plenty of room for you. Bring your wife, if you like."

"Thanks, but not when I'm working. Where do you park?"

"Landmark Aviation. What time shall I pick you up?"

"I'll arrange my own transport, thanks."

Stone gave him directions to the house.

"It may be late in the day before I'm there."

"All right, see you then." He hung up.

"Who was that?" she asked.

"Billy Barnett. We're going to have a houseguest from tomorrow night."

"For how long?"

"I don't know."

"Does this have something to do with Boris?"

"Turns out that Tirov's Western is being filmed at a place called Bonanza Creek Movie Ranch, which is only a few minutes' drive from here. Do you know it?"

"Yes. I've been out there. It's a good facility. Lots of movies have been shot there. Boris didn't mention it to me."

"I shouldn't think he would."

They had dinner and shared a good bottle of wine. By the time they had cleaned up the kitchen it was bedtime, and they were both a little drunk.

Stone went ahead to the master suite and turned on some lights. Bob came along and got into his bed. Then he growled.

"What is it?" Stone asked.

Bob growled again, but then thought better of it and put his head down.

Stone got Gala's pistol from her bedside table and pumped a round into the chamber. He turned on the outside lights, stepped out onto the terrace, the gun extended, and walked halfway around the house and back. No bears.

He went back inside, disarmed the pistol, and put it into his bedside drawer. He was more tired than he had thought, and still a little drunk, and he was out before Gala came to bed.

47

Stone was awakened by a loud bark from Bob. He sat up and looked at the dog; the room was lit by the moon. "Bob," he said softly, "go back to sleep. There are no bears." Then he heard another noise, one he had not heard since he was a boy at summer camp. He had been running down a trail and ran straight over a rattlesnake before he heard the rattle.

Now he heard the rattle again, and Bob started barking.

"What's going on?" Gala said, sitting up.

"Just stay where you are, and don't put your feet on the floor." He got out the pistol again and armed it. The rattling continued, and so did Bob.

Stone got on his hands and knees and crawled to the end of the bed. He could see it now, coiled to strike, hissing and rattling at Bob. "Bob, stay! Don't move." He found the head of a rattlesnake too small a target, so he got down from the bed and began inching his way toward the fireplace. The snake became aware of him and struck in his direction, but short.

Stone found time to wonder at the size of the thing; it was at least a five-footer. He made a leap for the fireplace and got hold of the poker. When the snake turned its attention to Bob again, Stone stepped forward and swung at its head. He felt a shock like connecting with a golf ball, and the snake began writhing uncontrollably. It took him half a dozen swings to connect with the head again, and then the reptile gave up and lay there, twitching. Bob approached it cautiously, then jumped back when it twitched again.

"My God in heaven," Gala said. "What next?"

Stone got the fireplace tongs, picked up the snake, and dragged it outside, surprised at how heavy it was. He could not reach around the body of the thing with one hand. He flipped open a box where a garden hose was stored, removed the hose, and packed the snake's body in it and closed the lid, to keep the coyotes out.

Back in the room, Gala was still sitting up in bed. "May I go to the bathroom now? I really need to go to the bathroom."

"Sure, go ahead." It was only when she had left the room that it occurred to him that there could be more than one snake in the house. He followed her down the hall, poker at the ready, listening for another rattle. Satisfied that there were no more reptiles in the house, he went back to bed, but left the pistol and the poker on the bedside table, within ready reach.

Gala went back to sleep immediately; it took Stone an hour.

*   *   *

Billy Barnett landed Peter's Citation Mustang at Santa Fe in the early afternoon, rented a nondescript car with a GPS, and drove away, not bothering to ask directions of anyone. He didn't want someone to remember having given somebody directions to the Bonanza Creek Movie Ranch.

He found Bonanza Creek Road, and soon came to the ranch. There was a place for public parking, and he left the car there and followed the signs to the tour bus, which was loading when he got there. He was dressed in khakis, sneakers, a tan windbreaker, and a baseball cap with no name embroidered on it, and cheap sunglasses. He paid the man at the bus door and went to the rear of the bus, where there were a number of empty seats. He didn't want conversation.

The bus was electric and drove slowly down the town's main street, while the driver pointed out the saloons, the sheriff's office, the hotel, the stable, the blacksmith's shop, and a corral with half a dozen horses in it. The driver mentioned that the gunfight at the O.K. Corral had been filmed there more than once.

The bus continued off the main street and it was revealed that some of the buildings were simply facades, with nothing behind them.

Then they went back to the main street and parked in front of the saloon, which turned out to be beautifully complete and heavily furnished with a large nude over the bar, a painting of Custer's Last Stand nearby, a huge mahogany bar, manned by a bartender in period clothes, and a poker game of movie extras in costume. A player piano ground away in a corner, playing "Oh, Them Golden Slippers," and the tourers were treated to a draft beer on the house.

"Are they not filming today?" Billy asked the bartender.

"Nah, shooting begins tomorrow, and the first three scenes will be shot on this set," the bartender replied.

"Where does the crew and cast live?"

"They're all staying in town at La Fonda, on the Plaza."

Billy wandered around the saloon, peering at the decorations. He found a hat rack with a gun belt and a six-shooter hanging from it. Keeping his back to the bartender, he took the Colt .45 out of its holster and checked the cylinder: loaded, but with blanks. He replaced the gun and went and watched the poker game for a couple of minutes; the extras were playing for real, it seemed.

The bus driver announced that he was about to leave and that no one could stay on the set. As the tourers filed out, Billy saw a script on a table near the door. He was last out, and he slipped it under his jacket, then got back on the bus. They were driven back to the parking lot, and as he got off the bus, Billy noted a truck arriving with a closed rear, and emblazoned with the legend COSTER'S ANIMAL WRANGLERS—Furry Creatures and Reptiles.

"Those folks supply coyotes and snakes and such," the driver said as Billy got off the bus.

Billy got into his rental car and drove back past the airport and to Tesuque, thinking all the way.

48

Billy got to Gala's house at dusk and was greeted by Stone Barrington at the front door. Stone led him to a guest room, and helped him with his bags, one of them quite large. "What's in here?" Stone asked.

"Stuff," Billy replied.

"Oh. Get settled, then find us in the kitchen, and we'll have a drink there before dinner."

Billy put his shaving kit on the sink and stuffed his large case into a closet, then he sat down for a few minutes and flipped through the script he had stolen at the ranch. There was a shooting schedule and a call sheet for the next day, too; probably belonged to one of the poker players. He tossed the script onto the desk, then went to find the kitchen.

"Before I offer you a drink," Stone said, "I want to show you something." He led Billy outside through the kitchen door, switching on an outdoor light along the way, then he flipped open the hose box. "Have a look at that."

Billy looked at the snake. "My God," he said. He reached into the box, took the dead snake by the neck and hauled it out, holding it up under the light. "I'm five-eleven, and this thing is six and a half feet," he said. "His head is the size of my fist, what's left of it, and look at those rattles!"

Stone told him how he had found the snake in the house. "Is it native to these parts? What do you think?"

"Could be," Billy said. "Do you want the skin?"

"Okay," Stone said.

Billy draped the carcass over a table by the pool, took a folding knife from his pocket, made a few deft cuts, and in one motion, stripped the hide from the snake. The rattles came off with it. "There you go," he said. He opened the door to the woodshed, hung the skin from a nail, stretched it tight and placed a piece of flagstone on the bottom. "Let it dry there, and you can have a pair of boots made from it." He closed the door and latched it. "The meat is very good deep fried. Do you want to keep it?"

"I don't think so," Stone said.

"Then let's leave it for the coyotes." He swung the carcass wide and tossed it into some bushes a few yards away. "They'll find it before morning."

They went back into the kitchen and sat in front of the fire with drinks, while Gala prepared dinner.

"Stone," Billy said quietly, "that species of rattler may be native to this area, but I don't think it got into the house all by itself."

"Why do you think that?"

"Well, first of all, it's a very big snake. A mouse might get in through a small opening, but I doubt if there's one big enough to admit that snake."

"A door left open, maybe?"

"I don't think so—you've got screens on all the doors. However, there's a snake wrangler working on the movie being made at Bonanza Creek, and a scene in the script with a big rattler."

"How do you know that?"

"I took the tourist tour of the ranch this afternoon, and I swiped a copy of the script from the saloon set. And I saw the snake wrangler's truck."

"So it's Boris."

"He seems to have ignored my warning. Perhaps I'd better give him another chance to listen."

"Dinner's on," Gala called to them, and their conversation ended.

The following morning, Billy set his large case on the bed, opened it, and removed the items he had borrowed from Centurion Studios the day before. He dressed in the jeans, shirt, leather vest, and boots and donned the weathered, sweat-stained Stetson. He reassembled the Winchester Model 1873 and loaded it with .44/40 ammunition, then slung the gun belt with its Colt .44 over his shoulder, grabbed the movie script, and walked out to his car.

He drove out to the Bonanza Creek Movie Ranch and

parked his car in the parking lot. The place was alive with the movie's cast and crew. He loaded the .45 and strapped on the Ojala holster and belt, almost universally used in Western films, then he put on his Stetson and left the car, blending in with the other cast and crew arrivals.

There was an elaborate breakfast table laid out by the caterers, and he helped himself to a pastry and a cup of coffee, then sat down on the front porch of the general store and watched and listened. He read the script carefully and picked the scene he needed, then he filed into the saloon with the others and took up a place at the bar, which was crowded with actors and extras. A woman with a clipboard approached him.

"You must be Baxter," she said. "You didn't sign in." She handed Billy the clipboard and a pen. "Right there," she said, pointing to an empty space in her list. "You want to get paid, don't you?"

"Sure," Billy said, and scrawled an indecipherable signature on the sheet.

The director came in and placed the actors for the scene, while the cameraman placed the lights. While they were working, Billy saw Boris Tirov enter the saloon and sit down in a folding chair with his name on it, one of a dozen that had been set out for members of the cast and production people.

Billy stood at the bar, bored, while they shot a scene from three angles and then did close-ups. The whole business took four and a half hours for, maybe, three minutes of usable footage, and Billy thought that was fast, if dull. They broke for lunch, which the caterers set up in the saloon, and he ate a sandwich at the bar. Nobody questioned his presence; this was a new shoot, and there would be people there that everybody didn't know yet.

After lunch, the cast were called outside, where the camera had been set up in the street. Tirov was now sitting on the porch of the sheriff's office, across the street, out of camera range.

"Okay," an assistant director said through a bullhorn, "this is the wide shot. Nobody fires until Brad takes the first shot." He moved among the dozen and a half cast members, placing each one. Billy was moved next to an empty hitching rail. "Other side of the rail," the young man said. "When the shooting starts, you can rest your rifle on it." Billy nodded, bent over and ducked under the rail. He was just outside the general-store set.

"Okay," the assistant director yelled, "this is a rehearsal—nobody fires."

They rehearsed the scene twice, and Billy moved down the rail for a better view of Tirov, across the street.

"This is a take," the AD shouted.

The director stood behind and to one side of the camera, watching a video monitor. He looked up and nodded to the AD, and the AD yelled, "Lights!" The lights came on. "Camera!"

"Speed," the cameraman replied.

"Action!"

Billy crouched and laid his rifle across the hitching rail. The principal actors began speaking their lines, and Billy panned right with his rifle and took a bead on Boris Tirov's left arm at the shoulder. Brad, whoever that was, drew his pistol and fired, and everybody else began firing, too. Billy squeezed off a round and saw Tirov spin in his chair and fall to the board sidewalk while a windowpane shattered behind him.

"Cut!" the AD screamed, and the firing came to a halt. "Hold your positions, take five for a lighting change!"

Billy crossed the boardwalk, entered the general store, walked through it and out the back door, past a privy, then he turned toward the parking lot and began walking, not too fast.

"Where you going?" somebody yelled from behind him.

Billy turned and saw the woman with the clipboard. "I'm not in this one," he called back. "I want to get something from my car." She nodded and he continued. He tossed the rifle onto the backseat, got in, started the car, and drove slowly out of the lot and onto the road.

When he got back to Tesuque, he sat outside the house for a minute, then found the call sheet with the hotel assignments and cell phones of the cast and crew. He called Boris Tirov's cell number. He had expected to get voice mail, but Tirov answered. "Yeah?"

"Listen to me," Billy said.

"Hang on," Tirov replied, then spoke to somebody else. "Yes, it hurts, but it's not bad. Just put some goddamned antibiotic cream on it, bandage it, and tell them to find out who's using live ammo!" Then he turned back to the phone. "Yeah?"

"Boris," Billy said softly, "I warned you, and you ignored my warning. Now you'll have to face the consequences."

Billy broke the connection, then went to his room and changed clothes.

49

The director of the Western assembled his cast and crew in the saloon standing set, the principals in the chairs and the extras standing at the back, and an enlarged photograph of the street scene, taken from the balcony of the hotel, was stapled to a wall. The AD used his megaphone. "All right, everybody, listen up!" The crowd got quiet.

The director stepped forward; he didn't need the megaphone. "Look at this," he said, pointing to the photograph with a pool cue from the set. "This is how we were set up this afternoon for our first exterior of this movie. Find your own positions and remember them. Now, somebody on this shoot loaded a weapon with live rounds, and, as a result, our executive producer took one in the upper arm." He indicated Boris Tirov, who sat, glowering, facing the crowd, his left arm in a sling and a whiskey bottle and shot glass on the table before him.

"This is against our procedures and policies," the director said. "Every actor on this shoot is an experienced performer and knows how we work. I exclude the crew from blame, because none of them had a weapon, so these remarks are directed at those who were armed. Anybody want to cop to loading live rounds?"

Nobody spoke. "I didn't think so." The director went to the photograph, took a black marking pen and drew two lines radiating out from Tirov. "Whoever fired the shot was within these lines, given the nature and position of Boris's wound. Kitty is going to call out the names of those who were well outside the lines, and when she does, I want each of you to step over to the bar and wait there."

The woman with the clipboard stood up and began calling names, and each person moved to the bar. They were left with sixteen people who had been armed and in a position to have fired the round. "Now," she said, "as I call your name, I want you to come up here and point out where you are in the photograph. She began calling names, and each actor took the pool cue and pointed to himself, while the AD marked his position. "Okay," Kitty said, "I think we know who our man is." She took the pool cue and pointed to the only unmarked man in the photo. "His name is Baxter, or at least that's what he said. Earlier in the day, production got a call from a man calling himself Baxter, saying he was sick in bed and couldn't make it to work. I didn't hear about it until this afternoon. Still, this guy signed in as Baxter. I remember him, he was sitting at the bar before the first scene was shot. After the incident, I noticed him leaving the general-store set. I asked him where he was going, and he said he wasn't in the next shot, and he was going to the parking lot to get something out of his car."

"Kitty," the director said, "can you tell us what he looked like?"

"Like every man in this room—cowboy clothes, six feet or so, slim. He wore his hat tipped forward, so you couldn't get a good look at his face. I checked with wardrobe—the real Baxter didn't check out a costume or weapon. Neither did his impersonator. This was very well planned."

The director spoke up. "Why do you think it was planned? How would he know Baxter was sick? How would he know to sign in for him?"

"You have a point. I asked him to sign in, and there was only one blank space, next to Baxter's name. But it was well planned enough for him to provide his own costume and weapons—he was wearing a six-gun, too."

"Is there anybody in the room who talked to the fake Baxter or got a close look at him?"

The AD spoke up. "I placed him by the hitching rail in front of the general store, but I wasn't really looking at his face. He was taller than I am, but then almost everybody here is." The crowd had a good laugh at the short AD.

"Anybody else have conversation with him?"

Nobody spoke.

"Boris, is anybody mad at you?"

"Not that I know of," Tirov replied. "At least, not mad enough to take a shot at me."

"Anybody else have anything—anything at all—to contribute?"

Nobody spoke.

"All right, then," the director said, "I'm going to assume that somebody brought the gun from home, and that it was already loaded with live ammo, and that this was an accident. I'm not going to call the police, because there is no reason to think that he was trying to kill Boris, and we'd likely lose a day's shooting. Boris agrees with me—in fact, it was his idea. So we're going to go back to work and right now. I want to get this scene done before we lose the light. Let's go! Assume your previous positions in the street."

Everybody filed out of the saloon and into the street.

The director approached Tirov on his way out. "Boris, do you really think this was an accident?"

"What else could it be?" Tirov asked. He had brought the bourbon with him and took a swig from the bottle.

"You'd think, wouldn't you, that in a crew this size *somebody* would have an oxycodone?"

"You'd think," Boris replied, taking another swig.

It was the director's private opinion that if everybody on the set had had a pocketful of pills, nobody would have offered Boris one. He was that popular with the crew.

B oris didn't resume his seat on the set. Instead, he went to his trailer, stretched out on his sofa, and got drunker. He had no intention of going to an ER, where a gunshot wound would be reported to the police, with all that that would entail.

There was a rap on the trailer door. "Boris?"

"Come in!"

A man entered. "Are you finished with my snake?"

"What?"

"You borrowed a six-foot rattler, remember? I handed it to you in its cage."

"Oh, that. It got away."

"How the hell did that happen?"

"I screwed up, okay? It got away from me."

"Where?"

Tirov waved a hand. "Out there somewhere. Just bill me for the fucking thing, okay?"

"That will be one thousand dollars. I raised it from a pup."

"Fine. Send me a bill."

"Don't ask to borrow any more animals." The man left.

Tirov took another swig of the bourbon and lay back on his sofa, swearing under his breath.

There was another rap on the door. "Boris?"

"Who is it?"

"It's Sam. Your director."

"It's open!"

The director came into the trailer. "I've had a conversation with a lawyer at the Directors Guild, and I have to report the shooting to the police."

"It wasn't a shooting, it was an accident."

"I'm sorry, I've already called them. You'd better sober up enough to talk to them."

"Oh, Jesus Christ, get out of here, or I'll fire you."

The director left, slamming the door behind him. "You just try that," he muttered under his breath.

50

Tirov was sound asleep and snoring loudly when there was a loud hammering on his trailer door.

"Mr. Tirov, Santa Fe County Sheriff's Office. Open up."

Tirov sat up on one elbow. "Open it yourself!"

Two men, one in a tan uniform and a Stetson, the other in a business suit, entered the trailer.

"Mr. Tirov, I'm Detective Rhea, and this is Deputy Smith, of the Santa Fe County Sheriff's Office," said the suit.

Tirov struggled to a sitting position and got his feet on the floor. "What do you want?"

"We're investigating a report of a shooting on your movie set."

"There was no shooting."

"Then how come your arm is in a sling?"

"It was an accident, not a shooting."

"How is it an accident that somebody was carrying a

loaded weapon on a movie set, where every weapon is supposed to be loaded with blanks?"

"I figure somebody brought his own weapon from home and forgot it was loaded."

"I'm sorry, sir, but that doesn't make any sense at all. Where would I find this extra, Tom Baxter?"

"He called in sick. I imagine he's at home, wherever that is."

"Then how did he sign the worksheet?"

"There was clearly an unauthorized person on the set. He signed the only blank space on the sheet, rather than get thrown out."

"Do you always have unauthorized persons mingling with your cast and crew?"

"It happens more often than you would believe. People are starstruck, movie-struck. Some of them would do anything to nuzzle up to our star, Brad Goshen."

"Did anybody nuzzle up to Mr. Goshen this morning?"

"How would I know? Ask Mr. Goshen."

"You're being uncooperative, Mr. Tirov."

"Oh? Tell me a question I haven't answered. How am I uncooperative?"

"Well, you're pretty surly."

"I have a gunshot wound, and I'm in pain, and since nobody in this company has a pain pill, I'm substituting bourbon. And there's no law that says I have to be polite to a cop."

"I'm sorry for your pain. We'll go talk to Mr. Goshen."

"Good luck with that. Between takes, he goes into his trailer and I'm told does some pretty weird stuff."

"Stuff? What kind of stuff?"

"I don't know what it is—some kind of yoga or meditation or something. The entire company is on standing orders not to knock on his door until we're ready for a take."

"We still need to talk to him."

"If you start messing around with our star, we're liable to lose a day's shooting. Do you know what that costs?"

"No, sir."

"Several hundred thousand dollars. I can tell you that Brad Goshen didn't shoot at me. I was looking at him at the moment I got hit, and he was doing his job. The bullet came from behind him somewhere, so he couldn't have seen the shooter. And he wouldn't have anything but blanks in his gun, because he didn't load it, our armorer did, so why don't you just leave the kid alone. Talk to the armorer, if you like."

"What's his name?"

"Frog."

"Frog what?"

"Frog the armorer—how do I know? Ask the production manager—that's who he reports to."

"What's the production manager's name?"

"Al."

"Al what?"

"I don't know that, either. I don't talk to the crew, I talk to the director or his assistant or the line producer, and they talk to everybody else. Ask the first person you see when you leave, which I'd like you to do right now."

"We may have more questions for you later."

"Not today, you won't. Now please leave my trailer,

and don't let the doorknob hit you in the ass on your way out."

"Thanks so much for your help, Mr. Tirov."

"Sarcasm doesn't suit you, Sheriff."

"Detective."

"It doesn't suit you, either, Detective. Next time, try charm."

"I don't do charm," the detective said, and slammed the door hard behind him. "Let's go find this Brad guy and annoy him," he said to the deputy.

"Sounds like fun."

"And if we don't start getting some joy around here, I'll get a search warrant and we'll turn over every trailer and truck in this goddamned cardboard town until we find that weapon."

"Can I watch?"

"No, but you can help. Come on." The detective stalked off in the direction of a cluster of trailers. He reckoned Brad Goshen would be in the biggest one.

B oris Tirov locked his trailer and yelled for his driver. "Bernie!"

Bernie popped out from behind the trailer. "Yessir?"

"Get the goddamned car. I want to go to the hotel."

"Yessir!" Bernie ran to get the car.

51

Billy Barnett drove back to the movie ranch in the late afternoon and parked in the public lot. The animal wrangler's truck was in its usual spot at the edge of the lot closest to the sets, and the engine was running, Billy assumed for the purpose of air-conditioning the cages in the back. He checked the driver's seat and found no one there; it took him less than a minute to pick the lock on the rear doors.

It was fairly quiet in the back of the truck; there was a kind of zoo odor, but it was not unpleasant. It took Billy hardly any time to find the perfect rattlesnake, about a four-footer, he estimated. He took a burlap bag from a stack, picked up a handling pole with a hook at the end, opened the cage and, after a little fumbling, got the snake into the burlap bag and tied a knot in it.

He got into his car, put the bag on the floor of the backseat, drove into Santa Fe, and parked his car on Water Street, behind La Fonda Hotel, where the movie crew was staying. He checked the call sheet and found the room number he wanted, then he took a cardboard box from a nearby trash bin and put the burlap bag inside it.

The hotel was a hive of tourists; the restaurants were full, the gift shop was crowded, and every time an elevator arrived in the lobby, half a dozen people got off, and another half dozen got on. He didn't want to be seen on an elevator, so he walked up the stairs five stories and found the room number. The hallway was deserted; he put an ear to the door and listened for half a minute, checked the hall for traffic again, then picked the lock.

Once inside he listened again for signs of occupancy and heard none. There was a large living room and a terrace overlooking the plaza. He saw a pair of feet on a chaise longue on the terrace, but they weren't moving. He thought the owner must be asleep.

He removed the burlap bag from the box and got an answering rattle for his trouble. As quickly as he could, he walked into the bedroom, pulled back the covers on the bed, then emptied the snake onto it, pulling the covers up again before it could escape. He stood there for a moment, waiting for it to quiet down, then he left, taking the bag and box with him. On the street again, he deposited them both in the same receptacle where he had found the box, then got back into the car and left. He was a couple of blocks away when an ambulance passed him going the other way.

*   *   *

Boris Tirov stirred as the late-afternoon sun found him on the terrace, and he began to perspire. He got up and went through the sliding door into the air-conditioned suite and into the bedroom, where he stripped off his clothes. In one motion, he pulled back the covers and lifted one leg to climb into the bed. The rattling froze him for just a moment; he didn't see the snake until it hit him on the thigh, then withdrew, remaining coiled and still rattling.

Tirov panicked and ran into the living room, looking for a phone.

"Front desk!"

"I've been bitten by a rattlesnake!" he shouted into the phone. "I need an ambulance right now!"

"What was that, sir?"

"Rattlesnake bite! Ambulance!"

"Yes, sir, right away."

Tirov hung up the phone and watched as the snake slithered from the bedroom and headed toward the terrace. The sliding door was still open a few inches, and it moved outside. Tirov ran across the room and closed the door behind it, then he began thinking about his predicament.

He went into the bedroom, treading carefully, lest there were more, undiscovered snakes. He grabbed a necktie from the closet, wrapped it twice around his leg and tightened it. He thought for a moment, What else? You were supposed to suck the wound, weren't you? But he couldn't reach his outer thigh to do that.

There was a loud knocking on the door, and he got up to answer it, holding the necktie in place. Before he could reach the door it opened, and a uniformed security guard walked in, to be confronted by a naked man with a necktie wrapped around his leg.

"Did you call an ambulance?" Tirov asked.

"Yes, sir," the man said, averting his eyes. "Where's the snake?"

"On the terrace. I want you to suck the poison out."

The man was appalled. "I'm sorry, sir, but I don't know anything about that."

"You have to suck the poison from my wound, or I'll die." He put one foot on a dining chair to make his thigh more accessible. "I'll give you a thousand dollars."

"I'm sorry, sir, that's outside my job description. Is there anything else I can do?"

"Do you have a knife?"

"I have a pocketknife."

"Make a cut where the fangs went in."

The man fumbled in his pocket, came up with a Swiss Army knife and selected a blade.

"Quickly!"

The man offered him the knife. "You'll have to do it yourself," he said.

Before Tirov could act, two men with a stretcher came into the room through the open door. "Where's the rattlesnake?" one of them asked, looking around nervously.

"On the terrace," Tirov said, then he began to get dizzy.

"You get him to the hospital," the guard said. "I'll deal with the snake. He grabbed a towel from the back of a chair and started toward the terrace.

Tirov hobbled toward the stretcher, feeling ill, then he fainted and fell into the arms of an EMT.

*   *   *

Billy Barnett drove north, turned off the main high-
way onto Tesuque Village Road, then he pulled
over, stopped, and got a cell phone from the glove compartment. He got the number for the *Santa Fe New
Mexican*, the local newspaper, and asked for the city
desk.

"City desk, this is Peg."

"The movie producer Boris Tirov, who is making the
movie being filmed out at the Bonanza Creek Movie
Ranch, has been bitten by a large rattlesnake and taken to
the hospital." He broke the connection, then made a similar call to the sheriff's office, then he tossed the phone into
the weeds beside the road and drove on to Gala Wilde's
house.

Boris Tirov woke up slowly on a gurney in an emergency room; a doctor was bending over him. "What
happened?" he asked.

"You were bitten by a rattlesnake," the doctor said.
"We've given you the antivenom and, since you're awake,
you're improving. How do you feel?"

"Sick," Tirov said.

"What's wrong with your shoulder?"

"Bullet wound to the arm—accidental shooting on a
movie set."

"We'll need to report that to the police."

"The sheriff's department has already investigated. Call them, if you like."

"You know," the doctor said, "I've been working in this ER for eight years, and this is the first time we've ever admitted a naked man with a rattlesnake bite and a gunshot wound."

"I'm happy for you," Tirov said.

52

Tirov stayed the night in the hospital, since the doctor insisted, and checked himself out the next morning. He drove out to the set and went to his trailer to pick up his script. He was surprised to find the door unlocked, and when he opened it, he found the place turned upside down. The drawers of his desk had been emptied onto the floor and clothes were everywhere.

The AD appeared in the doorway. "It's the same all over the lot," he said. "Every trailer and set has been searched. That detective had a warrant."

"Are we shooting yet?"

"We're having to put the saloon back together, using photographs to place everything correctly. We're about an hour away from starting."

"Tell the snake wrangler I want to see him. Now."

"Right." The AD trotted off toward the parking lot.

* * *

The snake wrangler was not amused to receive Tirov's invitation. He locked his truck and stalked off toward where the trailers were parked.

Tirov had made some progress straightening his trailer when the snake wrangler knocked on the open door. "You wanted to see me?"

"Yes. Are you missing any snakes?"

"Well, yeah. First of all, there's the six-foot rattler I loaned—pardon me, sold to you. Then there's another four-footer that's missing."

"Somebody put that one in my bed at the hotel. You have anything to do with that?"

"I did not. I found the back door to my truck unlocked yesterday, though, and Lizzie was missing."

"Who's Lizzie?"

"My four-foot rattler, the female. Did you get bit?"

"I did, spent the night in the hospital. You tell the security company I want a twenty-four-hour guard on your truck."

"Is Lizzie okay?"

"How the hell would I know? I put her—it—on the terrace of my room before the ambulance got there. You might check with the hotel. And don't you bill me for this one."

"Which hotel?"

"La Fonda, suite 500. You seen anybody hanging around your truck?"

"Nope. The crew don't park where I am. All I ever see is the folks getting on and off the tour bus."

"All right, get out of here."

The snake wrangler went gladly. He got out his cell phone, called La Fonda and asked for the manager.

"Yes?"

"My name is Simmons. I'm the animal wrangler on the movie being shot out at Bonanza Creek. I'm told you've got one of my snakes there."

"Describe it."

"Four-foot, diamondback rattler, female."

"We've got one answering to that description, though I can't vouch for the gender. We haven't known what the hell to do with it."

"I'll be there in half an hour and take her off your hands."

"We'd appreciate that. It's in a burlap bag inside a cardboard box. It bit one of our guests, and I wouldn't be surprised if he sued you. His name is Tirov."

"Yeah, I just had a conversation with him. Somebody who doesn't like him stole the rattler from my truck."

"From what I know of him, there's nobody who *does* like him. My staff were rooting for the rattlesnake."

"I know how they feel. I'll be there in half an hour."

"Can you check the suite for any more snakes?"

"I'm only missing the one."

"Thank God for that." The manager hung up.

*   *   *

Boris Tirov was seething, but he didn't know who to be angry at. The sonofabitch had entered his home, drugged him, and threatened him. Then there was the call after he was shot: Had the guy followed him to Santa Fe from L.A.? Whoever he was, he was working for Barrington; he knew that much.

Tirov went to the set and found them nearly ready to shoot. The director approached. "Boris, I can't work like this."

"Like what?"

"You getting shot, the police tearing up my trailer and my sets."

"You think I have anything to say about that?" Boris demanded.

"I guess not."

"Then get your ass in gear and fulfill your contract."

The man went back to work.

A man approached him, an extra in costume. "Mr. Tirov?"

"Yeah?"

"My name's Tom Baxter. I—"

"Are you the guy who called in sick?"

"Yessir. I figured you wouldn't want me infecting anybody else."

"You have any idea who pretended to be you?"

"No, sir, I don't. Wouldn't nobody I know do something like that."

"Then go back to work and leave me alone."

"Yessir."

Tirov turned away. "I'm going to have to end this once and for all," he said aloud.

"Sir?"

Tirov turned to find the extra still standing there. "I said, go back to work!"

"Yessir!" The extra fled.

Tirov sat down in his chair and began to contemplate the end of Stone Barrington. It made him feel better.

53

During a break, while the first scene in two days was being shot, the film's publicist approached Tirov.

"Boris," she said, "I have a request from the *Santa Fe New Mexican* to interview you. I recommend you give the interview, as it will be good local publicity."

Tirov sighed. "When?"

"She's outside. What about now?"

"Where outside?"

"On the front porch. I got her some lemonade."

"All right," Boris said, heaving himself to his feet. He had discarded the sling as his wound improved, and he checked himself out in the mirror behind the bar before going outside. He walked out to the front porch and found a very attractive young woman sitting in one of the chairs, sipping from a glass of lemonade. "Good morning," he said to her. "I'm Boris Tirov."

"Good morning, Mr. Tirov, I'm Christy Mayson, *Santa Fe New Mexican*. Would you like some lemonade?"

Boris sat down. "Don't mind if I do," he said.

She filled another glass from the pitcher on the table and handed it to him.

"What would you like to know?" he asked. His eyes wandered down to her body and up again.

"Tell me what attracted you to this story," she said.

"Well, I read the novel." This was a lie; Tirov never read anything longer than a single-page synopsis. "And I liked the story."

"How would you describe the story?"

"Without giving away too much, I'd say it's an adult Western, rather than a family one."

"So you expect an R rating?"

"We're working on that. The ratings people have asked for a little toning down here and there—nudity and violence, some of the language. It's my view that the old West has had too much of a cleaning up. The real West was a violent place, and the inhabitants were a profane bunch."

"How about the women?"

"In a town like the one in our movie, most of the women were whores."

"No wives, no families?"

"Perhaps those belonging to the local merchants. The rest were for rent by the hour, or less."

"And do you feel it necessary to your story to portray them that way?"

"I like realism. How about you?"

"Within limits. I don't see the necessity of making a

film that takes the lowest view of all its characters, especially the women."

"Ah, a feminist, huh?"

"Of course."

"What do you mean, 'of course'?"

"What woman isn't a feminist these days? Don't you favor equal pay for equal work?"

"There's no equality in the movie business. There's only who draws the audiences in, and that's usually the male stars, especially in Westerns. Can you remember a Western where a woman was the star?"

"One or two."

"Do you remember what the grosses were?"

"No."

"I can tell you, they bit the dust, first week out. In the movie business we learn from our mistakes."

"What about your female star in this picture, Helen Beatty?"

"She plays a whore."

"Does she get the same salary as Brad Goshen?"

"Of course not, haven't you been listening?"

"Does she appear on fewer pages of the script than Mr. Goshen?"

"I take it you've read the script—you tell me."

"She has two more pages than Goshen."

"You sure about that?"

"I can count, Mr. Tirov."

"Call me Boris, Christy," he said, looking her up and down again.

"I prefer Mr. Tirov and Ms. Mayson, if you don't mind."

Tirov shrugged. "Why would I mind?"

"Mr. Tirov, you have a reputation in the film community of being obstreperous—"

"What's that? My English is not perfect."

"Surly and aggressive, especially with women. Does that help?"

"Who said that about me?"

"Every single person I've talked to who knows you or has worked with you, and that's probably a couple of dozen. I try to do my homework."

Boris felt his temperature rising. "Then you've been talking to the wrong people."

"Whom should I talk to? Give me some names, and I'll call them. I want to be fair."

"I won't have you bothering my friends."

"You don't seem to have many," she replied.

"Why would you say that?"

"Is it true that there have been two attempts on your life during this shoot? And your shoot is only a couple of days old?"

"Nonsense."

"Well, you've been shot and had a rattlesnake put in your bed. Do you consider those friendly acts?"

"I don't know where you get this stuff."

"From the Santa Fe County Sheriff's Office and the staff of your hotel. Are they lying?"

"The gunshot was an accident while shooting a gunfight scene."

"But great care is taken, is it not, to load all the weapons on your set with blank cartridges?"

"Somebody made a mistake."

"And how about the snake in your bed? It didn't make its own way into La Fonda."

"A prank gone wrong."

"Isn't it true that the snake came from that wrangler's truck over there?" She pointed.

"I don't know where it came from."

"Do you have any objection to my talking to your former wife, Gala Wilde? I understand she lives in Santa Fe."

"That would be an invasion of her privacy and mine."

"I've been hearing rumors of a very large rattlesnake being put in her bedroom, and someone seems to have gone out of his way to attract a bear to her property."

"What is all this about snakes and bears? I thought you came here to talk about my movie."

"I just want to hear your side of these stories," she said. "I thought you'd welcome the opportunity to set the record straight."

Tirov got to his feet, upsetting the table holding the lemonade. "Let me set you straight, you fucking little bitch. This so-called interview is at an end, and if you print any of this stuff I'll sue your paper. You tell your editor that." He stalked back into the saloon.

The publicist came running out. "Christy? What happened?"

"He didn't seem to want to answer my questions," she replied, brushing the lemonade off her skirt. "Thanks, I've got everything I need." She set off for the parking lot and her car.

54

Christy Mayson got back to her desk to find a note from her editor: "See me." She glanced in his direction and found him away from his desk, so she put her notebook beside her computer, got a blank page on her screen, and started her story.

TWO ATTEMPTS ON LIFE
OF MOVIE PRODUCER

Christy could type as fast as she could think, and she did so now. In twenty minutes she had a seven-hundred-word piece. She reread it quickly, made a few minor corrections, typed in her boss's e-mail address, and pressed the Send button.

"Didn't you get my note?"

She looked up to find him standing in her doorway. "I did, but you weren't at your desk when I got in, so I wrote my piece. Just sent it to you." She pressed the Print button and handed him the hard copy. "There you go."

Her editor, whose name was Chuck Ellis, glanced at the headline. "Holy shit! This was supposed to be a piece designed to get the tourists out to the Bonanza Creek Movie Ranch!"

"Please finish reading it."

He did so. "You know, I had a call from the tourist office an hour ago. They were worried about something exactly like this."

"Don't worry, the tourists will be flocking to the ranch when they read that."

"What are your sources for all of this?"

"The Santa Fe County Sheriff's Office, members of the cast and crew of the movie, employees of La Fonda, the snake wrangler, and for the part about the rattlesnake in Gala Wilde's bedroom, a source who prefers to remain anonymous. And the quotes from Boris Tirov are, word for word, from my notes. And I recorded them." She held up a tiny digital recorder and pressed a button. "Let me set you straight, you fucking little bitch," Tirov was saying. "It's a solid piece," she said.

"I don't like using anonymous sources."

"Who does? But when it's a choice between getting a front-page story while keeping someone's name out of it and not getting the story at all, which way do you come down?"

He threw up his hands.

"I come down on the front page," she said. "Every time."

"Okay, okay, we'll run it tomorrow morning."

"Thanks, Chuck. Stop by anytime." He had been stopping by her place in the evenings a couple of times a week for the past six months, and she wanted him to know that he could continue to do so.

The following morning, breakfast was delivered to Boris Tirov's suite at seven AM, and the tray set on his lap as he sat up in bed. The Santa Fe paper was placed on the tray with the headline in plain view, upper right-hand corner of the front page. He grabbed the paper and read it, continued on page 3, then he threw it across the room, spilling his orange juice in the effort. Tirov began screaming in Russian.

Stone Barrington, Gala Wilde, and Billy Barnett sat at the breakfast table while Stone read the *New Mexican* piece aloud. Gala's face was buried in her hands. "Oh, God," she said, "Boris is going to explode now."

"Tell me," Stone said, "is the anonymous source anyone in this room?"

"I wouldn't be surprised," Billy said, buttering his English muffin.

"I'm going to have to go around armed, now," Stone said.

"I think, perhaps, my work here is done," Billy said.

"You mean you're just going to light the fuse, then fly back to L.A.?"

"I'll stay on, if that's what you want, but I think my boss back at Centurion, who happens to be your son, would like me back soon. He expects to use his airplane this weekend, to fly up to their place in Carmel."

"Give me one more day, if you can."

"All right. How do you want to handle this?"

"I will place myself entirely in your hands, Billy. What would you like me to do?"

"I'd like you to have dinner and go to bed," Billy replied.

"Without you?"

"I may be feeling a bit dyspeptic this evening."

"Tell you what, why don't we send Gala over to her sister's for dinner tonight, then you and I can sort of hang around here."

"I don't think that's such a good idea," Billy said. "Why don't you both go over to the Eagle place and have dinner? I think it would be much better if you were not here this evening—and could prove it."

"I can't believe what I'm hearing," Gala said.

"Gala," Stone replied, "I'd be grateful if you would remember that you're not hearing anything at all."

"Suddenly, I'm deaf?"

"Perhaps you'd like to be in another room while Billy and I have this discussion."

"I think I'm going to go and have a long soak in a hot tub."

"What a good idea," Stone said.

After breakfast, Stone drove out to the airport, asked which hangar his airplane was in, then drove to it. He unlocked the forward luggage compartment, removed a small leather case, and tossed it into the car.

Back at Gala's house, he went to the study, unlocked the little case and removed a startlingly small .45 pistol, reduced from 39 ounces to 21 by its maker, Terry Tussey. He threaded the holster and a magazine case onto his belt, shoved another magazine into the pistol, and holstered it. He reflected that he should have felt safer, but he didn't.

55

Boris Tirov was back on his set on time that morning, and he made a special effort to be affable with everyone and charming to the more important members of the cast and crew. He settled into his on-set chair a few minutes before shooting and called his L.A. attorney.

"Good morning, Boris," the man said, sounding weary.

"Good morning, Kim. I'd like you to file a lawsuit today."

"Who are we suing *this* time?"

"A newspaper called the *Santa Fe New Mexican*, a reporter named Christy Mayson and her editor, whoever that is."

"And what are we suing for?"

"Libel."

"Boris, I've explained American law on this subject to

you more than once. We will have to prove actual malice to win. Are you personally acquainted with this reporter?"

"Yes, I met her yesterday when she came to the set to interview me."

"Do you have a sexual relationship with her?"

"No, but that's not a bad idea."

"And I assume that you don't know her editor, since you can't come up with his name."

"That's correct."

"It's going to be, practically speaking, impossible to prove actual malice on the part of two professional people, one of whom you just met and the other, you don't know at all. Are the allegations they made about you true?"

"Get on the Internet, go to the paper's website, and read the article," Tirov said. "Call me when you've filed the suit."

"I'm not licensed to practice in New Mexico. I'll have to find a local attorney to bring the suit."

"Then do it." Tirov hung up.

Kim Kopchinsky found the newspaper article and read it. He found it plausible that two attempts had been made on Tirov's life—he had often been tempted himself, but the man did pay his legal bills on time. The part about putting a rattlesnake in his ex-wife's bedroom did not seem too far-fetched, given his previous experience with his client during the divorce proceedings, and the part about having another rattlesnake put in his client's bed seemed just, if not legal. He called Tirov back.

"Yeah?"

"Boris, I've read the newspaper article, and I've noticed that both the Santa Fe sheriff and hotel employees have been cited as sources. There is one anonymous source, for the part about the rattlesnake in your wife's bedroom, but having witnessed your behavior during the divorce, I find it completely plausible that you would do such a thing. Now, it's one thing to represent you in career and divorce negotiations, but it's quite another to file a frivolous lawsuit against a reputable newspaper, and I am unwilling to sully the good name of this law firm by being a party to such an idiotic proceeding."

"Are you willing to be fired right now?"

"I'd be proud to be fired by you, Boris. I might even take out an ad, bragging about it. Go fuck yourself." Kopchinsky hung up the phone, feeling unaccountably clean.

Boris could feel his blood pressure going up. He got out of his chair and walked into the street, headed for the armorer's trailer at one end. He walked up to the open window through which the man issued and accepted firearms.

"Morning, Mr. Tirov," the man drawled. "What can I do you for?"

"Good morning, Frog. Give me a shotgun," Tirov said.

"What kind did you have in mind?"

"What do you mean, what kind?"

"I've got twelve- and ten-gauges, both antiques, with open hammers. That do you?"

"How about something sawed off?"

The man disappeared into his trailer and came back with a weapon sporting about eight inches of barrel. "How 'bout this 'un?"

"Fine. Give me a box of ammo."

"All we got is blanks."

"I want a box of live ammo for that shotgun."

"Coupla things, Mr. Tirov. First of all, you load this weapon with live ammo, and you're breaking the law. It's a felony to possess a shotgun with a barrel shorter than eighteen inches."

"Then how come you've got one?"

"This ain't a shotgun, it's a prop, unless you load it with live shells. Second thing is, this place ain't a firing range, it's a prop business, and we don't stock no live ammo—at all, for any weapon. I've already been accused of issuing live rounds to whoever shot you, and I didn't like it much."

"You're fired," Tirov said. "Get your ass off my set."

"Tell you what, you round up the thirty-four folks I've issued firearms to and tell 'em to bring their weapons down here, and when they've done that and checked 'em in, I'll get my ass off your set. Then I'll call my union rep and my lawyer, and this shoot will be shut down before the sun sets. Oh, and good luck staging all them shoot-outs in the script without no weapons. You'll have to find somebody in L.A. who will replace mine."

Boris stared at him for a long moment, trembling with rage, then he swallowed it and said, "Sorry about that. Carry on."

"Yessir, I'll do that, because I signed a contract, but don't you bother calling on me for work in the future."

Boris turned and walked away, seething. His internal rage gauge was threatening to blow its top off, and he had to relieve the pressure. There was only one way to do that.

56

Gala knew as well as Stone and Billy that Boris was coming for her, and probably for Stone as well. Boris didn't know Billy, of course, or he would be coming for him, too.

There were times when she still regretted the divorce. She had loved Boris, when he was in good temper, and the sex had been just fabulous. She still sometimes woke up in the night in the middle of a dream about Boris, and turned to Stone, who was always willing, for release.

Twice since the divorce, she had succumbed to Boris; if he walked into the house right now she would be unable to trust herself with him. Many times they had fucked on the kitchen island in this house, because they couldn't wait to get to the bedroom. It made her wet just thinking about it.

Stone came into the kitchen, where she was sitting in front of the fire, and made them both a drink.

"This thing is coming to a head, isn't it?" she asked.

"That's up to Boris," he replied.

"I think the newspaper article will be enough to set him off. He reaches a point where he's so angry that he can no longer control himself. He appears to be cool and calm when he's actually boiling inside. He becomes more, not less, calculating, and eventually, more violent. He told me that once, when in that state, he killed a man with a steak knife in the middle of a restaurant, then sat back down and finished his steak. That was in Russia, when he was still under Petrov's protection and he could do whatever he wanted."

"He's not in Russia anymore," Stone pointed out, "and there's no Petrov here to protect him."

Billy came into the kitchen and sat down.

"Can I get you a drink, Billy?"

"Thanks, but no. I'm going to fly back to L.A. tonight. Peter needs the airplane tomorrow morning. My bags are already in the car. I just wanted to thank you both for your hospitality. You've made me very comfortable here."

"You must come back and bring your wife whenever you can, Billy," Gala said. "You'll always be welcome."

"That's very kind of you, Gala, we'll take you up on it one of these days." He turned toward Stone. "You going to be okay here on your own?"

"I'll be fine," Stone replied. "You've been just great, Billy, and I appreciate everything you've done." The two men shook hands, and Billy left.

"I don't understand," Gala said. "What is Billy doing?"

Stone turned to her. "Here's how it goes. Billy needed

a break from work," he said. "You invited him to visit Santa Fe and stay at your house. He was a quiet house-guest, read a lot and took walks. Sometimes he went into Santa Fe to take a look at the town. He was polite and charming, and you were happy to have him. Tonight, he left the house, went to the airport, and flew back to Los Angeles. Those are the things you need to remember—just those things. Do you understand?"

"Of course, whatever you say."

"Now, let's have some dinner and go to bed."

B illy drove out the front gate, then pulled over to the side of the road, got out his phone and called Land-mark Aviation. "This is Billy Barnett. I'm in a Citation Mustang, which is in your hangar."

"Yes, Mr. Barnett, what can we do for you?"

"How late are you open?"

"Until nine PM."

"Please pull my airplane out of the hangar, top it off—Jet A, negative Prist—and leave it on the ramp for my late departure. Charge the fuel to my credit card on file."

"Of course. What time will you be departing?"

"As soon as I can get there."

"We'll have it ready for you, Mr. Barnett." She hung up.

Billy drove down a side street off Tesuque Village Road and worked his way around until he was behind Gala's house. He left the car in a side road, climbed over the fence, and walked toward the rear of the house. He stopped, checked his weapon, then climbed into a tree that gave him a good view from about twelve feet up. Then he made himself as comfortable as possible, braced between two limbs.

Billy was a patient man and, when he chose to be, a still one. He did not move for insects or noises in the night, nor to scratch himself when he itched. He closed his eyes and let his imagination wander; he sometimes had good ideas when he did that. All he had to do was wait, and he was good at waiting.

S tone and Gala finished their dinner and did the dishes together. Stone took Bob out for a brief walk, and when the dog had done his duty, went back inside.

Gala was already in bed when Stone got back, and she held out a hand. She wanted him.

He undressed, switched off the lights, and got into bed. She was ready for him, and they turned their attention to each other, pleasing each other slowly. When they were sated, she said, "I've been such a fool."

"Why? That's such an odd thing to say."

"Oh, never mind. Go to sleep. I'll tell you about it tomorrow."

Soon, he went to sleep.

57

B oris got into his car and drove around for a while, looking forward to his approaching task.

When it was done, he'd take Gala back—no, he'd summon her, and she would come. He was sure of that. He hoped he'd have enough time with Stone Barrington before he died, so that he could reveal, under torture, the identity of the man he had sent to frighten him into staying away. He would reserve special treatment for that man.

He had no doubt that his plan for the night would work, but he had brought along the weapon that Sergei had supplied to him, with its very effective silencer.

He wished he could call Viktor Petrov and tell him about his plans, as he had done when they were fast friends years ago. Viktor had loved hearing his plans, then reading the investigative reports of the beatings and killings to see how the details matched. Sometimes Viktor had insisted that Boris recite them to him over drinks, followed by sex with two or more women.

After he had summoned Gala once more, he would give her everything she loved, then shoot her in the head with Barrington's gun. He smiled at the thought.

It would be nice to get back to work on his movie, but then he remembered something: he had one more killing to look forward to before he could enjoy the film: the reporter Christy Mayson, at the *New Mexican*, would receive a visit from him. The fact that she hated him made the thought even more entertaining.

Later, when his film was done shooting and he had returned to L.A., he had others to attend to: that twerp who ran the admissions committee at the country club; Leo Goldman, at Centurion, and maybe Bacchetti, the new head of production there, too. Then there was Barrington's kid, the director, just for the hell of it. He would be a busy man for a while.

He parked on Upper Canyon Road, to enjoy the view of the city's lights; he even dozed for a while. Then he awoke and found it to be a little after one AM. Time to go.

Billy Barnett stirred in his tree; there was a scuffling and growling sound coming from the bushes near his hideout, then there was a high bark and more scuffling. It was the coyotes or other animals, come for the snake's carcass that Billy had left for them. From the inside of the house he heard Bob bark.

Stone sat up in bed. "What is it, Bob?"

Bob growled, then went to the door and looked outside, toward the noises. "It's only coyotes, Bob," Stone said quietly. "Get in your bed." Bob reluctantly returned to his bed and put his head down. The coyotes were quiet now.

Stone searched for sleep again and found it.

Boris Tirov checked his weapon, abandoned his car, and headed for the rear fence of Gala's house. Conscious of the dog's presence in the house, he got over the fence very quietly.

Billy Barnett opened his eyes. It was time; someone was nearing the rear of the house. He watched without moving.

Billy Barnett could see Tirov from where he sat, and he knew what would come next. He watched as the man picked the lock on the kitchen door, then stood by the door.

Billy let himself down gently from the tree. He wanted to be at the open back door when Stone emerged from the bedroom, as Tirov no doubt wished him to. It was Billy's hope that Stone would have an opportunity to shoot Tirov, instead of requiring himself as backup. He was certainly prepared to kill Tirov if it became necessary, but then he would have to leave his own weapon at the scene for the police to take from Stone, and he liked the weapon.

Billy watched as Tirov picked up a handful of gravel and threw it at the portal outside the master bedroom, some of it striking the back doors, then he stepped into the kitchen and hid behind the kitchen island. The dog, Bob, began to bark ferociously, throwing himself at the back doors. Stone would be getting up, now.

Then Billy heard something crashing through the brush where he had thrown the rattlesnake meat. He turned and pointed his weapon in that direction, and he was astonished at the size of the thing that emerged. It looked more like what he thought a grizzly should, not a black bear. It made for the kitchen door, moving quickly, headed for where it no doubt knew food could be found.

Tirov heard the noise, too, and turned to face it as it came through the door. He fired two quick rounds at the roaring hulk before it overwhelmed him.

58

ob's furious barking woke Stone. Gala was not in bed. Stone reached for his .45 on the night table, but it wasn't there. He rolled over to Gala's side and searched her bedside drawer; her pistol was gone, too.

"Bob, be quiet," Stone said, and the dog obeyed for a few seconds. The kitchen was two rooms away, and some sort of noise was coming from there, but he couldn't place it. Then came a sound that he recognized: the unmistakable roar of a bear.

This was followed by two gunshots—loud, but not his .45.

Stone got out of bed, stepped into slippers, and let himself out the outside door, leaving Bob barking again, shut in the bedroom. He ran along the back walkway, and as he got through the kitchen door he heard Gala scream at him.

"Stone! Stop!"

He stopped and saw the bear wrestling with some-body, a man. Gala was a few steps away, pointing her gun.

"Boris!" she screamed. "Get out of the way!"

The bear had his jaws locked onto Boris, between the shoulder and the neck. Stone started to move toward them.

He felt a hand on his shoulder. "Don't," Billy said from behind him. "Let this play out. It'll be over soon."

"Boris!" Gala screamed again. "Get clear! I don't want to shoot you!"

Tirov's feet were off the ground, now, as the bear reared back and shook its head.

"Are you armed?" Billy asked.

"I was, but not anymore. Gala must have taken it."

Gala turned and saw Billy and Stone. "No, don't shoot! You'll hit Boris!"

"In just a minute, Boris isn't going to care," Billy said.

The bear had taken Tirov to the floor and was savag-ing him. Tirov was moaning and making gurgling noises.

"Gala," Stone said, as quietly as he could, "where is my gun?"

She looked baffled for a moment, then reached into the pocket of her robe and took out the weapon. Stone strode over and took it from her.

"Don't shoot Boris," Gala pleaded. "I've already shot the bear twice."

Stone racked the slide on his little .45, swept Gala aside with an arm, and walked toward the bear and Tirov. She tugged at his sleeve. "Don't shoot Boris, please!"

Stone pushed her away again, then walked over to the

beast and shot it twice in the head. It collapsed on top of Tirov and lay still.

"I think that did it," Billy said.

Gala ran over, buried her hands in the bear's fur, and tried to pull it off Tirov.

Stone pulled her gently away, and Billy joined him.

"Gala," Billy said gently. "That bear weighs about three hundred and fifty pounds—you're not going to budge him."

"But Boris could still be alive," she protested.

Billy took her pistol out of her hand and set it on the kitchen island. He reached around the bear and found Tirov's wrist. "He has no pulse. He's as dead as the bear."

Gala rested her head on Stone's shoulder and wept loudly.

Billy opened kitchen drawers until he found a box of plastic bags. He pulled one over each of his feet and tied a knot in it.

"Now listen, both of you," Billy said. "You've handled this very well, but it's time to call the police. It's also time for me to leave, but remember, I left earlier tonight. We'll talk tomorrow, Stone. Good night, Gala."

She answered with a sob.

Billy walked toward the rear of the property, sticking to the flagstones as far as possible. He made his way to the fence, climbed it, and went to his car. He sat down in the car, pulled off the plastic bags and put them into the door pocket, then started the car and drove away. Five minutes later he turned onto the Santa Fe bypass, which led to the airport.

*   *   *

S tone picked up the phone and dialed 911.

"Nine-one-one operator. What is your emergency?"

"Is this call being recorded?"

"Yes, sir."

"Good, because I'm going to say this only once. There is a bear in the house, and it has attacked an intruder and killed him. I have shot and killed the bear. We need the police and an ambulance for the man, and whatever kind of vehicle is needed to remove a *very* large bear." He gave his name, the address and phone number, then hung up.

He led Gala to the sofa and sat her down. "The police or the sheriff will be here soon. Take some deep breaths. When they arrive, tell them exactly what happened, except for the part about Billy being here. Do you understand?"

She nodded. "Why didn't it kill the bear when I shot him?"

"Because you shot him in the back with a .380 caliber, and that wasn't powerful enough. I shot him twice in the head with a .45, and that would have stopped a rhinoceros."

Stone sat down beside her to wait.

59

Gala sat up, leaving him with a wet shoulder. "There are some things I have to tell you," she said.

"Perhaps it would be better if you wait until morning. We still have the police to deal with."

"No, I have to say it now, while I have my courage up."

"What could you possibly say to me that requires courage? You know you can tell me anything."

"It's about Boris."

"I don't see any need to discuss him ever again."

"I have a need. Please listen to me."

Stone sighed. "All right, you have my undivided attention." That was, perhaps, an overstatement, given that there were two corpses, a man and a bear, in the room.

"Boris and I had a difficult marriage, and an even more difficult divorce."

"I think I'm already aware of that."

"Still, there was some part of me that still wanted him."

Stone moved over on the sofa so that he could face her. "Which part of you was that?"

"Part of my heart, I guess you'd say."

Stone stared at her, and a couple of things tucked away in the back of his mind suddenly came to the forefront. "Are you sure that's the right body part?"

"All right, that part of me, too. Especially that part."

Stone was thinking about the screen of his iPhone, and the merging of a green dot with a yellow dot. Twice. "Let me guess—the day you went riding and encountered Tirov in the wood?"

Gala nodded. "Yes."

"And when you went to London and had lunch at Claridge's?"

"Yes. On my way out, I ran into Boris in the lobby and went with him to his suite."

"I see."

"I know I was unfaithful, and I'm sorry."

"You never pledged your faith to me, we never got that far."

"Nevertheless, I felt unfaithful."

"And yet you fucked him. Twice."

She nodded. "Again, I'm sorry. I don't expect you to forgive me."

"I'm glad. I wouldn't want to disappoint you."

She started to speak again, but she was interrupted by the doorbell. "We'll talk more later."

"I'd rather not. I've heard enough," Stone said. He got up and went to the front door.

60

A man in a sheriff's uniform and another in a suit stood there. The man in the suit said, "I'm Detective Rhea, and this is Deputy Sheriff Smith. You have an emergency?"

"I'm Stone Barrington. Please come in. The emergency is over, but there's a lot to deal with." He led them to the kitchen. "The man under the bear broke into the house, but I think that before he could do anything further, he was attacked by the bear. We've had a bear here before."

"Do you live here, Mr. Barrington?"

"No, I've been visiting for a few days. This is Gala Wilde, whose house this is."

"Why are there two guns on the island, there?" the detective asked.

"We both fired at the bear. Gala got here first and shot her twice in the back with a .380. I arrived and shot her twice in the head with a .45."

"That would do it," the deputy said. "Who's the guy under the bear?"

"His name is Boris Tirov. He's Ms. Wilde's ex-husband, who has been harassing and threatening her since their divorce last year."

"I read about him in the newspaper," the detective said. "And I interviewed him after he got shot on his movie set. He struck me as crazy."

"He struck me that way, too," Stone said. "He's been threatening me, as well. He thought I cost him a deal at a movie studio."

"Are you something in the movies?"

"No, I'm an attorney in New York. I serve on the board of a movie studio in Los Angeles."

"Ms. Wilde," Rhea said, "you got anything to add to Mr. Barrington's account of things?"

Gala shook her head.

The detective looked at his watch. "We ought to have an ambulance here any minute now. I don't know what the hell we're going to do with that bear. I've got a man working on it, though. Maybe the three of us can get it off Mr. Tirov, so we can check his vital signs?"

"It's worth a try," Stone said. "She must weigh three hundred and fifty pounds."

The three men stood on one side of the bear, grabbed its legs and, with a great deal of effort, rolled it off Tirov.

"That's a he-bear," the deputy said, pointing. He picked up Tirov's wrist. "No pulse."

Two EMTs carrying a litter came into the kitchen. They set it down and regarded the mauled man before them. "Damn," the older of the two said. "Once I saw the body of a guy who had been mauled by a tiger. It wasn't as bad as this." He knelt beside Tirov and pressed a stethoscope to the unwounded side of his neck. "Deceased," he said. "How long, you reckon?"

"Maybe fifteen minutes," Stone said. "I checked his pulse after I shot the bear."

"There'll be a crime scene investigation team here pretty soon," Rhea said. As he spoke, a team of others arrived, carrying luggage.

"Hey, Tom," their leader said to Rhea.

"Hey, Mack. This is Mr. Barrington and Ms. Wilde. That fellow over yonder is named Boris Tirov."

"Is this how you found him?"

"Nope, he was under the bear when we got here. We had to move him to see if Tirov was still alive. He wasn't. Hope we didn't mess up your scene too much."

"You did what you had to do," Mack said, then he started taking pictures with a digital camera and taking measurements. When he was done he stood back. "You charging anybody, Tom?"

"The DA will have the final say when he reads my report, but I doubt very much if anybody will be charged. I mean, the bear's dead."

"I've got a front-end loader from the county coming to deal with that carcass," Mack said. "Maybe if everybody grabs a handful of hair, we can get it out the door. You want the hide, Mr. Barrington? Make a nice rug."

"No, thanks," Stone said. "I'd like to forget it as soon as I can."

The front-end loader arrived and made it around the

house. Six men grabbed what they could and dragged the bear outside and onto the loader's scoop. They went back inside, and the EMTs loaded Tirov's bloody corpse onto their litter and departed.

Rhea handed Stone a card, and Stone gave him his and Gala's contact information.

"You going to be around for a while, Mr. Barrington? There might be an inquest."

"I've got to go to New York this morning," Stone replied, "but if you need my testimony, I'll come back."

"Well, I guess the cause of death is clear enough, unless the coroner finds some bullets in Tirov. No human being could have done what that bear did to him."

Stone saw them to the front door and came back to the kitchen, where Gala was still sitting on the sofa. "God, what a mess," he said, looking around at the bloody kitchen. "You go to bed, and I'll tidy up here."

Stone was still wide awake. He found a mop and bucket and some cleaning fluids and started in.

The sun was well up when he finished. He showered and dressed, packed his things, and got Bob and himself some breakfast. When he was ready to go, he found a pad and wrote a note.

Gala,

I confess I'm baffled by the things you told me last night. For the life of me I don't understand how you

could want both Tirov and me, and I don't find it
flattering or even acceptable.

I'll leave the Range Rover at Landmark
Aviation. You can send for it when you get up.

I thank you for the good times.

Stone

Stone got Bob and his bags into the car and drove to the airport. On the way he called Fred and asked him to meet them at Teterboro. Half an hour later they were climbing out of Santa Fe, headed east. The skies were clear all the way, and he had a good tailwind. He made it to Teterboro nonstop, landing with an hour of fuel reserve.

Fred was there with the car to meet him. "Good flight, sir?"

"A perfect flight," Stone replied.

Bob came down the steps and flung himself at Fred. They all got into the car and headed home.

S tone had spent most of the trip trying to put Gala out of his mind. He hadn't succeeded, but he had time.

Fred pulled into the garage, and Stone got out. Joan came through the inside door.

"There's someone here to see you," she said. "He won't give me his name. He said those people in Palm Beach sent him."

"Dicky Chalmers?"

"Right. He's waiting in my office."

"Send him in." Stone walked into his office and set his briefcase on the desk. He poked through the messages and found one from Dicky Chalmers.

I'm sending you a client—you'll like him.

Stone looked up and found a rather seedy young man standing in his doorway. He appeared to be in his late twenties or early thirties and was dressed in the current youth fashion. Stone thought of it as "adolescent lumberjack": jeans, checkered shirt, tail out, vest, hoodie, scraggly beard, and unkempt hair.

"I'm Laurence Hayward," he said. "Richard Chalmers said I had to see you."

"Had to?"

"I'm being pursued," he said.

"Who's pursuing you?"

"*Everybody.*"

Oh, God, one of those, he thought. "Well," Stone said, "you'd better close the door and sit down."

To be continued . . .

Author's Note

I am happy to hear from readers, but you should know that if you write to me in care of my publisher, three to six months will pass before I receive your letter, and when it finally arrives it will be one among many, and I will not be able to reply.

However, if you have access to the Internet, you may visit my website at www.stuartwoods.com, where there is a button for sending me e-mail. So far, I have been able to reply to all my e-mail, and I will continue to try to do so.

If you send me an e-mail and do not receive a reply, it is probably because you are among an alarming number of people who have entered their e-mail address incorrectly in their mail software. I have many of my replies returned as undeliverable.

Remember: e-mail, reply; snail mail, no reply.

When you e-mail, please do not send attachments, as I never open these. They can take twenty minutes to download, and they often contain viruses.

Please do not place me on your mailing lists for funny stories, prayers, political causes, charitable fund-raising, petitions, or sentimental claptrap. I get enough of that from people I already know. Generally speaking, when I get e-mail addressed to a large number of people, I immediately delete it without reading it.

Please do not send me your ideas for a book, as I have a policy of writing only what I myself invent. If you send me story ideas, I will immediately delete them without reading them. If you have a good idea for a book, write it yourself, but I will not be able to advise you on how to get it published. Buy a copy of *Writer's Market* at any bookstore; that will tell you how.

Anyone with a request concerning events or appearances may e-mail it to me or send it to: Publicity Department, Penguin Random House LLC, 375 Hudson Street, New York, NY 10014.

Those ambitious folk who wish to buy film, dramatic, or television rights to my books should contact Matthew Snyder, Creative Artists Agency, 9830 Wilshire Boulevard, Beverly Hills, CA 98212-1825.

Those who wish to make offers for rights of a literary nature should contact Anne Sibbald, Janklow & Nesbit, 445 Park Avenue, New York, NY 10022. (Note: This is not an invitation for you to send her your manuscript or to solicit her to be your agent.)

If you want to know if I will be signing books in your city, please visit my website, www.stuartwoods.com, where the tour schedule will be published a month or so in advance. If you wish me to do a book signing in your locality, ask your favorite bookseller to contact his Penguin representative or the Penguin publicity department with the request.

If you find typographical or editorial errors in my book and feel an irresistible urge to tell someone, please write to Sara Minnich at Penguin's address above. Do not e-mail your discoveries to me, as I will already have learned about them from others.

A list of my published works appears in the front of this book and on my website. All the novels are still in print in paperback and can be found at or ordered from any bookstore. If you wish to obtain hardcover copies of earlier novels or of the two nonfiction books, a good used-book store or one of the online bookstores can help you find them. Otherwise, you will have to go to a great many garage sales.

Fresh off the runway at Teterboro,
Stone Barrington arrives home to find an
unexpected new client on his doorstep,
anxiously soliciting his help. But everything
is not as it seems, when the client reveals
the true nature—and value—of his recent
turn of fortune. Stone quickly learns
that easy money isn't always so easy . . .

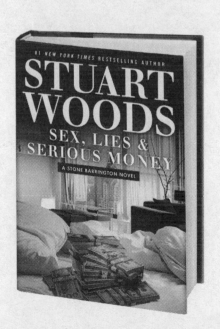

PUTNAM
EST 1838

Penguin
Random
House

1

Stone Barrington landed at Teterboro Airport, having flown nonstop from Santa Fe, with a good tailwind. He and Bob, his Labrador retriever, were met by Fred Flicker, his factotum, at the airport. Bob threw himself at Fred. After a moment's happy reunion they were transferred to Stone's car.

Stone had spent most of the flight trying to put Gala Wilde out of his mind after their breakup. He had not succeeded.

They arrived at Stone's house in Turtle Bay and Fred pulled into the garage. Stone got out of the car to be greeted by his secretary, Joan Robertson, but Bob got there first and did his happy dance.

"There's somebody waiting to see you," Joan said.

"Anybody I know?"

"Apparently a friend of somebody you know in Palm Beach."

Stone's acquaintance in Palm Beach was not wide. "Dicky Chalmers?"

"Right."

"Give me a minute, then send him in." Stone went into his office, rummaged among the mail and messages on his desk and found a pink message slip.

Stone, I'm sending you somebody you will find interesting.

Dicky.

Stone looked up to see a young man standing in his doorway: late twenties or early thirties, unkempt hair, scraggly beard, dressed in a current style Stone thought of as "adolescent lumberjack"—checkered shirt, tail out, greasy jeans, sneakers, hoodie, top down.

"Mr. Barrington?"

"Come in," Stone said, "and have a seat."

"Your friend Richard Chalmers suggested I should see you."

"How are the Chalmerses?"

"Dicky and Vanessa are very well."

"Do you have a name?"

"Sorry. I'm Laurence Hayward." He spelled both names.

"Larry, to your friends?"

"Laurence, if you please." He sounded vaguely English when he said that.

"Laurence, it is. I'm Stone, and this is Bob." Bob came over and sniffed the young man, accepted a scratching of the ears, then went to his bed and lay down. "How can I help you, Laurence?"

"I'm being pursued," Laurence replied.

"Pursued by whom?"

"Everybody."

Oh, God, Stone thought, not one of those. He took a deep breath. "Well, Laurence, why don't we start with your telling me about yourself?"

"What would you like to know?"

"Sixty-second bio."

"All right. I'm thirty years old. I was born in West Palm Beach, Florida. When I was eight, my mother, who was the manager of a small hotel in our community, was swept off her feet by an Englishman, who was an investor in the hotel. She subsequently divorced my father, married the Brit, and he took the two of us to live in England, where, except for summers, when I visited my father, I grew up. In fact, I became, for all practical purposes, English, including my accent."

"I thought I caught a bit of that."

"My American accent comes back when I'm here."

"Go on."

"I was educated at my stepfather's old schools, Eton and Oxford, and after I graduated, I became a tutor at Eton, later an assistant master, teaching English and art history. My stepfather has a successful advertising agency, and I had no interest in a career in his company or any other business."

Fred knocked on the door and stepped in. "Shall I take your bags up, sir?"

"Please, Fred. Oh, and this is Mr. Laurence Hayward."

"How do you do?" Laurence said, becoming English, and they shook hands.

"Fred, what is Laurence's accent?" Stone asked.

"Eton and Oxford, I should think," Fred replied.

"Thank you, Fred. You can take the bags up. I'll be here for a while."

Fred departed.

"That was remarkable, the way Fred picked up on my accent."

"Fred is very good at speaking and recognizing British accents of all sorts," Stone said. "On with your bio."

"I took a leave of absence from Eton and came home to Palm Beach a couple of months ago, after my father fell ill. He had moved to the island from West Palm some years ago as his legal practice grew."

"What sort of legal practice?"

"Real estate. He spent most of his day closing sales and mortgages. Did quite well at it, and used the job to find good investment opportunities in real estate. He died three weeks ago."

"I'm sorry for your loss."

"Thank you. He was good friends with the Chalmerses, who were his neighbors until they bought the big house on the beach, and they visited him often during his illness. I've known them most of my life."

"All right, let's get to the pursuit part."

"A week or so ago, I bought a lottery ticket, then forgot about it. Then I saw the winning number in the local paper, and I remembered I had one. I checked the numbers, and they matched. I called in at the lottery office in West Palm Beach, and this morning, after some days for them to investigate and see that I was who I said I was, I received the check. I also learned that, in Florida, there's a state law against concealing the identity of the winner.

I've quickly learned that a great many people have an untoward interest in lottery winners, thus the pursuit. They released my name early this morning, and when I left their office, I was surrounded by media people and others who had come to beg for money. I got out of there as quickly as I could, and when I turned on the car radio, I heard my name on the air. I drove to Palm Beach International Airport, where I had taken flying lessons, and somebody I know there found me a seat on an executive charter flight to Teterboro, for only five thousand dollars."

"What kind of airplane?"

"A Gulfstream 450."

"How did you do in the lottery?"

Laurence reached into a pocket and handed Stone a crumpled envelope. "There were two other winners, in Texas and Washington, state, so I got only a third after they took out the taxes."

Stone opened the envelope wide enough to read the sum. "Very nice," he said. "What are you going to do with it?"

"There are some things I'd like to buy, and Dicky thought you might advise me on how to invest the rest of it."

"What do you want to buy?"

"Well, I think I'll need some clothes."

"Good idea," Stone said drily.

"Oh, I know I'm not appropriately dressed for the Upper East Side of New York. My good clothes are all in England and Palm Beach. I'll need some suits and jackets, I think."

"Anything else?"

"Perhaps a car?"

"What sort of car?"

"A Porsche, perhaps."

"Good choice."

"Oh, and I'd like to buy a New York apartment."

"That seems within your means, depending on the neighborhood," Stone observed. "What sort of apartment did you have in mind?"

Laurence produced a folded newspaper page and handed it to Stone. It was half a page from the real estate section of the previous Sunday's *New York Times*. "This one," he said.

"Oh, yes, I saw this. It's the penthouse of an old hotel on Park Avenue that has been remodeled and gone condo. Problem is, Laurence, the asking price for the apartment is twenty-two million dollars, but your check is for six hundred and twelve thousand. Do you have other means I'm not aware of?"

"Perhaps you'd better have another look at the check."

Stone removed the check from the envelope, read it and gulped. *"Six hundred and twelve million dollars?"*

"You missed a few zeros the first time," Laurence said.

"And this is a third of the prize?"

"It was the biggest Powerball ever."

2

S tone took another deep breath.

"The limo driver from Teterboro this morning recognized me," Laurence said. "I can't go anywhere. It's crazy."

"How long has this been going on?"

"Since this morning—that's when I went to the lottery office."

"I heard it mentioned on TV, but I didn't get the details."

"It seems that a lot of other people did."

"All right," Stone said, "we've covered the clothes, the car, and the apartment. What else do you have in mind?"

"Art and American antique furniture," Laurence replied. "Dicky and Vanessa turned me onto that—their house is full of it. There's a big show on at the armory on Park Avenue."

"Is that it?"

"For the moment. Oh, and I'd like to write a nice check to Habitat for Humanity. I volunteered to help build half a dozen of their houses during my summers in Palm Beach."

"Good. Here are the things I think you should do, starting tomorrow morning. First, we need to get that check into a bank, because every day you wait will cost you considerable income in interest. Then we need to get you introduced to some investment advisors, then I want to introduce you to a young partner at my law firm, Woodman & Weld. His name is Herb Fisher, and he will handle all the details of your plans. You will also need an accountant."

"What bank do you recommend?"

"M&T Bank, which has a branch in my firm's building, and which owns an investment company called Wilmington Trust. They were, originally, the DuPont family bank, and they handle the investments of high-end clients. You certainly qualify as that. Also, they have a branch in North Palm Beach, and your accounts should be based there, in order to protect you from being taxed as a resident of New York State. It helps that you were born in Florida. Did your father own a home there?"

"Yes, on Australian Avenue. It was his only home, and he had put it into a trust for me."

"Good. Another thing is, to protect your anonymity, we should set up a Florida corporation in which you can hold large assets, like your apartment. Think of a name for it."

Laurence thought about it. "The LBH Corporation—my initials?"

"Fine." Stone looked at his watch. "We need to get you a disguise, in the form of some barbering, I think."

"Okay."

He buzzed his secretary. "Joan, see if José at Nico's can take a new customer immediately—haircut, shave, mani-pedi, facial. Book him in as Mr. Jones."

"Okay."

"I need all of that?" Laurence asked.

"All of it. I'm going to set up a viewing of your prospective apartment tomorrow, and you need to look as though you can afford it."

Joan buzzed. "They can take Mr. Jones in fifteen minutes."

"Fine. Get Fred to drive him and wait for him. Laurence, do you have any other clothes?"

"I've got a blue blazer and some khakis."

"Where are they?"

"Right here, in my bag."

Stone held up the lottery check. "And I think we should put this in my safe overnight."

"Fine."

"Do you have any cash?"

"About seven thousand dollars. My father kept it in his safe. I used the rest to pay for the airplane ride."

"Let's put six thousand of it in the safe, too. A thousand ought to get you through the next day or two."

Laurence opened his bag, a small duffel, and handed Stone a thick wad of money, secured with a rubber band. "I've got a thousand in my pocket." He went to change, and Stone opened his safe and secured the check and the cash.

Laurence came back looking more presentable. "I think I'm going to need a secretary. And I guess I should ask about your legal fees."

"Oh," Stone said, handing him a printed sheet of paper. "This is a list of mine and my firm's legal fees. Please look it over when you have a chance."

Laurence scanned the document, folded it, and put in in his pocket. "I can afford you," he said.

"Good. I'll see what I can do about the secretary. Fred is waiting out front with the car. He'll bring you back when you're done at Nico's. You can leave your bag here."

"I guess I'll need a hotel room, until I have an apartment."

"You can bunk here. I've got a lot of extra room."

"Thank you."

"Get going. I'll start setting up our day for tomorrow."

Laurence left and Stone called Herbie Fisher.

"Herbert Fisher."

"It's Stone. I have a new client for you."

"Okay, who?"

"One Laurence B. Hayward, of Palm Beach, Florida."

"What does Mr. Hayward do?"

Stone thought about that. "Let's call him an investor, which he will be, starting tomorrow. And get us a meeting tomorrow morning at nine, nine-thirty, with Conrad Trilling, at Wilmington Trust."

"Can I mention Mr. Hayward's net worth?"

"Let's surprise him. Tell him to go ahead and set up a checking account." He gave Herbie Laurence's address in

Palm Beach. "The account should be at their North Palm Beach branch. Tell him we'll be making a large deposit, and ask him to call somebody at American Express and get Mr. Hayward a Centurion card instantly. He'll need a Visa card from the bank, too, and an ATM card. He's got a couple of hours before they close."

"Okay, anything else?"

"Mr. Hayward is going to need a secretary. Anybody we can steal from the firm without putting anyone's nose out of joint?"

"Funny you should mention that. You remember that one of our senior partners died about three months ago?"

"Frank Penny?"

"Right. His secretary is Margery Mason. They've kept her on to clean up Penny's affairs, and she's about done."

"Dark hair, going gray, mid-forties, on the plump side?"

"That's the one, and they've been slow to reassign her. The partners seem to go for the more fashionable-looking women."

"She's ideal. Talk to her, will you? Find out what she's making, so we can top it."

"Right."

"Oh, and set up a Florida company for Laurence called the LBH Corporation, to house some assets."

"Right away."

"He wants to buy an apartment in the old Fairleigh Hotel, on Park Avenue, that went condo. Get ahold of their prospectus and have a look at their standard contract. We should be ready for a quick closing, if he likes the place."

"Is he, by any chance, considering the one that was featured in the *Times* real estate section last Sunday?"

"How'd you guess?"

"Magic. I hear the apartments have gone quickly, but they're having trouble moving that penthouse. Most of the apartments are two, three bedrooms and three or four to a floor, but the penthouse takes up the whole fifteenth floor. My advice is, haggle."

"Absolutely. I'll have Mr. Hayward at Wilmington Trust at nine tomorrow morning. Meet us downstairs."

"Will do. Are you going to tell *me* Mr. Hayward's net worth?"

"I'll surprise you, too. And he likes to be called Laurence."

Stone buzzed Joan. "Please call Theresa Crane, a personal shopper at the Ralph Lauren store on Fifth Avenue at, what is it—Fifty-fifth?"

"Close enough."

"And set up an appointment for Laurence Hayward"—he spelled it for her—"at, say, ten-thirty AM tomorrow."

"Right. Anything else?"

"Yes, be prepared for anything, and be prepared to handle it fast."

"What else is new?" she asked.

"Oh, and ask Helene to get the big guest room on three ready. We'll be dining tonight in my study."

FROM #1 *NEW YORK TIMES*–BESTSELLING AUTHOR

STUART WOODS

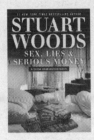
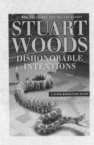

STUARTWOODS.COM

f StuartWoodsAuthor